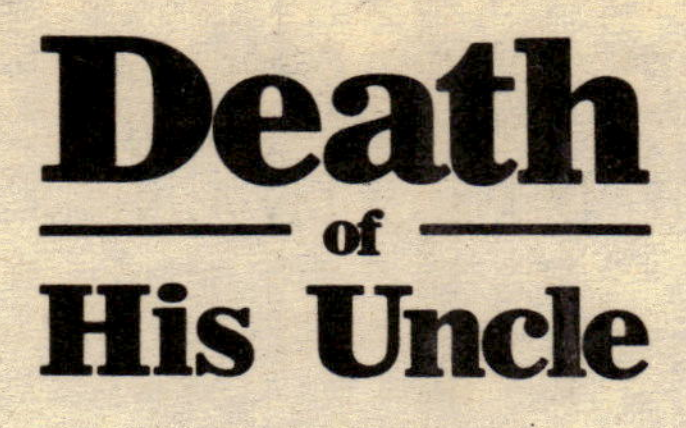

C. H. B. Kitchin

Also available in Perennial Library
by C.H.B. Kitchin:

DEATH OF MY AUNT

Death of His Uncle

C. H. B. Kitchin

PERENNIAL LIBRARY
Harper & Row, Publishers
New York, Cambridge, Philadelphia, San Francisco
London, Mexico City, São Paulo, Sydney

A hardcover edition of this book was first published in England in 1939 by Constable & Co., Ltd., and is fully protected by copyright under the terms of the International Copyright Union. It is here reprinted by arrangement with Francis King, the Executor of the Estate of C. H. B. Kitchin.

First PERENNIAL LIBRARY edition published 1984.

Library of Congress Cataloging in Publication Data

Kitchin, C. H. B. (Clifford Henry Benn), 1895–
Death of his uncle.

Originally published: London : 1939.
I. Title.
PR6021.17D36 1984 823′.912 83-48362
ISBN 0-06-080683-4 (pbk.)

---

84 85 86 87 88 10 9 8 7 6 5 4 3 2 1

1.
Thursday, June 10th

HAD it not been for my inability to mash potatoes on Thursday, June 10th, I think it quite possible that I might never have embarked on this third case of mine.

I had intended to dine alone in my flat that evening, but through a muddle on my part, my housekeeper failed to come in and cook my dinner, and I was faced unexpectedly with the task of preparing my own meal or going to my club or a restaurant. My first impulse was to go out, but a visit to my larderette, which was well stocked, made me feel ashamed. I reminded myself of friends who could preside gracefully over a four-course dinner party, cooked and served by themselves. I had long toyed with the idea of learning a little cookery, and this evening seemed designed for my first attempt. I found two cutlets, some bread, some butter, a pot of cream, a tin of peas and some potatoes. The crockery and cutlery were clean, and waiting for me. I hadn't even to wash up afterwards. Mrs. Rhodes would do that when she came the next day.

It was the sight of the pot of cream which decided me. Why not mash myself some potatoes, using cream in a way which would astonish Mrs. Rhodes?

I set to work with a cookery book open on the small kitchen table. First soak the potatoes. I did. Then peel them. This took me a long time. They were full of distasteful impurities which I chipped out extravagantly. Boil the potatoes. I boiled them. Meanwhile the cutlets were in the oven taking their chance. Next mash the potatoes vigorously, till a cream consistency is reached. I mashed for a few minutes, with little result. Then I poured in some cream. Perhaps, I thought, the cream would soften them and do my mashing for me. It didn't. Instead, there was a dubious smell, and, on opening the oven, I found that my cutlets were not all they should be. I took them out for an airing, and mashed again, with growing despair, until the telephone bell rang. 'If only,' I thought, 'it could be someone who would ask me out to dinner!'

It was.

'Can I speak to Mr. Malcolm Warren, please?'

'Yes. Speaking. Who is that?'

'This is Dick Findlay. Don't you recognize me?'

'Oh, Dick? This is a surprise.'

'I rang up your office this afternoon, about five, but they said you had left.'

'Yes, I went to get my hair cut.'

'Oh, you needn't excuse yourself. Stockbrokers have their hair cut every day.'

'Where are you?'

'I'm telephoning from a call-box off Piccadilly. I was hoping to get hold of you to come and dine to-night, if you've nothing better to do.'

I reflected hurriedly. I was never very eager to dine *tête-à-tête* with Dick Findlay. He was excellent as a fourth at bridge, or as a stop-gap invitee for a theatre party, when someone has let you down, but alone, unleavened by company, he was apt to be tedious. No, 'tedious' is quite the wrong word. I really meant that when I was alone with him I felt I was playing a permanent second fiddle. Just that touch of the bully about him, despite all his charm, whimsicality, wit and fitful generosity.

All this flashed through my head, while he said persuasively:

'*Aux Trois Pommes.*'

The *Trois Pommes* is a restaurant which gives one the very best French food. Perfect food, perfect wine, perfect service, an agreeable *dêcor* and no band. Set against this my messy mashed potatoes.

'When?' I asked.

'As soon as you can get round. Don't bother to make yourself smart. I'll go round myself at once, and drink a cocktail till you arrive. Don't be long.'

I said I should be with him in twenty minutes, and he rang off.

I had first met Dick Findlay at Oxford. A year my junior, he made a reputation for brilliance almost in his first term. He excelled, superficially, at everything. He was a scholar, but bore his scholarship lightly, even contemptuously. He was said to be a fine tennis player, and when he first came up, he played for his college at football. He joined the O.U.D.S., and was given some good parts in their plays. He could outdo the aesthetes at their own game, burnt incense in his room, had bowls filled with oranges (for decorative purposes only) and collected Aubrey Beardsley's drawings. And all the time, you felt he had his eye on a sports car or a private aeroplane. A dazzling creature—apparently without a background. One hardly heard of his public school. He had a father who lived vaguely abroad. How unlike me, I felt, with my background of a Somersetshire vicarage, my amiable step-father, my dear domesticated mother, my two sisters, my circus of uncles, aunts and cousins, from which it seemed impossible that I should ever emancipate myself.

I wonder if Oxford still breeds these versatile butterflies. Probably not. Nowadays, the young are so serious.

They seem to think it a sin to be comfortable, either physically or mentally. A self-tormenting impulse. Is it because they were all born during the war?

I think I have made it plain that I really never liked Dick very much. Jealousy, on my part, no doubt. He achieved the limelight too easily, and all the time I had the feeling that he was a second-rate person with a second-rate brain. And I had a specific grudge against him, which I may as well disclose, even if it shows the pettiness of my own character.

During my undergraduate days, I had one humble parlour trick. I could improvise on the piano in the styles of the great composers. I was pedantic in my method and heavy in my touch, but my musical friends—those who were really musical and not only interested in light luncheon music—seemed to enjoy my little performances, and gave them perhaps too much encouragement. 'This,' I would say, after suitable pressure, 'is a Beethoven Air with Variations. This is a César Franck Choral Prelude. This is a Brahms Intermezzo'; and though I must admit that one day, when my hostess had asked me to 'try some Bach,' an American, perhaps misunderstanding the situation, said, 'Waal, if that's Bach, it's the poorest Bach I've ever heard,' I usually had a mild success and was asked to play again.

Dick also played the piano. He had a velvety touch, a sense of syncopation, knowledge of half-a-dozen modern harmonies and considerable technique, provided he was allowed to bring it out in little bursts. The first time I heard him was after I had held the stage for twenty minutes with a free fugue in Beethoven's last manner. He was gracefully reluctant to go to the piano, and urged that his music was lamentably low-brow and that he couldn't stand comparison with a serious performer. Eventually, of course, he allowed himself to be persuaded, and sat down.

'I should like,' he said, 'if I may, to parody Warren parodying Beethoven.' And he did, introducing deliberately one or two gross mistakes such as I was only too prone to make, and later some ingenious little runs, which, though they were not Beethoven, were obviously beyond the scope of my fingers. Then suddenly he turned the whole piece into a sophisticated jazz. A triumph—but too much at my expense.

Of course, we came to terms. I couldn't afford not to come to terms with him. He knew far too many of my friends, about whom he said witty things to me, just as he said witty things about me to them—things that were often a little too true to be funny. He would also disarm criticism by saying witty things about himself. He used people as stepping-stones, and seemed to go from strength to strength, though he was too wise to injure those whom he had out-distanced. To do him justice, I don't think he wished to injure anyone. He simply liked being liked, and, if possible, admired. It may have come home to him as a shock, after a time, that people found it easier to admire him than to like him.

Then when he was talked of as a possible President of the Union, came eclipse—or, at any rate, decline. His mysterious father, who lived abroad, died suddenly, leaving, it was said, nothing but debts. Dick had accumulated debts of his own, too. In desperation, he had to turn to his father's brother—'a pawky little widower'—who lived in 'some ghastly suburb.' We weren't even told which suburb. Uncle Hamilton—I learnt his name later—played up well. He offered Dick a home in the 'ghastly suburb,' and sufficient money to take his degree, living the while in moderate, if unostentatious, comfort. There were relatives, too, on Dick's mother's side—the two sides of the family had always disliked one another—who offered him a job in their factory when he should have finished with Oxford. He was reading science—I suppose the idea had been that he would go to the factory sooner or later, and apparently the factory had a scientific side. Dick said, contemptuously, that his mother's family made chemical fertilisers—he used another word for them—amongst other things.

So Dick's life suddenly became earnest, and play had to yield to work. He took the change fairly well, outwardly, though he was never quite the same after it. 'Well, well,' he once said to me, 'all this posing is all right when you're twenty, but there isn't much to be said for it when you're twenty-one.' 'Did you pose?' I asked him. 'My dear fellow,' he answered, 'what do you think? Of course I posed, and did it very well.'

I asked him if he hadn't always intended to go into the factory, and he said it was there as a last resort, if nothing better turned up. He had hoped to have a year or two in which to look round, perhaps to take up free-lance journalism, or write a successful play. Now there was the factory and nothing but the factory. He must make good there. It was a little distressing to see him so changed—as it has been phrased, 'on the road from Oxford to London.'

But when he reached London, he didn't fare too badly. He seemed to give satisfaction in the factory, and fairly soon obtained a living wage. The factory was in the direction of Croydon, but it had offices in the City, and I used to meet Dick there for luncheon from time to time. I liked him better than I had done in Oxford. Adversity had tamed his brilliance. I might even say it had turned the tables, for, thanks to my Aunt Catherine's will, and a little good luck in my business, I was now in a position of host, while he was an agreeable guest. At bridge he was especially useful, and I'm afraid there was a period in which I regarded him chiefly from this angle. When hard up for a fourth, I would say to myself, 'Oh. Dick Findlay will do,' and he did. He developed an interest in horse-racing, and gave me two Derby winners. From time to time, he asked me to do little deals for him on the Stock Exchange—generally with success. He was an ideal client, gave clear instructions, never asked for advice, and paid promptly. None the less, I was always a little nervous that he might let my firm down. When I went away for a holiday I used to say to my senior partner, 'Now mind, if Dick Findlay asks you to buy ten thousand Mexican Oilfields, you're not to do it!' But he never attempted anything of the sort.

He was still living with his 'pawky' uncle, Hamilton Findlay, in South Mersley, one of London's outermost south-western suburbs, and I went there once to dinner. Once was enough. It was a dismal evening and it clearly embarrassed Dick to have me there. I imagine it had been a command invitation, and that the uncle had said: 'You keep mentioning this Malcolm Warren. Let's have a look at him,' while poor Dick couldn't reply: 'I'm not particularly keen on his having a look at *you!*'

The house was an ugly, late-Victorian building, with gables and spikes on the roof—considered a small place, no doubt, when it was built, but relatively big now that it was surrounded by modern houses. A good deal of the land had no doubt been sold for building at some time or another, and Uncle Hamilton now had rather less than an acre. I think he must have bought the property cheaply; for it was of the kind to make any house agent despair. There was nothing to commend it, except roominess. If a thousand pounds had been spent on it, I dare say it could have been made into quite a pleasant retreat for a City man, but Uncle Hamilton hadn't spent the thousand pounds. The inside was only fairly clean. The furniture was late Victorian with a few gimcrack additions from a later period. The garden was mostly lawn studded with a few rose beds, in which Uncle Hamilton showed a desultory interest, and such landscape effect as might have existed was spoilt by a big old-fashioned garage—complete with inspection pit, I was told. However, even this was useless, as, at that time, neither Dick nor his uncle had a car.

What a background for my brilliant friend of the Oxford days! And what an uncle! Hamilton Findlay had his nephew's physique but none of his good looks. His eyes were small and dull blue. His complexion was reddish. His grey-black moustache was so straggly that it looked as if it had been badly gummed on for amateur theatricals. Even an unobservant person could have seen that he wore a wig—an old wig, probably, since there was no touch of grey in it, as there was in the moustache and eyebrows. The only kind things I could find to say about him were that he was dressed with fair neatness and that he looked clean and healthy.

He made himself moderately agreeable to me, and it was easy for me to talk to him, because he clearly wanted to talk about the Stock Exchange. I was wondering whether I should get him as a client, when he announced with needless emphasis that for the last thirty years he had done all his Stock Exchange transactions through his bank. 'I have always found it a very satisfactory method,' he said, 'and I never speculate. However, I always enjoy hearing a professional broker's views.'

I gave him mine, for what they were worth, while Dick tried to make conversation with his cousin, William Hicks, who was the fourth member of our dinner party, if such it could be called. Dick had warned me about Bill Hicks in the train, as we were travelling down to South Mersley. 'He's the strong silent man incarnate,' he said, 'and so dull that he makes you scream. He's a nursery gardener.' I suggested that gardeners were usually very pleasant people, and he said: 'Oh, I dare say Bill's pleasant enough. We've never got on. Cousins. You know what it is. He went through the war, and I didn't. I went to Oxford, and he didn't go anywhere. I made a marvellous circle of friends. I don't think he knows anybody at all beyond a few people in the village near his nursery, and two or three farmers. But you'll see for yourself.'

'How does he get on with your uncle?' I asked.

'I don't think either of them cares twopence about the other,' he replied. 'But he lets Uncle Hamilton have rose trees at half price.'

'Why?'

'Oh, I suppose Uncle Hamilton sometimes sends a tiny cheque to Aunt Grace. She's Bill's mother, and lives with him.'

'He isn't married, then?'

'No.'

I confess that when I met Cousin Bill, I found him as uninteresting as the dinner, which, by the way, was eatable, but little more. I can't remember his saying anything at all, except once, when the conversation came round to roses. Then he described, in a dull, deep voice, how his father—also a nursery gardener, I gathered—had tried to produce a really good white rose, with the pure white of Frau Karl Druschki, the perfect form of, say, Mabel Morse, and the vigorous but neat habit of Shot Silk. He went through the newer white roses one by one, pointing out the faults in each of them. His chief complaint was that most of them weren't really white. And the few that were really white had other defects. It was a not uninteresting lecture, but Uncle Hamilton, who, perhaps, had heard the story before, listened impatiently, and finally cut Cousin Bill short by saying: 'Well, I bet it cost your father a lot of money. And he didn't produce anything to beat Clarice Goodacre. You stick to the commercial side of your business, and leave the fancy stuff alone. Now what about some coffee outside, before we start bridge?'

The maid brought tepid coffee to us in a small brick building in the corner of the garden. It was a fine day in mid-July. 'We call this the *loggia,*' Dick whispered to me, with a smile.

Uncle Hamilton began to talk about the merits of his house, which he said he wouldn't exchange for any other house in the district. It wasn't overlooked, but it was handy for the station. There was a bus stop only two minutes away, and yet you hardly heard the traffic. He couldn't understand why people paid three and four thousand pounds for band-boxes near the Garden City. Tied up with every kind of restriction, too. You couldn't even put up a piece of trellis without permission from the Garden City architect. I asked a few questions about the Garden City, and Dick said it was a vast semi-philanthropic foundation. Uncle Hamilton snorted. 'Reeks of Socialism,' he said, and led the way indoors.

By ill luck I had him as my partner for all four rubbers. He played badly and cantankerously, and sometimes abused me for things I hadn't done, or couldn't have done. 'Why on earth didn't you lead a heart, young man?' 'I hadn't got a heart,' I would reply. 'And you might have known I hadn't, because . . .' Sometimes I retaliated quite vigorously. Dick enjoyed our wrangles, though he may have been a little afraid that I should go too far.

We played for a halfpenny a hundred, and I lost elevenpence-halfpenny. Dick gave me a halfpenny change for my shilling with mock solemnity. After a whisky-and-soda, I said goodbye to my host and thanked him for a pleasant evening. Dick walked with me to the station. Apparently Cousin Bill's station was on a different line.

'Well, Malcolm,' Dick said, when we were out of earshot of the house, 'you now see how the poor live! I promise I won't inflict that on you again. Next time we'll dine in town.'

I protested that it hadn't been so bad.

'Oh, it isn't too bad,' he said. 'I've got a bed-sitting-room upstairs. There wasn't a chance of showing it to you. I've had it quite nicely done up. It's not like those ghastly rooms you saw downstairs. And the house is fairly convenient for the factory. As long as I've got to go there, I might as well live in South Mersley as anywhere. But—well, it's a bit of a come-down, isn't it?'

It was. As I said good-night to him I felt quite sorry for him, and thought how much more agreeable he was than when we first met—and he parodied my parodies of the great composers.

This expedition of mine to South Mersley took place some three years before the evening when I mis-mashed my potatoes. In the intervening period I had met Dick on an average about once every two months. He had had a rise in salary and had bought a large second-hand two-seater car, with an enormous luggage recess in the back, which impressed me. He still lived with Uncle Hamilton in South Mersley, though he talked of striking out for himself. Despite my growing sympathy for him, I still regarded him more as an acquaintance than a friend—an acquaintance with whom I was not altogether comfortable. Hence my hesitation when, out of the blue, he asked me to dine with him *Aux Trois Pommes*. But I was committed to that now. . . .

I found him in the little bar of the *Trois Pommes* drinking a dry Martini. He looked well and handsome, and there was a touch of bravado in his manner which reminded me of him as he used to be when he was younger. On my way to the restaurant I had wondered what had induced him to ask me to dinner so suddenly. He used to entertain me about once for every three times that I entertained him—a fair proportion having regard to the difference in our means. It wasn't quite 'his turn' yet. Perhaps he found himself stranded in London, and had tried other people first. But he had rung up my office as early as five. The fact that I tended to ask myself why he should want to see me showed how little we were close friends.

Over a cocktail we talked spasmodically about some friends with whom we had spent a week-end in April—the last time I had seen him. Then we went into the restaurant. He ordered boldly from the menu, and pressed me so hard to have caviar, which I adore, that I couldn't bring myself to refuse it.

'Look here,' I said, 'we must make this a Dutch party.

'Nonsense,' he said. 'You're my guest. You must let me do my little bit sometimes. Besides, I'm unusually well off at present—thanks to the Derby. I hope you got Midday Sun* all right? I'm frightfully sorry I tipped you Le Grand Duc, but when we last met—'

Racing carried us through our first two courses. When this subject began to languish, I said: 'How is Uncle Hamilton?' He stiffened momentarily, and said: 'Well, that really brings me to the point. Uncle Hamilton has vanished, and I want your advice. That's why—oh, I don't mean that!—that's one of the reasons I was so eager to get hold of you to-night.'

'My dear Dick, I'm so sorry—and greatly flattered. You ought to know by now that my advice won't be much use. I'm a stockbroker, not a detective. Do you need a detective, by the way? If you do, I know a very agreeable one.'

I was thinking of Detective Inspector Parris, whom I had met during my eventful Christmas at Beresford Lodge in Hampstead.†

'I don't think I want a detective—at least a professional one—yet,' he said. 'But I think I'm quite right to call in an unprofessional one—like you.'

'But I'm not even that.'

'Well, you've been in two murder cases, and they must have given you some kind of experience, which— By the way, I'm not implying that this is a murder case, or anything of the sort. But I'd better give you the facts at once—when we've ordered the rest of our dinner. Waiter!'

He chose an expensive Bombe—he always had a sweet tooth—and I chose a savoury. Then he began:

'Uncle Hamilton has vanished. By that, I mean, he went away for the week-end, and hasn't turned up again, and hasn't written or telegraphed to say he was detained. The story really starts with our domestic arrangements. As you may remember, my uncle runs Tylecroft with a staff of two, Mrs. Pressley and her ill-favoured daughter, Sibyl, who waited on us that memorable night when we had the

*Midday Sun won the Derby of 1937, Le Grand Duc coming in third.
†See *Crime at Christmas*.

honour of your company. It's too small a staff, really. That's why the house always looks a bit dingy. But Uncle Hamilton doesn't believe in spending twopence where a penny will do. Some weeks ago—oh, it must have been in April—Mrs. Pressley announced that her niece was being married on June 5th, that's last Saturday. The wedding was to be somewhere in Essex, where she comes from, and was a great family event. Could she and Sibyl go to it, and have the week-end off? Uncle Hamilton wasn't at all pleased—he hates anything that upsets his habits—but he said rather grudgingly that the Pressleys could go. After all, he would probably find it hard to get another couple who would suit him so well, at the mean wages he pays.

'It was arranged that they should go after luncheon on Friday—last Friday, June 4th. And they did go. While they were away a local "help," a Mrs. Garlick, was to come in the mornings and "do" for us, leaving cold suppers ready for evenings. We've had Mrs. Garlick before in spring-cleanings and other emergencies. As you know, we don't exactly live *en prince* when the Pressleys are available, but I can assure you that if the Garlick takes their place, life becomes a thousand times more horrible. Compared to Mrs. Garlick, Mrs. Pressley is the head chef at the Savoy. My uncle grumbled a bit, but I suppose he was going to put up with it, as he's done once or twice before—last year, for instance, when Mrs. Pressley's father died. Then, some weeks ago, he surprised me by saying he was going to spend the week-end of the Pressleys' wedding in Cornwall.'

'Why were you surprised?' I asked. 'It seems a fairly reasonable thing to do, doesn't it?'

'Not quite, where Uncle Hamilton's concerned. He's most frightfully set in all his habits. I've never heard of his going to Cornwall before. And it seems a long way to go just for the week-end. I should have thought the expense of the railway fare would have deterred him.'

'Does he never take holidays?'

'Oh, yes. Unadventurous, regular little holidays. He goes away for a week in the spring, during spring-cleaning—always to the same boarding house in Folkestone, and for a fortnight or three weeks in August, when the Pressleys have their yearly holiday. Then he goes to some seaside place on the East Coast, usually with his friend, Dr. Fielding, who's a keen chess-player, like my uncle. Dr. Fielding is coming into my story in one minute. So you see I had the prospect of a solitary week-end at Tylecroft, with only Mrs. Garlick to look after me. I made one or two unsuccessful efforts to cadge invitations, and then was reduced to asking an artist I know—I don't think you've met him, his name is Woodwell—if he'd like to have a motor-run with me to the Norfolk Broads. He said he was fixed up, but when I told him of our domestic crisis at Tylecroft, he offered to lend me his mews-flat in Chelsea while he was away. I wasn't frightfully keen to spend the week-end in London, but rather impulsively I accepted his offer and said I'd be glad to have the flat from Friday night till Tuesday, the day before yesterday. Oh, I've forgotten to tell you that for some reason or other, the Pressleys weren't expected back till the Tuesday morning. I told my uncle about the arrangement, and he was a bit sniffy, as he always is when I plan to leave what he calls my 'comfortable home,' but he didn't make any actual objection.

'Well, the Pressleys left after lunch on the Friday, and on Friday evening I had a cold supper with my uncle at Tylecroft. I should have liked to go straight to London when I'd finished my work, but I thought my uncle might not be too pleased if I did. He'd want me to be there to make coffee for him. Mrs. Garlick, of course, would be there to get his breakfast on Saturday morning.

'We had our meal, I made the coffee, and we were sitting in the loggia—you remember it, don't you?—when he surprised me by saying that he was frightened of missing his train the next morning, and thought he would like to spend the night at a hotel in London. In view of the probable discomforts which Mrs. Garlick would inflict upon him, it was quite a reasonable idea, but I should have thought that the extra cost would have deterred him.'

I interrupted him.

'Beyond deciding to go to Cornwall for the week-end, this was the first thing your uncle did which was not quite true to type?'

'Yes, I think it was.'

'I think it's always helpful,' I said, 'to notice anything which is slightly "out of character."'

'Ah, there speaks my little detective! But let me tell you the rest of the story. When my uncle suggested going to a hotel in London, I volunteered at once to drive him there in my car. This pleased him, as it saved him the fare. He had already done most of his packing. I went upstairs and put my few things together, came down and got the car out, and helped my uncle to shut up the house. Then we drove off.'

'What time was this?'

'Oh, about nine, I suppose. On the way, my uncle said he'd like to see the flat I was going to stay in, and we stopped there and I took him in. He didn't like it at all and said it was cramped and unhealthy—a poor exchange for Tylecroft. Then, about half-past ten, or a little later, he said he must be going. I urged him to let me drive him to his hotel, but he said he couldn't think of troubling me any more—a most unusual attitude, this. In the end we compromised and he agreed that I should drive him most of the way and put him down in Westbourne Terrace, which, of course, was handy for Paddington. I had assumed that he would stay at the station hotel, but it occurred to me that he might be wanting to find a cheaper place and was ashamed to let me know. So I drove him half-way up Westbourne Terrace, and put him down. He got out, I wished him a pleasant journey, and he walked on towards Paddington, carrying his bag. That was the last time I saw him. And I haven't heard from him since.'

He paused and a waiter, who had been hanging round, came up with the bill. We were the only diners left in the restaurant, which does not provide suppers, and for some time there had been signs of impatience behind us, swishings of tablecloths, clatterings of cutlery, lights turned out, and so on. I felt rather uncomfortable, and suggested to Dick that we should continue the story in my flat. He agreed, though he said that there wasn't much more story to tell.

'Oh,' I said, when we had got into a taxi, 'if you really want me to help you I shall have to ask you a lot of questions. I must get the background of all this into my head. I must be able to *visualise* it all as part of a natural process—as flowing from the general scheme of your and your uncle's lives.'

He laughed and said: 'Really, Malcolm, you might be writing an essay in a philosophical paper!'

'Well, those are my methods!'

'So you've really decided to interest yourself in the case?'

'You've made it so interesting, though I can't help wondering. . . .'

'What?'

'Oh, nothing much. But I shall, sooner or later, have to ask you some impertinent questions.'

'I know exactly what question you're thinking,' he said. 'You want to ask me about Uncle Hamilton's sex-life!'

He laughed again, embarrassingly.

'That, no doubt, will transpire, among other things,' I answered, a little prudishly. 'But first you might just round off your story for me. You'd got to the point when the figure of Uncle Hamilton was seen, for the last time, walking with his bag in the direction of Paddington. What did you do?'

'Turned the car round, drove to Chelsea, garaged it, and went to my own humble lodging. Oh, one little detail, though it's of no importance. We'd forgotten to tell Mrs.

Garlick—to leave a note for her, I mean—that there would be nobody at home the following morning. She knew, of course, that I wasn't going to be there, but she was expecting to have to take Uncle Hamilton his early tea and cook him one of her horrible breakfasts. Uncle Hamilton thought of this during our drive to London, and asked me to telephone to Mrs. Garlick next morning, just in case she got in a flutter. He also asked me to remind her to do some shopping for Mrs. Pressley on Tuesday morning. Dr. Fielding was coming to dinner that night—you remember my mentioning Dr. Fielding, my uncle's chess friend—and it was necessary to have some respectable food in the house ready for Mrs. Pressley to cook when she got back from her beano.

'This was just a piece of fussiness on my uncle's part, as I'm sure the Pressley arranged all this with the Garlick before going away. Of course I said I'd telephone, though, as a matter of fact, I forgot all about it.'

'This is important,' I said, 'because it shows that your uncle had every intention of being back on Tuesday night.'

'Yes, it does. Of course he may have forgotten the engagement later.'

'That would be quite "out of character," wouldn't it?'

'Yes, quite.'

'Well, here we are.'

We got out, I paid the taxi and showed Dick upstairs into my sitting-room. He went at once to the piano and played a few brilliant little passages, while I got out the drinks. His fingers seemed to have lost none of their agility.

'Do you play at home?' I asked.

'Yes, when my uncle isn't about. Music irritates him.'

Then we both sat down in easy chairs.

'Let me finish off first,' he said, looking at his watch. 'I spent my week-end in London, and went back to Tylecroft on Tuesday, finding the Pressleys installed there again, but no Uncle Hamilton. Half-past six, seven, a quarter-past seven. Mrs. Pressley became agitated. Had I had any message from Mr. Findlay? None. Had she? None.

'Dr. Fielding was expected any minute. What was she to do about dinner? Keep it hot, if she could, I suggested, at any rate till eight. Then we'd better have it, whether my uncle had arrived or not. He must have missed his train.'

'Out of character?'

'Out of character, in the highest degree. I've never known him to miss a train. He isn't even late for the train before the one he wants to catch. Dr. Fielding arrived at half-past seven.'

'What sort of a man is he?'

'He's the sort of man whom, when we were at Oxford, we should have thought of as simply non-existent. Drab, featureless, dead almost. Of course one has to be more tolerant as one grows older. What one loses in brilliance, one is supposed to gain in human understanding. Quite frankly, if you had produced a father like Dr. Fielding in Oxford, I should have regarded you as utterly damned. And, by the way, you might have thought the same of me, if I had produced an uncle like Uncle Hamilton.'

The whisky is making him long-winded, I thought, but I let him go on.

'Dr. Fielding is simply an old fogey. I suppose he was a doctor once, but he hasn't practised since I've known him, which is ever since I've been living at Tylecroft. He doesn't even produce medical *dicta.* Perhaps he was a doctor of botany, or philology. You can't tell. His conversation is so colourless. He's an indifferent but devoted chess player. I know that because my uncle, who isn't really much good, usually beats him. It wouldn't be like Uncle Hamilton to play against anyone who was too good.

'I imagine Dr. Fielding has private means. He lives in a small house in a row not far away from us. I've dined there two or three times. Dull evenings, like so many that I've had to spend these last fourteen years. But this isn't a moment for self-pity.

'As I said, Dr. Fielding arrived at half-past seven. I did the honours as well as I could. Offered the sherry and so on. I asked him if my uncle had mentioned the trip to Cornwall to him, and he said he had. He agreed with me that my uncle must have missed the train. We kept the conversation going till eight, when Sibyl brought in dinner. Every minute I expected a telegram. None came. We ate dinner. Dr. Fielding is rather greedy and doesn't talk much when he's eating. As a matter of fact, Mrs. Pressley had performed above her usual standard. Then we had coffee in the loggia. Dr. Fielding criticised my uncle's rose-beds. He's a bit of a rosarian too, though his own little garden is frightful. I told him Cousin Bill supplied the roses at half price. He asked for the address of Cousin Bill's nursery.'

'What is it, by the way?' I asked.

'Cantervale Nurseries, Sedcombe, Surrey, about twenty-five miles south-west of South Mersley. But why on earth do you want to know?'

I answered truthfully that I hadn't the vaguest idea.

'Nine o'clock came, then half-past nine, then ten. Then, mercifully, the old man seemed to have had enough of my society, and went away. I sat up, playing the piano, till eleven, twelve, one. Then I thought it unreasonable that I should be kept out of bed any longer. I left the front door unbolted and went to bed. After all, I had to work the next day. If Uncle Hamilton must arrive in the small hours, he must let himself in. He had his latch-key. It was bad enough that he should have left me to entertain his friend. I got up next morning. No uncle, no telegram, no letter. I went to work and came home as usual, and found Mrs. Pressley very worried. This was yesterday. Somehow, it seems longer ago than that. This morning—the same story. Mrs. Pressley very worried indeed. Ought I to go to the police? I said I thought it was hardly time for that yet, but that I had a friend who's been connected with the police—that's you, Malcolm!'

'Good lord!' I said.

'And that I'd try to get in touch with him. I got away from my business rather early and rang you up at five in your office. They told me you were going home via the barber's, and I waited till I was sure you'd have got home and rang you up again, when I got hold of you. And here we are. That's my story. What am I to do?'

I refilled both our glasses, to gain time. The truth was I hadn't any idea what he ought to do, except, perhaps, take Mrs. Pressley's advice and go to the police. And I felt I must at once disabuse him, if he thought that my two experiences of crime had given me any specialised knowledge as to its detection.

'I'm not a detective, I'm a stockbroker.'

I repeated the phrase with emphatic variations for his benefit.

'Well, then, as a man of the world, Malcolm—hang it all, I haven't got too many friends now—real friends, I mean.'

This appeal both touched and flattered me.

'Do you think there's a case for doing anything at all?' I asked.

'Perhaps there isn't—yet. But, clearly, there must be a time limit. I mean, we couldn't go on like this for a year, or even a month. The money question alone would make that impossible. The Pressleys' wages, and so on. I'm quite willing to do nothing for some days, but I must decide how long I ought to wait. That's one of the things I want you to advise me about. Suppose your partner in the City didn't turn up one morning, and continued not to turn up, how long would it be before you took some kind of action? Of course, you'd ring up his home the first morning, to ask if he was ill. But suppose they told you he'd set out for the office as usual?'

'Oh, then, I suppose, we should call in the police almost at once. But your uncle's disappearance isn't quite so conclusive. After all, we don't quite know—I mean, there is the question of his private life to be considered, isn't there? Except for his engagement with Dr. Fielding there wasn't any call for him to—turn up to time, shall we say, like one's partner in the office. You've got to allow him rather more latitude, or run the risk of interfering in his private affairs, which I take it wouldn't be good policy.'

I thought this rather a clever point to have made, and Dick seemed to think so too.

'I must get the background clear,' I went on, 'before I can value these facts which you have told me. I want to *feel* them taking place, not merely to know they have taken place. In other words, I want to know all about your family and your home life at Tylecroft. That would take a long time, but perhaps you can give me an outline.'

'I was born of poor but honest parents,' he began. 'No, even that isn't quite true. They weren't particularly poor, and I've never been very sure about my father's honesty! No. I had two quite rich grandfathers. My mother's father founded the fertiliser business in which I've been working. It was quite a small affair in his day, and he left each of his three daughters what used to be called a modest competence. One of my two aunts on this side of the family married an American, and died in America ten years ago, without issue. She left all her money, such as it was, to her husband. The other one lived as a spinster in England, and died three years ago and left me a thousand pounds. The rest went to friends and charities. My mother died when I was six, and left all her money to my father. Meanwhile, my two uncles on this side of the family, Uncle George and Uncle Herbert, came into the business, which prospered a good deal, especially after they took in a cousin of theirs. Uncle Herbert died soon after the war. Uncle George died last Christmas and the business is really run now by this cousin, whose name is Bagshaw, and his son. Both the Bagshaws are very able.'

'Didn't Uncle George leave you anything?' I asked. 'Excuse the question. It may just be relevant.'

'Not a bean. He had masses of daughters. Besides, my mother's relations always disapproved of the Findlays. I don't think Uncle Hamilton has met Uncle George since my father's death, when it was arranged definitely that I should go into the business. Now for my father's side, which I know better. My paternal grandfather made his money by importing something—I think it was ladies' shoes—and left each of his three children about twenty thousand pounds. Of course, it wasn't so difficult in those days, with no income tax or death duties to speak of. The three children were my father, Uncle Hamilton, and Aunt Grace. I've mentioned them, as a matter of fact, in order of juniority. My father was the youngest, and Aunt Grace is the eldest, with Uncle Hamilton in the middle. To take my father first. He was a financier. You may well ask me what that means. It means anything. I imagine that when he married my mother, he had a fairly steady kind of job. At all events, we lived well, in rather a grand house in Hampstead. Then, as I've told you, my mother died when I was six. I think it must have broken him up. There's no doubt that he and my mother were very much in love with one another. Two years later, we left Hampstead and my father took a small house near Orpington, more countrified than it is now, of course. I had a nurse-housekeeper to look after me, and soon went to a little boarding school. My father was away from home a good deal. I think, even then, he had begun to find consolation in women and wine. I remember that when I was about twelve, he told me that he couldn't afford to send me to Eton, for which I'd been entered, and that I should have to go to a very minor public school in the south of England. Really, it was hardly a public school at all. At that age, I didn't care twopence, but how very quiet one was about this sort of thing at Oxford!

'In due course I went to my so-called public school. It wasn't bad. I was good at games and found work easy. Some of the masters were quite cultivated and took an interest in me. It was easy to be a success there. The competition wasn't severe. Meanwhile, we gave up the house near Orpington, and so far as we had a home, it was at a private hotel in Chislehurst. My father now began to go to Paris a good deal, and when I went up to Oxford, where, as you know, I got a scholarship, he said he was going to live in Paris, which he found both cheaper and pleasanter than England. He was still dabbling in finance, trying to bring off "deals" and get a commission on them. Sometimes they succeeded, but more often they failed. As time went on, I think he lost grip on everything. He took me abroad once or twice, and I met some interesting people—people, that is to say, quite outside the scope of the Findlays or my mother's family. I was precocious and fairly intelligent, and tried to make myself as cosmopolitan as I could. When I came up to Oxford I found that my sophistication carried me quite a long way. I'm afraid this all sounds rather odious. Oxford simply went to my head.'

'You went to Oxford's head,' I said generously.

'Oh, no! A little circle of forty or fifty people. I cut no serious ice there. Well, you know the next chapter. My father died towards the end of my second year and left nothing. The family business became a reality which I had to face. Uncle George offered to take me in, provided I got a first in schools. I had to work, and did, and got my first and the privilege of entering Garvice and Bagshaw on probation at a salary of a hundred a year. This brings me to Uncle Hamilton, doesn't it?'

He looked at his watch again.

I refilled his glass, and told him I could put him up for the night if necessary. He said he still had over an hour before he needed to start for the last train, if I could bear him for so long. I said I could, and he went on:

'It's always hard to judge one's own father, but I think he was probably an able man in his way, and rather a fascinating character. Uncle Hamilton has always seemed to me to be just the opposite. He started life by going into house building—suburban building—and I think if he had been clever at it, he ought to have made a fortune. He didn't, probably because he had small ideas and would never take a risk. However, I suppose it was something that he didn't lose his money.'

'Is he really a rich uncle?' I asked.

'That depends upon your standard. I should think he's worth about forty thousand—made mostly by saving, I should say. He married before I was born, but his wife ran away with someone else after six months. She's been dead a great many years. He settled at Tylecroft just after the war, and completely retired from building in 1920, since when he's done nothing. I don't know if his mind is filled with ecstatic contemplation of the nature of the universe, or is just a vacuum. I suspect the latter. Oh, he has his good points! I think he genuinely admired my father, who used to despise him almost openly. He was certainly very kind when my father was dying, and I suppose it was good of him to give me a home, though a small allowance would have been more to my taste. While my father was alive, I didn't see very much of him. I remember very vividly an Easter holiday I spent at his house when I was sixteen. I was at a romantic age—you know, those dreamy romantic periods one has in adolescence—and spent my time reading everything I could. The visit lingers in my mind as having been marked by a warm spring rain which beat against my bedroom window, while I sat reading and thinking mysteriously like one on the threshold of a dream-world. The peach blossom was very lovely that year between the showers. Uncle Hamilton left me completely to myself. Twice only he gave me a shilling to go to the cinema. That was my first prolonged contact with him. The next one was after my father's death, a contact which lasted till I dropped him in Westbourne Terrace on Friday night.

'Even when I first went to his house as a penniless orphan, he didn't bully me. He doesn't bully. He nags over absurd little things that can't matter to anyone. Of course, I have sponged on him. Even these last eight years, when I've been paying thirty shillings a week, I've been sponging. You'll ask me, I know, why I stayed on at Tylecroft, while latterly, at all events, I could have afforded a *pied-à-terre* of my own. Well, the least creditable reason first—he would never have forgiven me if I'd left. In a kind of dim way, he likes to have me about his place, and, well, I have expectations, you know. But, apart from this, staying there did give me a good deal of pocket-money. I have been able to take trips abroad, which I adore, and to run a car, and do a certain amount of entertaining in London, though I know I've never done my fair share. As for Uncle Hamilton, I've just managed to rub along with him. He knows that if he nags me too much I shall go away, which he doesn't want. And I know that if I don't let myself be nagged up to a point, he'll cut me out of his will. And I don't want that. I'm speaking very frankly, though I dare say you could guess all I'm telling you. If you ask me whether I have any real affection for him, I shall simply have to say I don't know. You see, I started with him at such a disadvantage. My life took such a sudden jolt for the worse when I had to go and live at Tylecroft. And it had promised to be such a delightful affair.'

He sighed wistfully. If there had been more time, I should have enjoyed him as one enjoys a novel, but there were one or two points I felt had to be cleared up.

'Have you ever known your uncle to be, shall I say, amorously entangled?'

Greatly to my surprise, Dick showed the suspicion of a blush.

'Good heavens, no,' he said. 'Uncle Hamilton is far too set in his ways. I remember when I first began to work in London, he gave me a lecture on the perils of the streets, more, perhaps, from the medical than the moral point of view. Mind you, Uncle Hamilton is a perfectly normal man. I've seen his eyes glisten in what old ladies would call "an unpleasant way" when he's been served by a pretty shop-assistant. It is possible that when on holiday he has sometimes shaken a loose leg. But hardly during the last ten years, I should say. At all events, his home life is dismally respectable.'

'I was only wondering,' I said, 'whether this trip of his to Cornwall—'

'Exactly,' he said. 'But I'm afraid not. Still, it might just be possible. Now, have I given you enough of Uncle Hamilton?'

'I think so. For the present.'

'Well, then, I'd better polish off Aunt Grace, the eldest of Grandfather Findlay's three children. She's quite a nice old lady who married a nursery gardener named Hicks. A pleasant, cultivated nursery gardener, but he couldn't make money, and died just when he'd lost all of Aunt Grace's fortune. Since Cousin Bill has taken a hand—he's the strong silent man you met at Tylecroft that awful evening—they've been doing rather better, but according to Uncle Hamilton even Cousin Bill is more interested in botany than in selling geraniums at a shilling a pot, and the Hickses are still very hard up. Aunt Grace used to like my father, but she could never abide Uncle Hamilton. She's very plain-spoken. She thinks me rather a worm for having gone on living at Tylecroft. Cousin Bill has no use for me at all.'

'You said Cousin Bill was a bachelor.'

'Yes. A few years ago he was engaged, but the girl died, poor thing, after the doctors had had a lovely time with her. It was all very sad. Cousin Bill became stronger and more silent than ever.'

'I was wondering,' I said, 'if you oughtn't to have consulted Cousin Bill instead of me.'

He gave me a look of surprise, and thought for a moment before speaking.

'It just shows you,' he said, 'what terms I'm on with

Cousin Bill, that I haven't even thought of asking his advice.'

'Don't you think you should?'

'Perhaps. But if there's nothing in this affair, or if, as you seem to suggest, Uncle Hamilton is kicking over the traces for once in a way, it would be a frightful mistake on my part to go calling a family council yet awhile. I'm quite sure Uncle Hamilton would rather I kept his peccadilloes (if any) to myself, than blabbed about them to Aunt Grace and Cousin Bill. Besides, Malcolm, do have a heart! As I said before, I haven't many real friends now, and it is a relief to talk things over with someone like you, who do understand me up to a point, even if you did once describe me as "meretricious." Your judgment is worth ten of Cousin Bill's, who can't even make a nursery garden pay.'

He spoke quite passionately. One could put some of his fervour down to whisky, but he really did seem to want my help. I thought for a few minutes before answering, while he looked at me with anxiety.

Finally I said: 'I will try to help you as much as I can, Dick. But tell me this first. Have you any kind of plan in your own mind?'

'Well,' he said, 'I had thought we might go to Cornwall together for the week-end, just to see if Uncle Hamilton did go there, or for that matter, is still there. My word, it would be fun if we found him with a flaming *cocotte!* We should have to be discreet, of course. This is the only plan I've been able to think of.'

'Cornwall! The county's about a hundred miles long, isn't it?'

'Oh, didn't I tell you? Uncle Hamilton mentioned the town he was going to—Falmouth. We could explore the Falmouth area and inquire at the hotels there. What do you think of the idea?'

'Like you, I can't think of anything better,' I answered. 'While you were talking to me just now, it occurred to me that perhaps we ought to make inquiries at the hotels near Paddington, and start from there. But if your uncle said he was going to Falmouth, that seems the obvious place to begin with. You know, Dick, I think we ought both to sleep over this. Perhaps you'll find your uncle safely at home when you arrive. I may have some brighter ideas to-morrow. I suppose you couldn't have lunch with me in the City?'

'Yes, I could,' he said. 'I shall be going to our City office to-morrow.'

'Well then, come round to my office about one, and we'll go out somewhere. I feel, after to-night, that it ought to be the Savoy. Meanwhile, I'll sound my partners as to the possibility of my being away on Monday and Tuesday, just in case we do go to Falmouth. How long did you think of staying there?'

'I thought we'd motor down in my car on Saturday, and come back on Monday or Tuesday, according to circumstances.'

'Can you get away from your business all right without telling them why you're going, I mean?'

'Oh, yes. In any case, Uncle Hamilton means nothing to my directors, now that Uncle George is dead. I doubt if the Bagshaws know of his existence. Well, Malcolm, thank you very much. It's funny how each of one's real friends, one's few real friends, seems to have a special niche in one's life which no one else can fill. There's no one else I could have talked to as I've talked to you to-night, on this particular subject. You've been a great comfort.'

'You said I once called you meretricious,' I remarked, as he went out into the hall, 'but you've called me many worse things than that in your day.'

He laughed, and said: 'Oh, *non sum qualis eram.* That's been made pretty clear to you by now, hasn't it? Don't come down with me. Good-night, and many thanks. Till to-morrow at one. *Au revoir.*'

When he had gone I sat in my arm-chair for a quarter of an hour, thinking, not of the 'case,' but of Dick himself, and how he had changed since I first knew him. And mingled with these thoughts was the image which he himself had suggested, the image of Dick as a boy of sixteen, sitting by a bedroom window at Tylecroft, his head full of dreams and half-forbidden books, while the spring rain beat perpetually against the peach blossom on the wall.

2.
Friday, June 11th

When I was at school, and had to do Latin Verses, I used to find that if I slept on them they would be almost 'done' when I awoke the next morning—not necessarily well 'done,' but sufficiently knocked into shape to serve up to my form master.

It was with something of this sort in my mind that I let Dick's problem 'cook' all night in the 'oven' of my subconsciousness. When I awoke however, the first thing I recalled from our long conversation of the night before was an apparently aimless scrap of information—the address of Dick's cousin, William Hicks: Cantervale Nurseries, Sedcombe, Surrey. I had an almost blank notebook by my bed, and wrote the address down in it, resolving to dedicate the notebook to the 'case.'

But was there a 'case'? While I was sipping my morning tea, another thought occurred to me. So far, the only real ground for assuming that there was a 'case' lay in Uncle Hamilton's failure to turn up for dinner with Dr. Fielding on Tuesday night. Was it not possible that Uncle Hamilton had written both to Dr. Fielding and Dick or Mrs. Pressley, saying that he was extending his holiday, and cancelling the dinner. It was perhaps too much to suppose that both letters must have been lost in the post. Well, one letter would have been enough. He could have said to Dick or Mrs. Pressley, please ring up Dr. Fielding and put him off till next week. Even so, it wasn't necessary to assume that this one letter had been lost. Perhaps it was never posted, either through absentmindedness on Uncle Hamilton's part or through the carelessness of someone, a hall porter or a chambermaid, to whom he gave it to post. I resolved to ask Dick if his uncle was absentminded. But even if he wasn't, I could fall back on a careless hall porter.

I became quite convinced that when we went to Falmouth we should come across Uncle Hamilton ambling round the harbour, or sitting on the beach. Of course, every day he failed to turn up, the situation became a little graver. He certainly ought to write another letter towards the end of the week, and it would be too much of a coincidence to suppose, if such a letter were not received, that it had been written, but again had not been posted for some innocent reason.

When I was in my bath I expected to hear the telephone any minute, with Dick at the other end telling me that his uncle had written, or returned in person. But the telephone, which is specially fond of ringing when I am in my bath, did not ring that morning.

I reached the office, and while I performed my dull little tasks there, I still expected Dick to ring up and say that all was well. I was hoping he would, for despite the way in which he had both flattered me and won my sympathy, I was not greatly looking forward to our Cornish trip. With another companion I might have enjoyed it, but I still had misgivings about spending forty-eight hours or more in Dick's exclusive society.

I had to answer the telephone several times, but no Dick spoke to me. Instead, it was Miss A., asking why she hadn't got the interest on her War Loan (which she had sold six months before), Colonel B., complaining that our commission was too high (yet we had charged him the minimum allowed), and Lady C., whose daughter wanted to put twenty-five pounds into tin shares (but, of course, they mustn't be speculative).

I took the opportunity, during the morning, to make sure that I could be away from the office on Monday and Tuesday, without inconveniencing anyone. Luckily my partners decided that they could refrain from Ascot till the Wednesday. At five minutes to one I went downstairs and waited in the vestibule. I felt that Dick, in his rather nervous condition, wouldn't want to run the gauntlet of the office upstairs. He arrived exactly to time.

I said, 'Well?' and he said, 'Still no news. Mrs. Pressley's getting rather out of hand. She wants me to go to the police at once. I still think we ought to nose about in Cornwall first, don't you?'

I agreed, and as we walked to the restaurant I told him my idea of the lost letter, or the letter which had never been posted. He said it would have been quite "out of character" for his uncle to forget to post a letter, but admitted that we couldn't rule out forgetfulness on the part of a hall porter. But, even so, his uncle wasn't the person to give his letters to other people to post. 'He is incapable,' Dick said, 'of behaving in the rather lordly way in which you or I might behave. He can hardly bring himself to leave his hat and coat in a cloak-room. When he travels, he likes to carry his own bag. Not, of course, because he thinks it wrong to demand personal service from other people, but because he's suspicious and afraid that someone will do him down. The fact that his envelope had a stamp on it would have been quite a sufficient incentive to make him post it himself. In his view, all strangers are capable of stealing three ha'pence. That's why, of course, the little man could never really pretend to be a gentleman.'

This last remark shocked me a little, but I had to admit that from a psychological point of view Dick was probably quite right. Uncle Hamilton wasn't the type to say airily to a flunkey: 'Here's a shilling. Please see that this letter goes at once'—as Dick himself would have done in his salad days. No. The letter had either been lost in the post, or it had never been written. To Cornwall we must go.

During our indifferent luncheon—and nowadays luncheon in the City is apt to be a most indifferent meal—we made arrangements about the expedition. He suggested calling for me at nine with his car. Was that too early? No, I would make an effort. He suggested we should stay at the Greenbank Hotel, and I asked him if we ought to wire for rooms. He said he didn't think it necessary, as the holiday season was still a long way from beginning. I asked him what we should do if we found his uncle was staying at the Greenbank. He said that before taking rooms we must make sure that Uncle Hamilton wasn't there. Another reason for not wiring beforehand. Besides, the Greenbank was too good for Uncle Hamilton, and, being down by the harbour, was at the opposite end of the town to the parts which Uncle Hamilton might be expected to visit—the rather characterless area of the bathing beaches.

I asked him if Uncle Hamilton would tend to stay in a pub or a boarding house, and he replied, 'boarding house,' with great conviction. No hotel could be too boarding-housy for Uncle Hamilton's taste. I said I supposed Uncle Hamilton was a teetotaller, though I remembered a modicum of alcohol eking out the evening I had spent at Tylecroft. But apparently it wasn't so bad as all that. Uncle Hamilton drank a little sherry, cheap claret, sweet port, and a whisky-and-soda before going to bed. He disapproved of cocktails, white wines and liqueurs. I foresaw that in course of time I should get to know as much about Uncle Hamilton's habits as a personal maid does about her mistress. It seemed a pity that the object of my study was so unworthy.

We sat talking over our coffee till a quarter-past two, and I said *au revoir* to Dick by the Old Broad Street entrance of the Stock Exchange. The afternoon, like many Friday afternoons, was uneventful.

Before dinner that day I had to go to a cocktail party given by one of my clients, who lived north of the Park. I arrived there about half-past six, having called at my flat and changed into a less shiny suit. It was a big party; I knew hardly anyone, and as so often in the houses of the rich, the cocktails were bad. I was thankful to make my escape at a quarter-past seven.

On the way home I passed the end of Westbourne Terrace, and an impulse came over me to walk up it, as Uncle Hamilton must have walked up it when Dick had said goodbye to him. It was really the morbid curiosity of the sightseer who goes to see the house in which a tragedy has occurred, even though no trace of the tragedy is visible. Indeed, I could hardly hope to find the spot where Uncle Hamilton stepped out of Dick's life marked with a cross, like one's bedroom on a picture postcard.

I walked the whole length of that broad thoroughfare on the western side of the road. Dick had been coming from South London and must therefore have driven on the western side. Needless to say, I found nothing in the nature of a 'clue,' nor was I seriously looking for one. At the end of the street, however, it did occur to me that by walking on vaguely in the direction of Paddington Station I might see an hotel in which I could conceive Uncle Hamilton spending the night. There was no harm in making sure that he did spend the night in the neighbourhood of the railway, even if I couldn't trace him to the train he was supposed to have taken to Cornwall on the Saturday. I resolved that if I saw a really suitable hotel I would go in and make inquiries. It would give me a little practice in detection, which I badly needed. Perhaps my cocktails, weak though they were, emboldened me.

I have always maintained that when an ordinary member of the public is confronted with a crime or a mystery he bases his conduct on the detective stories he has read. I have read a good many detective stories and find them a sedative for the nerves. Oddly enough, what I like in them isn't so much the puzzle of the plot, still less sensational hairbreadth escapes, but precisely the element which you would least expect to find in such stories—the humdrum background, tea at the Vicarage, a morning in an office, a trip to Brighton pier—that microscopic study of ordinary life which is the foil to the extraordinary event which interrupts it. A good detective story, I have found, is often a clearer mirror or ordinary life than many a novel written specially to portray it. Indeed, I think a test of its goodness is the pleasure you can derive from it even though you know who the murderer is. A historian of the future will probably turn, not to blue books or statistics, but to detective stories if he wishes to study the manners of our age. Middle-class manners perhaps. But I am old-fashioned enough to enjoy the individualism of the middle class.

I hoped very much, as I wandered round the purlieus of Paddington, that if by a lucky chance I succeeded in finding Uncle Hamilton's hotel, the porter or receptionist would live up to detective-story standards, just as I hoped that I should live up to the standard of a detective, be nippy with my half-crown (which in detective stories never fails to work wonders), put my questions ingratiatingly but firmly, and not look too sheepish if I met with a rebuff.

I passed two or three dirty-looking hotels without going inside. They seemed too 'pubby' for Uncle Hamilton. Then in a side street I came across the Strafford Royal, drab but respectable, so far as I could tell from the facade. I went up a flight of indifferently cleaned marble steps, through a swing-door into a lofty dark hall. No one was in sight, and I rang a big brass bell, which said 'press,' by a little glazed enclosure. A voice in the darkness said, 'Who can that be, Flo?' and a moment later a small henna-haired lady darted in and sat on a stool behind the glass partition, as if she had been sitting there for ever.

Was it a case for the nimble half-crown? I thought not.

'I'm sorry to bother you,' I said, 'but have you a Mr. Hamilton Findlay staying here?'

'Hamilton Findlay,' she said, probably trying to sum me up. 'No, we've nobody of that name.'

She produced a book and gave it a quick glance.

'I believe he arrived here late last Friday night,' I suggested.

'Last Friday night,' she repeated, consulting another book. 'Oh, but he left early on Saturday morning. Here's the name.'

She showed me the hotel register, and I saw under the heading, 'Friday, June 4th,' the rather copperplate signature: E. Hamilton Findlay.

'That's quite right,' I said as determinedly as I could. 'That's the gentleman I want to see. May I ask if it was you who received him?'

'No,' she said. 'He didn't arrive till after ten. It would be Timpson, the porter, who let him in.'

'I wonder if I could have a word with Timpson,' I said tentatively. (*Have a word with*—that's a real detective-story phrase.)

'Well, I dare say you could,' she said rather sniffily, 'though I'm sure I don't quite know what your business is.'

'I'm a friend of Mr. Findlay's,' I answered, improvising hurriedly, 'and I thought he was still here. I see, now, there was a misunderstanding. I should be very grateful if you could fetch Timpson for me.'

'Well, I suppose I can,' she conceded. 'Will you wait here?'

I waited, full of eagerness to try my half-crown on Timpson. After a few minutes he arrived—an elderly little hunchback. Evidently, the henna lady didn't find me interesting enough to come with him.

I displayed my half-crown at once, blushing as I did so.

'I wonder if you could give me any information,' I

asked, 'about my friend Mr. Hamilton Findlay, whom, I'm told, you admitted here last Friday night, a week ago to-day. Do you remember?'

The hunchback scratched his head, and turned up the register.

'E. Hamilton Findlay,' he said laboriously. 'A little bald man with horn spectacles?'

'No,' I said, 'that doesn't sound very much like him.'

He meditated for a moment and said: 'Oh, I remember. It was getting on for eleven, or maybe it was after. A gent with a bag which he carried himself. Tallish. Wore a wig, I thought. Can't remember much else.'

'Yes,' I said. 'That's the man.'

'Well, he went straight to No. 9. Said he was leaving next morning from Paddington by the 8.15 for Cornwall. Asked for breakfast in his bedroom at a quarter-past seven. I said that would be a shilling extra, but he said all right. I showed him up to his room, and that's the last I seen of him.'

'You weren't here when he left the next day?'

'No, not on Saturdays. Miss Elder would have been here to take the cash. She's the young lady you saw. Would you like to see her again?'

My heart failed me. I gave Timpson the half-crown, with which I had been making excessive demonstrations, and said: 'No, if you say he went the next morning, that's good enough for me. Thank you very much, and good-night.'

I walked quickly through the swing-door and down the steps, almost as if I were a guilty party. Then, as I moved at a more contemplative pace towards the Park and home, I began to congratulate myself on my beginner's luck. Or was I really rather good? No, I wasn't very good. I had only traced Uncle Hamilton into the hotel. I hadn't traced him out again. That was because I was frightened of the supercilious henna lady. She could never have unnerved a real detective. Still, for the time being there didn't seem much need to pursue this investigation much further. In twenty-four hours I should be trying my skill in Cornwall, and if I was able to trace Uncle Hamilton there I could certainly assume that he had travelled from Paddington by the 8.15.

Half-way across the Park I sat down on a seat, took out my notebook, now grandiosely entitled 'Warren's Third Case,' and wrote:

Friday, June 11th.—Discovered that Hamilton Findlay arrived at Strafford Royal Hotel, Paddington, 'getting on for eleven or maybe after' on the night of Friday, June 4th. Had Room No. 9. Ordered breakfast in it, and announced his intention of catching the 8.15 for Cornwall the next morning. Witness, Timpson, hotel porter. Possible further witness, Miss Elder, assistant manageress. Saw Hamilton Findlay's signature in visitors' book. Slightly shaky copperplate.

Then I walked home, had an excellent little dinner cooked by my housekeeper, Mrs. Rhodes, read a depressing book about international affairs, did *The Times* crossword puzzle, and went to bed.

3.

Saturday, June 12th

DICK FINDLAY called for me with aggressive punctuality. Indeed, he hustled me so much that I forgot to pack my bedroom slippers. But this is of no consequence. Dick was excited, almost gay, and eager to be off. He said he had asked Mrs. Pressley to make some sandwiches, so that we needn't waste time stopping for lunch. If only I'd hurry, we should get to Falmouth by half-past four. He added as he put my suitcase into the huge luggage compartment of his car, that Mrs. Pressley was getting quite out of hand. She had declared that morning that if she had no word of Uncle Hamilton by Tuesday night she would go to the police herself.

'I don't blame her,' Dick said. 'It's quite beyond a joke now. Apart from everything else, I've had to provide the money for the household bills.'

I didn't produce my piece of news till he had got through Staines and had a fairly clear road. Then I said: 'Your uncle spent the night of Friday the 4th at the Strafford Royal Hotel, Paddington.'

He was so taken aback that he almost failed to get round a corner.

'How on earth did you discover that?' he asked.

'I have my methods,' I said with banal classicism. Then, of course, I told him exactly what I had done. He professed a lively admiration, and said that he would certainly leave the investigation of the Falmouth hotels entirely to me. In any event, it was better that I should undertake it, in case his uncle happened to be there in the flesh. He would never forgive Dick for spying on him. If I were confronted by him, I should have to make what excuse I could. And it wouldn't matter very much if I wasn't convincing—not being the poor relation.

As road conditions improved, we talked less. Dick kept the Packard going at nearly seventy miles an hour from Stonehenge onwards. I hadn't seen Stonehenge before, and thought it looked insignificant from the road. It was a pleasant day, despite an excess of cloud, and I enjoyed the desolate country which we passed. Dick explained that there was not one really big town between us and Exeter. By taking the northern route we missed Salisbury, Shaftesbury, Yeovil, Crewkerne and Chard, and didn't rejoin the main road, A 30, till a few miles before Honiton. Ilchester and Ilminster were in no way formidable to the motorist.

We stopped for a few minutes between those two towns and ate our luncheon—horrible fatty beef sandwiches, and some bread and cheese. I wished that I had thought of asking Mrs. Rhodes to try one of her delicious mayonnaise effects. She is almost as clever as the Americans at producing savoury sandwiches. Then I reminded myself that real detectives set no store by the palate when on the chase.

We reached Exeter about half-past two, and crawled through the bottle-neck. I thought I had never seen a town with so crowded a main street and so many traffic lights, each one of which made us stop.

'Exeter,' said Dick, 'is the last outpost of civilisation.'

'On the contrary,' I answered. 'Civilisation begins after Exeter, the moment we cross the Tamar and get into Cornwall.'

We both seemed to know Cornwall up to a point. Dick confessed to having spent a romantic week-end in Falmouth the year before. But he didn't really like the county, while I did. I asked him if he knew of any previous visit to Cornwall on the part of Uncle Hamilton. He said he knew of none. Uncle Hamilton was a most stereotyped traveller.

'I'm beginning to think,' Dick said, 'that there simply must be a lady in the case. On the other hand, he may have seen a railway advertisement, and been seized with sudden impulse. Perhaps we do yield more to sudden impulses as we grow older.'

Having safely crossed the Tamar we touched eighty over Bodmin Moor. A heavy bank of clouds to the west made me glad that I had brought my mackintosh. I foresaw us spending Sunday trudging drearily about in the rain as I went incompetently from hotel to hotel. I said as much to Dick, and he replied: 'You are a wet blanket, Malcolm. Don't you see that this is your great chance? If you make good, you'll be able to set up as a private detective, and leave the Stock Exchange. Besides, it's very good for you to be jolted out of your fixed habits. You're growing prematurely old.' I said I thought there was nothing to be afraid of in old age, which seemed to promise the kind of happiness I wanted. 'Already,' I said, 'I loathe the energetic fanaticism of youth. I'm building myself up for the contemplative life. Have you forgotten Aristotle's "Ethics"?'

He reminded me that he had taken a science school, not Greats, and I thought to myself, I'm not sure that I really like scientists. It was probably those beef sandwiches disagreeing with me.

But when we had passed Truro, and were driving along the edge of the tidal water by Perranarworthal, only half a dozen miles from Falmouth, I began to feel as excited as I imagined Dick to be. After all it was a kind of chase, this hunt for the missing uncle. It would make another Catherine's death and my experiences during a Christmas in Hampstead.* Not for nothing had I inscribed my notebook with the words, 'Warren's Third Case.' If only I could live up to my hitherto undeserved reputation. In my first two cases I had been 'in at the death' in a very real sense. Could I hope for a similar stroke of luck? But why think of death on this occasion? In all probability we should unearth nothing more than a domestic scandal. I should run across Uncle Hamilton in the dining-room of an hotel, and by his side would be sitting a 'flaming cocotte,' to use Dick's phrase, devouring strawberries with gross red lips.

The Greenbank Hotel, our destination, is almost at the very beginning of Falmouth as you approach the town from Truro. Dick drove the car a little way beyond the front door and asked me to see to the engaging of rooms, with the proviso that we were not to stay there if by any chance Uncle Hamilton was in residence.

Accordingly, my first question to the receptionist was: 'Can you tell me if you have a Mr. Hamilton Findlay staying here? I think he arrived last Saturday, just a week ago.'

To my relief the answer was in the negative. No Mr. Findlay had arrived the previous Saturday, or since then.

'Oh,' I said, 'I had hoped to find him here. But it can't be helped. I wonder if you can let me have two rooms? My friend is outside with his car.'

We were lucky enough to be given two adjoining rooms facing the harbour, with a bathroom just across the passage. Dick came in with the porter who carried our luggage, and after unpacking and washing we had tea in the lounge. It was now about a quarter-past five. I should have liked to sit there for some time, looking through those long windows at the broad waters and the boats, but Dick was eager to be up and doing.

'I told you we shouldn't find Uncle Hamilton here,' he said. 'The kind of hotel he'd go to is right at the other end

*See *Death of my Aunt*, and *Crime at Christmas*.

of the town. There are about twelve of them where you may have to inquire. I think I'd better drive you to the promenade, and hang about till you report progress.'

'What am I to do if I do find him?' I asked.

He hesitated a moment, and then said: 'If by any awful chance you meet him face to face—well then, I suppose, you'll have to say that you're down here with me, and that we are looking for him. That will be a pity if he's here on an unofficial honeymoon, but we must risk that. I should give him a chance of saying that he did write home and that the letter must have gone astray. That's the theory you produced yesterday, you remember. But even if the worst happens, and he thinks we've come down here to spy on his romance, we just can't help it. We *have* come here to find him, after all.'

I agreed somewhat ruefully. I didn't relish the task of interviewing a whole series of haughty ladies in glass cages, and saw no great reason why Dick shouldn't do the work himself, but he reminded me again that our object was to find Uncle Hamilton without letting him know that we were looking for him. I was a stranger to him, in spite of our one meeting, and stood a much better chance than Dick of making a get-away.

When we had driven through the narrow main street of the town, and emerged the other side on the 'visitors' quarter,' Dick stopped the car on the promenade and suggested that I should make my expedition on foot. The whole promenade seemed to be lined with hotels and boarding houses. Dick advised me to leave the big and probably expensive ones alone, for the time being, and to concentrate on those which looked thoroughly respectable but cheap.

For a few minutes I walked up and down surveying them from this point of view. The first one at which I called was the St. Griffian. Here, as at our own hotel, the Greenbank, I met with an efficient negative. I apologised for troubling the lady, and passed on to the next building, which was entitled Ocean Glory. Here, to my consternation, the porter with whom I was talking responded to the name Findlay at once.

'Yes, sir,' he said. 'He arrived last Tuesday. He's still here, and I think I saw him go into the smoking-room about ten minutes ago.'

'Tuesday?' I said. 'I thought it was last Saturday, but—'

While I spoke he turned up the visitors' book.

'No, sir, it was Tuesday. Mr. H. Findlay. I'm quite sure you'll find him in now, if you'll just come across the hall with me. What name shall I say, sir?'

'Er, Warren,' I answered, 'but really—'

There was no escape, and I followed the porter through the hall. At the end of it was a door bearing the legend 'Smoking-room' in white letters on the brown paint. He opened it and went inside, leaving me cursing my clumsiness on the threshold. After a minute he reappeared and said: 'Mr. Findlay will see you, sire, though he says he hasn't the pleasure of your acquaintance,' and opened the door ceremoniously.

I found myself face to face with a very tall man wearing pince-nez. It was true I hadn't seen Uncle Hamilton for three years, but I could hardly believe I had formed so inaccurate a memory of him.

'Mr. Hamilton Findlay?' I said tentatively, and he replied testily:

'No, sir; my name is Henry Findlay, not Hamilton. I think you must be under some misapprehension.'

I admitted at once that I was, and extricated myself from the hotel with apologies to the false Mr. Findlay, and a gift of half a crown to the porter. 'Next time,' I vowed, 'I won't be caught like that. I'll have a look at the visitors' book before I submit to a personal interview. What a fool I've made of myself here!'

As I returned disconsolately to the promenade, I found Dick waiting about for me. I told him quickly of my failures, and also of my resolve to look in the visitors' book before taking any action.

'It occurred to me that one ought to proceed like that,' he said. 'I meant to give you this before so that you could identify Uncle Hamilton's signature.'

He took a cheque, a cleared cheque, from his note-case and gave it to me. It was for nineteen pounds ten shillings, payable to E. Hamilton Findlay, Esq., and signed by Dick himself.

'It's my quarterly payment for board and lodging at Tylecroft,' Dick explained. 'You'll find my uncle's endorsement on the back. My bank always sends me my cleared cheques with my monthly account, and I brought this one in case it might be useful. What an idiot I was to forget it till now!'

I turned the cheque over and looked at the back, which bore the copperplate but rather spidery signature, 'E. Hamilton Findlay.' So far as I could remember it tallied exactly with the signature I had seen in the visitors' book of the Strafford Royal, Paddington. I told Dick so, and he said: 'Yes, it's an easy signature to memorise—like a senile clerk's, isn't it?'

'Well,' I said, 'I suppose I must go straight ahead. I rather like the look of this next place—what's it called? The Radnor. I think there's probably a bar where I can get a drink.'

'For that reason,' Dick suggested, 'I think it's most unlikely that you'll find Uncle Hamilton there. Look at that neon sign and those fairy lights. They'd put him off at once. I should give it a miss, and the one beyond, too, which looks much too big and expensive.'

'Oh,' I said, 'I think I may as well take them in order. I shall develop my technique soon, and shan't be so long. Will you wait for me here?'

He said he would, and I went into the Radnor, secretly relieved at the thought that Uncle Hamilton was unlikely to have stayed there owing to its comparative grandeur.

Instead of going at once to the reception office I sat down in a wicker chair in the lounge and asked a waiter to bring me a whisky-and-soda. When the drink arrived I paid for it at once, and gave the waiter so lavish a tip that he almost demurred.

'Oh, that's all right,' I said with a lordly air. 'But I'll tell you what you can do for me. You might let me see your visitors' book. The friend of a business acquaintance of mine was to have arrived here last Saturday, and I should like to get in touch with him if I can.'

'What name would that be, sir?' asked the waiter.

I tried to laugh convincingly, and said: 'Oddly enough, I simply can't remember, though I should know it if I saw it. I have an idea it begins with F—something like Francis, or Franklin, or Freeman. I've seen business letters from him, and I think I should recognise his handwriting.'

The more I talked, the more I feared that the waiter would think my story very thin, if not suspicious. But he was young, and had been well tipped, and volunteered to fetch me the book at once. Luckily there were only two old ladies in the lounge apart from myself, and they were sitting some distance away from me. I was not eager that anyone should overhear my conversation with the waiter, or observe him committing what was probably an irregularity. After all, a visitor's book is surely a confidential document.

When the waiter had fetched if for me, I turned up Saturday, June 5th. There were eleven arrivals, no Findlay among them, but there was a visitor named Franks. The waiter, who was looking over my shoulder, pointed to the name with a triumphant finger.

'No,' I said, 'I'm afraid that isn't it. It's something like the name, but the handwriting is all wrong. It's far too small and fiddling. I'm looking for a much bolder kind of signature. If you don't mind, I'll just go through the other pages to date.'

I turned over to Sunday, June 6th. Four arrivals. Still no

Findlay, but instead a name which caused me to feel no less surprise—William Hicks, Sedcombe, Surrey. What on earth was Cousin Bill, the nurseryman, doing there? According to the book he had stayed only one night.

'Do you remember this gentleman?' I asked the waiter.

'Yes, sir. I was here when he arrived, and got him to sign, as Miss Grayson was out. A big, well-made gentleman, isn't he?'

'Yes. As a matter of fact he's an acquaintance of mine, too. Do you know what train he came by?'

'Oh, he didn't come by train, so far as I know. He had a big car with him. Almost more like a commercial van than a car it was. He must have left fairly early on Monday morning, when I was off duty.'

'Well,' I said, feeling that I might have been unguarded in admitting that I knew Cousin Bill, 'he isn't the gentleman I was looking for. In fact, Mr. Freeman, or whatever his wretched name is, doesn't seem to have stayed here.'

I looked quickly through the remaining pages, gave the book to the waiter with another tip, and got up from my seat.

'I'm very much obliged to you,' I said, and then, seeing a manageress approaching through a side door, I left the building as quickly as I could.

Outside I saw no Dick, but assumed that as I had been rather a long time in the Radnor he had lost patience and gone somewhere for a drink. I decided not to wait for him, but went straight to the next hotel, which resembled the Radnor, though it was more tawdry and less clean—not at all the kind of hotel which Uncle Hamilton would have chosen.

I was received by so formidable a manageress that I hadn't the courage to tell her the story I had told to the waiter in the Radnor. Instead I just asked feebly for Mr. Hamilton Findlay. The lady turned over the pages of her book ungraciously and said that she had no such visitor. As she did so it occurred to me suddenly that if Uncle Hamilton had gone to Falmouth for some naughty purpose, he might have assumed a false name. Acquainted though I was with his real signature, I doubted whether I should recognise his writing if he had written anything but his real name. Still, I felt I ought to see the book for myself, and asked the manageress, through her *guichet*, if she would show it to me. Her reply was: 'Certainly not. We don't show our visitors' book to strangers. Besides, I've looked through it for you myself. We've had no Findlay here since Saturday, nor all this year, so far as I can remember.'

I went out feeling greatly depressed.

The next hotel was small but clean, a more likely hunting-ground. I was received by an agreeable young girl, and was bold enough to ask straight out if I might see the register. She allowed me to do so without hesitation, but it contained no Findlay, and no signature which was suggestive of his handwriting.

I looked back along the promenade, saw Dick's empty car, and decided that after two more failures I would 'strike,' go back to the car and wait for him. I had begun to feel a little self-conscious, popping into all those hotels and out again, like an unwanted commercial traveller, and hoped that nobody on the promenade was following my movements.

The next hotel was very small indeed—little more than a bungalow. I waited for five minutes in the tiny entrance-hall without seeing signs of life. Then a youth in flannel trousers and pullover open at the neck came downstairs, whistling loudly. I asked him if he knew where I could find the proprietor, and he said: 'No, I think Mrs. Reeves has gone out. Is there anything I can do for you?'

'I wanted to ask if I could have a look at the visitors' book,' I said. 'I rather think a friend of mine is staying here.'

'Is it Colonel Hitchcock, by any chance?'

'No,' I said with some doubt in my voice. After all, Uncle

Hamilton might have called himself Colonel Hitchcock, though it seemed a little "out of character".

'Well,' he said obligingly, 'I think I can get you the book. In fact, it's here on this table. But I don't think there have been any arrivals in the last fortnight—since I came here with my aunt, that is.'

He was right. The last entry was Miss G. Swinton, Nottingham, with Albert Swinton, ditto, written underneath, and the date was May 27th. I thanked him, and went once more on to the promenade.

The next hotel was separated from me by a broad road, Tregaskis Avenue, which ran inland at right angles to the sea. Instead of crossing it directly I walked up it a little way, and was disgusted to find that on both sides it was strewn with hotels and boarding houses, all of them quite suitable as abodes for Uncle Hamilton. The task seemed endless, and I felt confirmed in my resolve to abandon it after one more attempt.

The corner hotel, which faced both the promenade and Tregaskis Avenue, was called Trepolpen Lodge. As I went up the front steps I decided to employ the method I had used at the Radnor, though I could hardly hope to meet anybody as ingenuous as the waiter who had fallen so readily into my unskilful trap. However, I reminded myself that a generous tip was worth any amount of skill, and fumbled for a half crown in my trouser pocket, wondering if I should ever present Dick with a bill for my expenses.

The first person I met in the hall was a benign, military-looking porter—eminently tippable, I thought. I let my half-crown glitter between my thumb and finger.

'I'm looking for a business acquaintance,' I said, 'who I think is staying here, or was a day or two ago. I stupidly can't be quite sure of his name, though I know his handwriting quite well. I wonder if you could help me by letting me see your visitors' book for the past week?'

The porter looked at me searchingly for a minute or two, while I found myself blushing slightly.

'Are you sure you don't remember the gentleman's name?' he asked.

'Well,' I answered, 'I'm quite sure of it, I think it begins with F—Francis, or Findlay, or something like that. If I could see the entries—'

'We had a Mr. Findlay arrive here last Saturday afternoon. He left on Monday morning. A middle-aged gentleman with a wig.'

I nearly jumped with excitement.

'Yes, that must have been the person I mean. Findlay, of course, that was the name. E. H. Findlay, I think.'

Without speaking to me the porter went into a small office from which I heard the sound of voices—his and that of a presumed manageress. I was hoping I should not have to deal with the manageress as well, when he came out again, bringing the precious book.

'Miss Harpenden has no objection to your seeing it,' he told me, 'though she says it's a little irregular.'

With trembling hand I turned up the page allotted to June 5th, and there, heading the list of arrivals for the day, I saw, in a spidery copperplate, the name, E. Hamilton Findlay, South Mersley.

'That's my man without a doubt,' I said. 'But you say he left on Monday?'

'Yes, Monday morning,' he began; but at that moment a grey-haired female head emerged from the office and said: 'Ormerod, be as quick as you can, will you! I must get these accounts checked before seven.'

As the head withdrew, I quickly gave Ormerod my half-crown and searched for another.

'I see you're very busy now,' I said, 'and I ought to be going, too. But there are several things I should like to ask you about this Mr. Findlay. I wonder if I could call and see you later, say after dinner. I'm staying at the Greenbank.'*

I saw that this address made me rise in his esteem, and

*The St. Griffian, Ocean Glory, Radnor, and Trepolpen are imaginary hotels. The Greenbank is real, and most excellent.

went on, 'I should like a private talk if possible. As perhaps you've guessed already, the circumstances aren't quite usual.'

'Well, sir,' he said, 'all this sounds very mysterious to me, but if you like to be outside the staff entrance at 8.45, when I'm off duty, I shall be delighted to do anything I can to help you—that is, if you can satisfy me that the business is quite *bona fide*.'

'Oh, it's certainly that!' I said. 'I'm not acting in any way against Mr. Findlay's interests. Quite the contrary. But I'll tell you more when I see you at 8.45. Goodbye till then.'

As I spoke the grey-haired lady emerged from her sanctum, and I fled down the front steps, leaving the porter to make what explanations he could. Then, a little breathlessly, I made my way back to the car. As I had expected, Dick was sitting inside waiting for me. When I was half-a-dozen paces away from him I shouted, 'Found!'

He jumped out of the car, ran towards me and seized my arm.

'What! Is he here?'

'No; left last Monday. But he spent Saturday to Monday at Trepolpen Lodge.'

'And where is he now?'

'Now? Oh, I'm afraid I can't tell you that yet! But we may get more news after dinner, when you've got to interview Mr. Ormerod, the Trepolpen's head porter. Now take me back to our hotel for a drink, will you, and I'll tell you all my adventures.'

We got into the car, and as he drove back to the Greenbank I gave him a slightly serio-comic account of what I had done since he deserted me—intent on a drink for himself, I gathered.

Once or twice he was so excited that I had to caution him to look to his driving in the narrow main street, which had suddenly become as crowded as the promenade had been deserted.

When I told him that his cousin, Bill Hicks, had been

staying at the Radnor, he nearly ran into a motor-bus.

'Did you know Cousin Bill was holiday-making down here?' I asked.

'No, I didn't,' he replied, 'though I'm not sure some weeks ago that he didn't say something about having to visit Cornwall fairly soon. I think he has dealings with a nursery-garden here. He must have motored down with his nursery-van. I wonder if he came across Uncle Hamilton. I shall have to get in touch with him as soon as we get back, unless your porter is able to tell us a good deal more. Well, here we are. Let's have a drink first, then a wash, then dinner. Then I'll drive you round to the Trepolpen again.'

What with the long motor-drive from London, my exertions on the promenade, and an excellent dinner, I felt more inclined for bed than for further work that evening. However, it was clearly essential to have a talk with Ormerod, and Dick was quite right to whip me away from my coffee and drive me back to the junction of Tregaskis Avenue and the promenade. I had assumed that he would conduct the interview with Ormerod, and that I should be allowed to relax in a pub while he did so. But it was Dick who was to do the relaxing. 'You'll manage better than I should,' he said, 'and it'll only flurry your porter if two of us turn up to see him. I'm still rather frightened of seeming to spy on Uncle Hamilton.'

'But he's left the town,' I interrupted.

'I know, but he may be coming back, or the porter may still be in touch with him. There isn't much in it, of course, and I dare say it's simply a complex of mind, but, as you've started the ball rolling, I do think it will be better if you see things through. You've done splendidly so far. And, of course, you must let me provide you with ammunition.'

He gave me a pound and four half-crowns. I demurred a little, but gave in. After all, when it came to the point I should have been disappointed if I had had to be merely a listener while Dick questioned Ormerod, and I knew that if I was to do the questioning, I should be less self-conscious if Dick were not there to criticise me. Accordingly, we arranged that Dick should wait for me in the bar of the Feathered Owl—a pub at the far end of the High Street, which, he said, was quite amusing on Saturday nights—unless my researches occupied me till past closing time, in which event I was to make my way back to the Greenbank.

It was ten to nine when Dick dropped me at the Trepolpen, and I found Ormerod pacing outside the staff entrance in Tregaskis Avenue. He was wearing a blue lounge-coat over the trousers of his uniform.

'I was wondering if you'd turn up,' he said.

I apologised for being late, and blamed the Greenbank's excellent dinner. He suggested that we should stroll up Tregaskis Avenue to the top end, where there were a few seats in a small public garden. We were less likely to be interrupted there, he said, than if we sat on the promenade. I asked him if he wouldn't prefer to have a drink with me somewhere, but he replied that he was a teetotaller. Indeed, he did seem to be almost formidably respectable, and I felt no doubt that anything he told me would be the truth.

'I'd better tell you,' I began, as we walked up the hill, 'that I was deceiving you when I said I couldn't feel sure of Findlay's name. I remembered it perfectly, but I wanted to see the signature in your visitors' book, so to be certain I was on the track of the right Mr. Findlay. Already to-day I've been introduced to a complete stranger named Findlay, and I didn't want that to happen again. The truth is, I'm very worried about Mr. Findlay, who has failed to turn up and keep an appointment, and can't be traced at home. As you know, one doesn't like to rush off to the police in these cases. He may have perfectly good private reasons for staying out of touch with his friends for a time, and I dare say he wouldn't thank me for making these inquiries. So if, as I very much hope, Mr. Findlay does reappear in due course, I want to be able to rely on your saying nothing to him about me. You can regard me, if you like, as an amateur detective—a very amateur one.'

He paused in his stride and studied me for a moment.

'Yes,' he said; 'you don't look much like the real thing. But I think you look all right. You needn't be afraid that I shall let on about you, even if Mr. Findlay does turn up again. And it isn't as if I'm telling you anything he could mind you knowing. So far as that goes, I've really nothing to tell you. He just behaved like an ordinary visitor, rather quieter than some, though we don't get the rowdy sort at our place. If we sit here, we can watch the sunset. Our visitors are usually keen on sunsets and that sort of thing.'

We sat down on an iron seat in the middle of a triangular patch of public garden. Apart from a young man and woman walking arm in arm up the hill towards the great open spaces, we were alone. Indeed, this end of Falmouth seemed quite deserted, in contrast with the High Street and the part of town near the harbour. The clouds of the afternoon had largely dispersed, and there was a pink glow in the western sky which augured well for Sunday's weather. I felt I ought to have been more romantically employed than in listening to the hall porter's account of Uncle Hamilton's prosaic little actions.

He had arrived, the porter said, at half-past three on Saturday, June 5th. He came in one of the station taxis. His luggage consisted of an old leather suitcase. He carried a brown mackintosh over his arm, and wore a none-too-clean grey Homburg hat, and a grey lounge suit, which was a bit baggy for him. He was received by Miss Harpenden, the manageress, and his luggage was taken up to Room No. 15 by the hall-boy. He followed the boy upstairs, and seemed to remain there for a long time. At all events Ormerod, who was in or about the hall the whole time, didn't remember seeing him again till about five. Then Findlay came up to him in the hall and asked where he could buy a bathing-suit. He was now wearing a blue and grey check cap, which fitted badly over his wig, and it struck Ormerod that he would look rather comical in the water. However, he recommended him to try Jacka and Protheroe, a firm of gentlemen's outfitters at the nearer end of the High Street, and Findlay went out, presumably to that destination. The next time Ormerod saw him was in the lounge after dinner. Findlay had changed from his grey suit into a dark blue one—not a bad suit, but it didn't seem to fit him too well. He was sipping his coffee, and reading a paper. Ormerod then went off duty, and saw no more of him till the following morning about ten, when he asked if he could have some sandwiches instead of lunching in the hotel. Ormerod transmitted the order to the waiter, and, while the sandwiches were being prepared, Findlay consulted him about taking a long walk. He had a kind of hiker's knapsack with him, which he said he had bought the previous evening, and he was evidently intent on spending the day in the open air. There was every inducement to do so, as the weather was bright and hot. Ormerod suggested a route in the direction of Maen Porth, Mawnan Smith and Constantine, and in due course the sandwiches were stowed in the knapsack, and Findlay set forth, a jaunty if rather absurd figure in his check cap and grey 'citified' suit. As Ormerod observed to me, he was evidently a more sporty gentleman than he looked at first sight.

Ormerod was off duty all Sunday afternoon and evening, and said that if I wanted information about Findlay during that time, I should have to ask the hall-boy or one of the waitresses. The waiter was also off duty that evening.

The next and last meeting between Ormerod and Findlay occurred soon after nine on Monday morning. Findlay had breakfasted and paid his bill. He said he was bound for Truro that night, but would like to do part of the journey on foot, combining it, if possible, with a bathe. He asked if the hotel could send his suitcase by train to Truro Station, where he would call for it later in the day. When Ormerod told him that this could easily be arranged, he said he would like to cross over to St. Mawes by ferry and then to explore the coast beyond. Was there a nice quiet cove on the way, where he could have a dip? When you wear a wig, he said, you don't like bathing in a crowd. Ormerod suggested Brora Cove, which was pretty but not much sought after by bathers, owing to the rocks and rather treacherous currents. However, the sea looked smooth enough that day.

Here I interrupted Ormerod, and said: 'All this seems to be frightfully important. I do wish I'd brought a map with me. I suppose we couldn't go and look at one in the hotel.'

'I took the precaution of bringing one with me, sir,' Ormerod replied. 'I thought you'd want to see one. If we move over to that lamp, I shall be able to show you the walk I suggested to the gentleman, though, of course, I can't say if he took it or not.'

I complimented him on being so provident, and we walked a little way down the road to the nearest lamp-post, in the light of which Ormerod unfolded a dilapidated map.

'That's where we are, sir,' he said; 'and this is the way I advised Mr. Findlay to go. You see the ferry across there to St. Mawes? Then I suggested he should strike along that road which brings him out to the sea again there. Here's Brora* Cove, marked on the map. Oh, I should have mentioned that he asked me about Polgedswell Cove. That's not marked, but you can see it here—that little inlet just alongside Brora Cove. He said someone had told him what a beauty spot it was. I said, yes, artists seemed to like it, but it wasn't any good for bathing. It was too dangerous except in a dead calm. Now you see the road after touch-

*Do not get out the map. I have taken several liberties with the geography of Cornwall, east of St. Mawes and elsewhere.

ing Polgedswell Cove at one corner goes a bit inland and comes out to the sea again at Marthen. There was lunch to be had at Marthen, I said—as a matter of fact, my sister keeps the Green Swan there—but he said he'd asked the waiter for sandwiches. "Well," I said, "if you've had enough walking by then, you can get a motor-bus for Truro from there. If you want to go on, you can strike across to Brehan Well. That's a pretty village, too. The bus calls at Brehan before it gets to Marthen, going to Truro. That, I should think, is about as far as you're likely to get if you want to reach Truro to-night.' I told him that the last bus, except on Saturdays, left Marthen for Truro at half-past six. I wasn't sure of the times from Brehan, but I supposed it would be about half an hour earlier. Well, sir, that's more or less my story. Fred brought round the sandwiches, and Mr. Findlay, still in his grey suit and check cap, put them into his knapsack, which was a bit bulgy, I suppose, with his bathing things and a towel, and, after giving me the money to send his suitcase to the station and a shilling for myself, he says goodbye and away he goes.'

'I think you'd earned more than a shilling,' I said.

Ormerod shrugged his big shoulders.

'Oh, well, sir, we have to take the fat with the lean!' he answered, and began to fold the map away.

'I wonder,' I asked him, 'if you could possibly let me buy that map.'

'Oh, certainly, sir. I can get another on Monday. But it's pretty well worn. They cost a shilling new.'

I produced Dick's pound note, and said: 'Well, I shall be delighted to give you this for it, and all the kind help you've given me.'

He was almost too embarrassed to thank me, and I reflected that I had misjudged him in thinking that his mention of Uncle Hamilton's mean tip had been a hint to me. I also reflected, stingily, on Dick's behalf, that ten shillings would have done.

'Well,' I said, 'I ought to be getting back now. I suppose

that's my quickest way to the middle of town, isn't it, over the hill there?'

'Yes, sir. You don't need to come down to the promenade.'

As I put the map in my pocket a thought struck me.

'By the way,' I asked, 'was Mr. Findlay alone the whole time, so far as you know?'

'Absolutely alone, sir.'

'He didn't have any visitors? There wasn't a lady friend knocking about by any chance, was there?'

Ormerod seemed to bridle a little at the suggestion.

'Certainly not, sir. We don't have that sort of thing at the Trepolpen. Miss Harpenden would be down on it pretty quick, I can tell you.'

'Oh, I'm not suggesting anything of the sort! But when gentlemen of apparently regular habits suddenly fail to keep appointments, you begin to wonder a little.'

'No, sir,' he insisted. 'So far as I am aware, Mr. Findlay spoke to no one but the hotel staff all the time he was our guest.'

I held out my hand, and said: 'Well, as you know, I am very greatly obliged to you.'

He shook hands diffidently, said it had been a pleasure to help me, and he hoped very much I should soon find Mr. Findlay all right. Then he walked down Tregaskis Avenue to his hotel, while I set out for the Feathered Owl in the centre of the town.

I arrived there at twenty-five to ten, a little afraid that Dick would be too elated to take in my story, or recognise the skill I had shown—what skill after all?—in tracking Uncle Hamilton down. On entering the bar I saw that my worst fears were realised. Dick was in the middle, presiding over a little group of three girls, two sailors, and a seedy, middle-aged man who might have been anything.

He introduced me at once as 'my stand-offish friend,' and ordered more drinks. I knew Dick in those moods.

There was nothing to be done, except to take offence and go haughtily away, or to drink freely. I decided to drink freely. After all, one doesn't spend every Saturday night in Falmouth.

During a moment's lull in the crude but inoffensive banter with which I found myself surrounded, I whispered to Dick that I had a good deal of news, but he whispered back: 'Oh, that'll keep till we get to the Greenbank. It'll be closing time in twenty minutes. Let's enjoy this.'

His remark made me think that he was less drunk than I had supposed. However, he acted as if he were very much 'lit up,' and was clearly a great success with his new friends. He was indeed holding the floor just as he used to hold it at Oxford in the old days, though he had adopted different tactics to suit the different company. In a way I was glad to see him coming, even momentarily, into his own again, and felt I couldn't protest at his conviviality. He plied me so heavily with drink that when closing time came I was quite indignant, and declaimed volubly against the restrictions on our liberty which the war had brought us. 'If we have another war,' I said, 'I suppose we shan't be left with any liberties at all.' Fortunately, no one was impelled to debate this gloomy thought.

Though tired with a good deal of walking, I was glad to find that Dick had taken the car back to the hotel garage, anticipating that when he left the Feathered Owl he might well be too much 'under the influence' to drive. But the walk, instead of clearing my head, made me feel more muzzy, and, on reaching our hotel, I insisted on going to bed at once.

'You can't be tight,' Dick said. 'You were only there for half an hour.'

'I haven't got your capacity,' I replied, 'and even if I'm not tight, I'm absolutely exhausted. I'm going to bed at once. You can come and hear my story if you like, but I'm not going to stay up any longer for anyone.'

'Well,' he said, 'to show you that *I'm* not tight, I'll have one more drink in the lounge, and I'll look in on you when I come upstairs.'

A little envious of his stamina—after all, he had done all the driving that day—I went to my room, undressed and got into bed. When Dick came in, a few minutes later, I felt too sleepy to talk to him, but he naturally insisted on my making some attempt to tell him of my interview with Ormerod, and pored over the map with great eagerness. I was too dazed to study his reactions, or even to notice his comments, though I remember him saying, when I had to shut my eyes decisively: 'It looks to me, Malcolm, as if we shall have to go over this ground in the car to-morrow. I'll see the porter about getting the car over the ferry.'

'For the Lord's sake,' I said, 'turn out that light.'

He laughed, put the map in his pocket, turned out the light, and went away. I think I fell asleep almost before he had shut the door.

4.

Sunday, June 13th

I AWOKE at five, felt very sick, and was sick. During my spasms I thought of Dick bitterly. Dick, whose idiotic carouse at the Feathered Owl—or was it those vile sandwiches made by his uncle's housekeeper?—had brought me such distress. I resolved to spend all the following day in bed, and then to go quietly home by train—to abandon the case.

I got back to bed feeling miserable in mind and body, till a delicious drowsiness came over me and I fell asleep again. My sleep was peaceful, except for a quick dream that Dick came into my room, whereupon I told him that I was very ill, and that he must let me die in peace. He promised to do so, and went out. Once more a lovely blank.

When I next awoke, Dick was standing at my bedside, saying: 'Malcolm, do you know it's nearly twelve?'

I sat up in dismay, suddenly remembering the horrible events of the night. I felt limp, but not actually ill.

'Good heavens,' I said. 'Why on earth didn't you come in before? I've been frightfully ill in the night.'

'I came in at eight,' he answered, 'and you told me to go

away. I thought it best to let you sleep on, but we ought to be doing something now, if you feel better. I hope you do.'

'Oh, so you did come in. I thought you were just a bad dream. Yes, I think I'm fairly well now. If you'd order me a cup of tea and a little dry toast, I'll get up.'

He made one or two solicitous remarks, and I blamed both the sandwiches he had given me for lunch and the excessive drink he had given me after dinner—anything except my own silly stomach, which has a way of misbehaving, not only when I exceed with food or drink, but even when I am worried or excited. Indeed, the only bright aspect of my over-sensitive inside is that it usually recovers its equilibrium as quickly as it succumbs. Already I felt better.

'You send my breakfast up,' I told him, 'and I'll be downstairs as soon as I can.'

It must have been about one o'clock when I joined him in his car by the front door of the hotel.

He said: 'I've got them to make us some sandwiches.'

'Oh dear, no more sandwiches for me,' I interrupted.

'These will be better than those we had yesterday. Besides, I've brought some very dry biscuits for you. You can just nibble at them when you feel the pangs. I've been going over Uncle Hamilton's route very carefully, and find that with a car it's best to miss the ferry and go round by land and pick up his footsteps near St. Mawes. I suppose we may as well admit that we both have ideas in our heads as to what may have happened?'

'You mean—this bathing business?'

'Yes.'

'Was he really a bather? I should have thought he was rather too stuffy for that sort of thing. Forgive me for saying that, Dick.'

'No, you're quite right. But, oddly enough, he was proud of his swimming. He once won a swimming prize at school, and it gave him a superiority-complex. His difficulty was his wig. He was very wig-conscious, and didn't like bathing in public. I'm afraid it all hangs together only too well. However, let's be off.'

'Where exactly are we going?' I asked, as he drove towards Truro.

'I'm going round the Carrick Roads, making a big oval, as you'll see from the map, in the hope of picking up the trail from St. Mawes onwards. Of course we ought to question the officials on the ferry, but I can hardly believe they'd be able to help us. We should have to say: "Do you remember a rather dim man, a bit wiggy round the ears, who crossed last Monday?" Oh, Lord, Malcolm, that was in pretty bad taste, wasn't it, considering what we both think may have happened?'

I said nothing, nor did Dick, for a long time. It had, of course, occurred to me in theory that Uncle Hamilton's failure to return home might be due to his death while on holiday, but now that theory was replaced by practical investigation I felt rather shocked, just as in my two previous cases I had been shocked when I came into actual contact with death. I suppose a detective would have been quite different, like a surgeon confronted with some hideous malformation of the human body.

When Dick next spoke his voice had changed.

'If Uncle Hamilton was really drowned while bathing—' he said, and paused.

'His clothes should be somewhere,' I said, 'and the body should be washed ashore.'

'Are they always washed ashore?' he asked, and I answered: 'I suppose not always. . . .'

Another long silence.

It was a relief when we reached St. Mawes and began to drive along the actual route which the porter of the Trepolpen told us he had indicated to Uncle Hamilton. We went slowly along the narrow road, and came suddenly upon Brora Cove, a rocky inlet of the sea. There were a few grey clouds on the horizon, and I thought the water which lapped the little beach looked very chilly. Would Uncle Hamilton have braved that chilliness? Then I remembered that last Monday, in London at least, had been a blazingly hot day, more like July than the beginning of June. No doubt here in Cornwall the swirling sea had smiled and Uncle Hamilton, rejuvenated by that unwonted air, had, as in boyhood, seen the beckoning of the Oceanids in each little breaker as it crunched the pebbles, and heard the Sirens' Song—forgotten since what youthful reverie?—in each salt movement of the breeze. A mood of irresistible folly. Perhaps. And yet . . .

'We must get out and search here,' Dick said. 'I'll bring lunch in case we find nothing.'

We got out of the car and climbed down the rocky cliff, which had been cut into rough steps. Then, systematically, we made a tour of the inlet, going first to the western side and then to the eastern. It was easy to see at a glance that there was no heap of clothes on the shingle, but there were small caves and still smaller plateaux among the rocks which we had to search. In one of the caves I saw a fat man drying himself.

'The clothes might have been stolen,' I suggested to Dick, who agreed, and the fact that this little beach was not really so unfrequented as we imagined was brought home to me still more, when, having explored the whole area without result, we sat down at the apex of the inlet and began our lunch—sandwiches for Dick and very dry biscuits for me—and a party of three men and two girls carrying bathing things, towels and what not, invaded what we had taken to be our solitude.

'If it was like this last Monday,' Dick said, 'Uncle Hamilton wouldn't have bathed here.'

'What will you do,' I asked, 'if we find nothing in Polgedswell Cove? I suppose we're going to search that next.'

'Yes,' he said. 'If we find nothing there, I think we shall

have to go back to London to-morrow, and if there's no word from Uncle Hamilton at Tylecroft, I shall simply have to call in the police, telling them how far we've got. Then it's up to them and the family solicitor.'

We finished our little meal and watched the bathers, while we smoked. The women were hardier than the men, and I reminded myself that women are supposed to be covered with an extra layer of fat. I certainly had no desire to expose my skinny body to that inhospitable sea, and began to feel quite sure that Uncle Hamilton would not have bathed even in the heat of the previous Monday. However, I made no protest when Dick suggested that we ought to move to the scene of our next search.

Polgedswell Cove was even more forbidding than Brora Cove. It formed a narrow V, with a thin strip of rocky beach running round it. The road, which was little more than a track, lay forty or fifty yards away from the point of the V.

We climbed down rather more easily than we had done at Brora Cove, but the rush of water backwards and forwards along the gully was so terrifying that I felt I should be thankful when we were out of the place again. Dick suggested to me that to cut the search short we should each take one side of the cove. If either of us discovered anything, it would be quite possible to shout the news across the inlet. I agreed and started along the eastern side, while Dick took the western.

The beach, if one can so call it, and the cliff face were so cut up by projecting rocks, that I had to admit to myself that the most prudish bather would have found no lack of suitable spots for undressing, even if the cove had been crowded. But the further I went the more convinced I was that it would have been empty. Only a lunatic would have bathed there, and risked those jagged rocks and perplexing currents.

All along my side of the cove, and presumably along Dick's side also, there were recesses in the cliff, some of them only two feet deep though others took the form of miniature caves. I was exploring them rather timidly, fearing that at some time or other they had probably been put to a use of which no sanitary inspector could approve, when suddenly my eye was caught by a metal buckle glittering in semi-darkness, about nine feet under the cliff. I made my way to it, struck a match, and saw that it was the buckle of a big knapsack, neatly placed on the top of a pile of clothes. I was so startled that I almost tottered down to the beach, and hardly had voice enough to attract Dick's attention.

'Come here at once,' I said. 'There's something here you ought to see.'

When he heard me, he raced back to the end of the inlet.

'Have you some matches?' I added when he was opposite the road. 'There are only two left in my box.'

'I'll get a torch from the car,' he said.

I stood on guard by the entrance of the recess and waited. He reached me in less than four minutes, hardly panting at all from his exertions, and said:

'Well?'

'I think I've found your uncle's clothes,' I replied. 'Look there.'

I took the torch from him and directed its ray into the cave. He darted in, lifted the knapsack from the little heap which it was covering, and carried the heap and knapsack out into the light. Then we knelt down and made an examination.

The knapsack was empty except for a wig, which Dick recognised at once as being his uncle's.

'There it is,' he said. 'The last thing he'd take off, and hidden away self-consciously.'

The heap of clothing comprised the following items:

A vest.

A pair of pants.

A grey and white striped shirt, with bone studs back and

front and imitation gold cuff-links.

A white soft collar.

A shabby grey tie.

A pair of grey socks and frayed sock-suspenders.

A pair of very dusty black shoes.

An old grey 'City' suit consisting of coat, waistcoat and trousers to which scarlet braces were attached.

A blue and white check cap.

A bathing towel.

The shirt, socks and underclothes were all marked E. Hamilton Findlay. I was going to examine the coat when Dick suddenly stood up and said:

'Do you know, Malcolm, I'm not sure that we oughtn't to have left these things where we found them. In any case I think I'd better fetch a policeman at once. I suppose I shall find one in the next village—Marthen, isn't it called? If you wouldn't mind waiting here on guard, I'll be back as soon as I can. I'm sure the authorities would rather we brought them to the clothes than the other way about. Don't you agree?' I said I did, but asked him to be as quick as he could.

When he had climbed up the cliff again and started off in the car, I sat down by the clothes and lit a cigarette, feeling for a while rather shattered. Then my inquisitive nature asserted itself, and I took the coat, which was damp to the touch, and examined the breast-pocket in which, as I had expected, was sewn a tailor's label. This one was printed with the words, 'Johnson and Co., Ltd., 144, High Street, South Mersley,' and underneath the printing was written in black ink, 'E. Hamilton Findlay, Esq., 7 ix. '30.' So the suit was nearly seven years old. It seemed to have worn well, but Uncle Hamilton was probably economical and careful with his clothes.

The inside breast-pocket, where I had found the tailor's tab, contained a wallet, and I am afraid the sight of it was sufficient to banish any scruples I may have had; for I laid the contents one by one on the rock beside me.

They were: a two-shilling booklet of stamps, eight pound notes and three ten-shilling notes, three visiting cards bearing Uncle Hamilton's name and address in South Mersley, the return half of a third-class ticket from Paddington to Falmouth, a cutting from a newspaper on the pruning of climbing roses, and a folded sheet of paper torn from a cheap writing block. I recognised Uncle Hamilton's writing at once, and read the letter. It was simply headed 6 vi. 37 and bore no address.

DEAR WILLIAM,

I have been thinking over your suggestion, but can find no justification whatever for entertaining it. When your mother married your father she had quite a fair income of her own, and the position in which you and your mother find yourselves now is entirely due to your late father's improvidence. I admit you seem to have rather more business instincts than he had, but I am far from being convinced that you have the will to run your establishment on really commercial lines. In fact, I fear that if you found yourself in funds, you would at once waste your resources on some elaborate experiments such as your father used to undertake, to the detriment of his ordinary business. It is true that you may have the will and the ability to create a name for yourself amongst a few horticulturists, and possibly even to win some high award at the Chelsea Show, but that won't pay off the mortgage on your nursery and it certainly isn't an inducement to me to part with my savings. No, as I've said before, you must either run your establishment as a commercial proposition, leaving the fancy side of it to those more amply provided with this world's goods than you are, or you must give up your business, lock, stock and barrel, and get a job in some institution where your scientific interests might find scope for themselves. Do you know anyone at Kew who could help you, or at any of the agricultural colleges? I believe Dick once met the Professor of Botany at Oxford, but I doubt if he could give you an introduction. But I am quite aware that it isn't *advice* that you were applying to me for, and as I'm not disposed to give you anything else, I may as well conclude by signing myself,

Your affectionate
UNCLE HAMILTON.

As I folded up the letter and replaced it with the other things in the wallet, and put the wallet back in the breast-pocket of Uncle Hamilton's coat, it occurred to me that the manuscript I had just read was more like a draft than a finished product. So many words were scratched through, or interpolated. The date, too, interested me: 6 vi. 37. Exactly a week ago, and the very day when Cousin Bill was also in Falmouth. I could not help coming to the conclusion that Uncle Hamilton must have met Cousin Bill, by accident or design, on the Sunday afternoon or evening, a period regarding which the porter at the Trepolpen had not been able to give me any information, since he had been off duty. The letter, presumably, was a reply to some suggestion which Cousin Bill had made during the meeting. Probably Uncle Hamilton had written it the same night, in the lounge of the Trepolpen, or even in bed. Whether he had made a fair copy and posted it, I had no means of knowing, though I was inclined to think that he would hardly have had time before—

And here my train of thought brought me to the realisation: that I was mounting guard over the clothes of a man who was almost certainly dead. Poor Uncle Hamilton! I looked down at the grey sea twisting in and out of the rocks a few feet beyond me and shuddered. Better death by drowning than death by fire, I had always thought, but there, on that rather sunless afternoon, alone by the sullen waters of that narrow creek, I suddenly felt an exaggerated horror of what must have happened. Did *he* have, I wondered, that final moment of calm self-realisation which they say comes to the drowning, when the agony of the death-struggle is over and life at its last gasp, or after its last gasp, flickers one precious instant in the brain, snatching sweet memories from the past, and merging them into the final bliss of Paradise? Paradise! What figure would Uncle Hamilton cut there, poor stunted little soul? Was he even now being purged by solemn angels, initiated, with what spiritual dismay, into the ultimate purpose of the universe? Is there an ultimate purpose? Or was there nothing left? Nothing of Uncle Hamilton but those shabby clothes which I was guarding, and a battered, decomposing body, drifting with the tide. Or was he still *there*, somewhere, not greatly changed from what he was, living his old life in another dimension, which we cannot apprehend because we are bound up with the ceaseless flow of time, just as at the cinema we can't see the picture of five minutes ago because to our eyes no light is passing through it on to the screen. But the picture of five minutes ago is still a real picture. Granted the light, it could become vivid again even to us, and in any event it will be shown again at to-morrow's performance, the same picture, unaltered, immortal till the whole film perishes.

This, on the whole, tends to be my notion of immortality—that the past is not a mere matter of memory, but a real thing which lives, even though we, as we form a new past, haven't the eyes to see it living. We are still aged six, creeping furtively round the strawberry-bed and picking the ripe fruit through the mesh of the netting with our small fingers. We are still twelve, walking timidly up to the headmaster's dais—behind it there are rows of parents, whispering and applauding gently—to receive our first prize for Latin. We are still fifteen, waiting to be caned by the Games Captain for funking at football. How huge he seems with his long arms and slight moustache, though we have since outgrown him. We are still twenty-four, standing in the cold hall on Christmas Eve, counting the minutes before a motor-car arrives and brings—what was her name? We are still all these ages, some of them hell, while others of them are heaven. Nor do they become nonsense through having a simultaneous immortality any more than the cinematograph-film becomes nonsense when it is coiled up in its tin box and the tenth picture lies on the hundred and twelfth. But there is this difference. The great moments in life reach out to far more distant dimensions than the trivial moments. We may be immortal when bending down to tie up a shoe-lace at the age of ten, but we acquire a very much more profound immortality when, at the age of twenty, we feel the raptures of a first love affair.

I will not believe that the emotional intensity of a moment counts for nothing, even if, as the crude scientists have it, such emotion has its origin merely in a glandular stimulation, or is founded on illusion, a misconception of what the realist calls reality. It is through personal psychophysical experience that we attain immortality, and I am inclined to wonder whether, when the world becomes a stereotyped Utopia, it will any longer produce immortal souls, since all free personal experience will have given way to the precision of a machine—in itself utterly valueless.

At this moment in my reverie—was it an immortal moment?—I was startled by the frivolous toot of Dick's motor. In another minute I saw him and a policeman climbing down the cliff-side. I have now reached the age, referred to by Somerset Maugham in one of his plays, when policemen, instead of seeming like benevolent uncles, look like younger brothers.

The policeman who accompanied Dick along the beach to where I was sitting, looked very much like a younger brother. Dick introduced him to me as Police-Constable James of Marthen, and said that we were all to go to Polpenford at once to see the Police Superintendent there. Police-Constable James was a little shy, and beyond murmuring that he was sorry I had had such a sad wait by myself, said very little. Dick showed him exactly where I had found the clothes, and helped him to gather them together. I said nothing about my investigation of the breast-pocket in the coat, and the wallet. If my finger-prints were discovered, I could confess my guilty curiosity later. But there was no call to search for finger-prints. It wasn't a criminal case.

When we had driven to the Police Station in Polpenford, almost in complete silence, Dick and I were shown into a small waiting-room and left there while Police-Constable James went with the clothes into another room. For some minutes I heard the sound of muffled voices, and then James came back and asked us if we would mind coming to see the Superintendent.

The Superintendent was large and sleepy.

'Well, gentlemen,' he said after shaking hands with us, 'we are meeting under very sad circumstances, but I hope we shan't think any the worse of one another for that. Police-Constable James had given me an outline of the case, but there are a good many gaps which he can't fill in, and I think it would be best if you would both tell me your stories from the very beginning. I gather you've been doing a little detective work on your own, haven't you? Well, we often meet with that. Now, Mr. Findlay, when exactly was it that you first felt anxiety about your uncle?'

Then Dick told his story, much as he had told it to me on Thursday night in my flat, though he suppressed the 'psychology,' and touched neither upon his home life at Tylecroft, nor upon his relations with his uncle. Perhaps it was this omission which made the Superintendent say:

'Well, I must say, it seems a bit queer to me that you didn't get in touch with your local police in South Mersley, instead of coming all the way down here, and trying to ferret things out for yourselves. However, I dare say you thought of your trip as a holiday jaunt more than anything else. Go on, Mr. Findlay, please.'

'That's practically all I have to tell you,' Dick replied. 'My friend, Mr. Warren, was kind enough to do the actual investigation in Falmouth, and I think you'd rather he gave you his own version of what happened. I may mention, by the way, that one of the reasons I asked Mr. Warren to help me, apart from the fact that I've known him since we were at Oxford together, was his experience in police matters. He has had the unusual fortune of being involved in two cases of murder.'

This jolted the Superintendent out of his sleepiness, and he gave me a suspicious look.

'Only as a witness,' I said hurriedly.

The Superintendent snorted, and said: 'Well, I've no doubt that's not material, but it might be as well if you would recall the two cases to my mind.'

I did so, very briefly, and was perhaps a little disappointed to find that the Superintendent gave no sign of being acquainted with either of them. But as he noted the names of three persons involved, I thought it a little unfortunate that I seemed destined, in all innocence, to come into such frequent contact with the police. If I ever did anything shady, they would be on to me like a knife. However, it couldn't be helped. Dick clearly had to explain why he had 'called me in.'

Then the Superintendent asked me to tell my part of the story, and I did so, beginning with my discovery that Uncle Hamilton had spent the first night of his holiday at the Strafford Royal Hotel, Paddington, and ending with my conversation with Ormerod, the porter at the Trepolpen. The Superintendent had come across Ormerod, and said that he was a very reliable fellow. I wondered for a moment during my narrative whether to mention that I had accidentally learnt of Cousin Bill's residence at the Radnor Hotel during Uncle Hamilton's second and last night at the Trepolpen. But this fact, coupled with the letter, or draft letter, I had found in Uncle Hamilton's wallet, might easily arouse ugly thoughts in the minds of the local police, and give a twist to the whole case, which I thought quite unwarranted. Well, if it was to be so—if I had been unlucky enough to stumble into an affair with a more sinister aspect than that of accidental death—I wasn't going to start the ball rolling. I had no right whatever, at that stage, to make free with Cousin Bill's name, and the police could hardly blame me afterwards, if it turned out that they would have been glad to hear it from me.

When I had finished, the Superintendent looked at his notes for a few moments, and then said:

'Well, gentlemen, I am bound to admit that the evidence indicates that Mr. Findlay, Senior, met his death accidentally by drowning in Polgedswell Cove—the fourth fatal accident we've had there in two years. In fact, we've twice urged the Council to erect a notice board saying that the place is a death-trap for bathers. We can only regret that Mr. Findlay, Senior, didn't take Ormerod's advice. I suppose, not being acquainted with these parts, he couldn't bring himself to realise last Sunday how very dangerous those currents are, in spite of the sea looking quite calm. However, there's no use—'

I think he was going to say 'crying over spilt milk,' but he altered the phrase to 'going into that now,' and continued:

'I advise you, Mr. Findlay, to telegraph to your solicitor first thing to-morrow morning. There won't, of course, be an inquest, because, as yet, there's no body to hold it on. We shall naturally inform all the coastguards and the police in coastal districts. I shall be glad if both you gentlemen will be kind enough to give me your addresses, and let me know your movements, in case we have to get in touch with you.'

As he took down our addresses, Dick said:

'We had thought of going back to London to-morrow. Would there be any objection to that?'

'None at all,' the Superintendent replied. 'There's only one thing to be done before you go, and that is to collect the suitcase, which Ormerod said Mr. Findlay, Senior, had ordered to be sent on to Truro Station. I should like the contents checked in your presence, if you don't mind. One of my men will see to it with you. Perhaps you'd be kind enough to drive him round to the station?'

Dick said, 'Certainly,' and the Superintendent, after shaking hands with us and uttering a few words of commiseration, pressed a bell, and we were shown out into the waiting-room again. After a few minutes a constable joined us and said he had been ordered to collect the suitcase with us.

Dick drove us to Truro Station, and there, despite its being Sunday afternoon, the constable succeeded in extracting the suitcase from the luggage office. There was three and eightpence to pay. We next drove back to the waiting-room at the Police Station, sat round a table and tried to open the suitcase, which was locked.

'My uncle would certainly have locked it,' Dick said.

'And where do you think the key would be?' the policeman asked.

'At a guess, in some pocket in the suit Mr. Warren found this afternoon,' Dick answered. 'We haven't, of course, gone through the pockets.'

I blushed, though it was only the inside breast-pocket of the coat which I had investigated.

'I should think we ought to do that now,' the policeman said a little doubtfully, and he went out, presumably to consult with his superior.

'If the key isn't in the grey suit,' Dick said to me, 'it really will be rather mysterious.'

I answered, 'The key must be there.'

A few minutes later the policeman returned with Uncle Hamilton's grey suit, and went through the pockets one by one. The outside breast-pocket of the coat contained a white cotton handkerchief marked E. H. F. in indelible ink. The inside breast-pocket contained the wallet with whose contents I was already familiar.

As they were produced, one by one, I endeavoured to assume a look of blank surprise. I noticed that the constable neither read the draft letter to William Hicks, nor did he give Dick the chance of doing so. The side pockets of the coat contained nothing but a rather foul pipe and tobacco pouch, and a gold wristwatch, put there, I imagined, for security during Uncle Hamilton's fatal bathe. In the waistcoat pockets were a cheap pencil and two South Mersley tram tickets. The right-hand trouser pocket contained three florins, two shillings, five sixpences and a box of matches. The left-hand trouser pocket contained seven pennies, three half-pennies, and a key-ring on which were eight keys. The second key which the policeman tried on the suitcase opened it.

The following is a list of what the suitcase contained:

A sponge-bag, containing a large torn sponge, a nail-brush, a tooth-brush, a celluloid box with a used tablet of Pears soap inside, a shaving brush, a tube of tooth-paste, and a tube of shaving cream.

A small box containing a safety-razor with three blades.

A hair-brush, a comb, a clothes-brush.

A grey Homburg hat, folded flat.

A pair of bedroom slippers.

A pair of patent-leather evening shoes in a linen shoe-bag.

A pair of black shoes, also in a shoe bag.

Three white cotton handkerchiefs.

A stud-box containing studs and a pair of gold cuff-links.

A blue tie (new) and a grey tie.

Two pairs of socks, one grey and one dark blue.

Two clean shirts, white with a tiny grey stripe, with collars to match.

A set of thick underclothes.

A pair of blue pyjamas.

An old silk dressing-gown.

A green woollen waistcoat, with nothing in the pockets.

A blue serge suit—coat, waistcoat, and trousers, with a pair of newish braces attached.

The policeman took each article reverently out of the suitcase, placed it on the table and listed it laboriously. The ceremony seemed rather ghoulish, and to hide my discomfiture, I found myself making a copy of the policeman's list, while Dick replaced the articles in the suitcase. As he was folding away the trousers of the blue serge suit, the side pockets of which the policeman had already examined, I noticed a very slight stiffness in the hip-pocket and said, 'One minute, give me those trousers, will you?' Dick gave them to me across the table, not without surprise and, putting my hand into the pocket, I drew out a folded sheet of printed paper—a Southern Railway leaflet giving particulars of cross-Channel services via Dover, Folkestone, Newhaven and Southampton.

'That's a funny thing to find,' said the policeman, leaning over my shoulder and studying the document.

'It may have been in the pocket for years,' I said. 'It's only by the merest chance I happened to notice the bulge.'

'Well, it's dated March 31st, 1937,' he said, 'so Mr. Findlay can't have had it longer than that.' Then he turned to Dick and said, 'I suppose you can't throw any light on it, sir?'

'The only suggestion I can make,' Dick replied, 'is that my uncle may have thought of a trip to France instead of coming to Cornwall. He said nothing to me about going to France, and I should have thought he would have done, because he knew I've crossed the Channel a good many times.'

Meanwhile, I examined the document on both sides, to see if it bore the stamp of a travel-agency, but it didn't, and I had to be content with noting the serial number, printed in very small figures underneath the date—X 55/ L 37294d.

'Well,' the policeman said, 'of course I'll mention it to the Superintendent, but I don't suppose it's of any consequence at all. I must congratulate you, sir, on having such quick eyes.'

'Oh,' Dick said, 'I told you he was a detective.'

The policeman seemed a little puzzled by this remark, and to ease the situation I looked at my watch and yawned. In any case it was now nearly six o'clock. I had hardly had any lunch, and felt the need of a restorative.

'If you gentlemen would like to be getting back, I don't think I need detain you,' the policeman said tactfully.

'I'm quite ready for some tea,' I said, 'or even for something stronger. How about you, Dick?'

'Oh, I'm quite ready, too,' he answered. 'I was only wondering—but no, I'd better keep that problem for our solicitor. I shall be told at once, I suppose, if there is any news—I mean from the coastguard, and so on. The Superintendent has my address. Perhaps you'd remind him that I shall be there to-morrow night. We are both spending tonight at the Greenbank in Falmouth, but we shall be leaving about ten to-morrow morning.'

The policeman assured him that he would be informed as soon as any news came in, and we said goodbye and went outside to the car. Dick drove back to Falmouth rather slowly, and we hardly spoke on the way.

During the drive, I had felt that we should separate when we reached the Greenbank, and we did so, Dick going for a stroll in the town while I sat in the lounge, reading the paper and thinking vaguely over the day's events. Dick came back at half-past seven and after a cocktail we went in to dinner. I had a good appetite, but I thought it prudent to exercise self-restraint.

During the meal, and afterwards in the lounge where we had coffee, I wondered very much whether I should tell Dick about the letter written by Uncle Hamilton to Cousin Bill, but thought it fairer not to do so. However, I couldn't refrain from bringing his name into the conversation.

'I suppose you'll wire to Cousin Bill to-morrow?' I said.

'Yes,' Dick answered, 'I shall have to wire to him, and to my uncle's solicitors and to Mrs. Pressley. It was rather a coincidence Cousin Bill being in Falmouth during Uncle Hamilton's visit, wasn't it?'

'Do you think they had arranged to meet here?' I asked.

'Well, if they did, it was a most extraordinary rendezvous. Why not meet nearer home? Uncle Hamilton could easily have sent for Cousin Bill to come to Tylecroft, if he'd wanted to see him, and he certainly said nothing to me about expecting to see Cousin Bill in Falmouth.'

'But then, he didn't ever really tell you why he was going to Falmouth, did he?'

'The explanation seemed obvious. He was going away to tide over Mrs. Pressley's absence, just as I went away to tide over it.'

'But Falmouth is rather a long way to go—just for the weekend.'

'I agree,' Dick said, 'but evidently my uncle thought he'd like to venture rather far afield. I dare say he even thought of going to Paris. That railway pamphlet you found in his trousers suggests that. You never know, Malcolm, what caprices are going to enter the heads of old men.'

But I was still thinking of Cousin Bill.

'Ormerod, the porter of the Trepolpen,' I said, 'was quite positive that your uncle didn't see any visitors in the hotel. I wonder if he went to the Radnor and saw your cousin there?'

Dick looked at me rather searchingly. 'Are you indicating,' he said, 'that we ought to go to the Radnor and find out if Cousin Bill had any visitors?'

'Oh no,' I said, 'the obvious person to find out that from is Cousin Bill himself. After all, he's just as much interested in this as you are. I suppose you and he, or you and his mother, will be co-heirs of Uncle Hamilton's estate.'

For once I saw Dick blush, as he said, 'Oh, it isn't time to begin thinking of that aspect yet. But you're quite right, it's just as much Cousin Bill's affair as mine. I must have a good talk with him over the telephone to-morrow night. Well, I'm going for a stroll now. I shall probably drop into the Feathered Owl. Would you like to join me there and repeat last night's performance?'

'Certainly not,' I answered, 'it made me far too ill. I shall sit here for a time and then I shall go to bed. I hope to be asleep before you come in, so don't disturb me. I'll tell them to send me up some tea at half-past seven to-morrow morning, so that I shan't oversleep. We start for home about ten, don't we?'

He said we did, wished me good-night, and went out.

For a while I sat alone in the lounge and meditated rather sleepily. Then, having given my instructions about early morning tea, I went up to my bedroom, did some preliminary packing—I loathe packing in the morning—and got into bed. Then I took my notebook, which I had entitled 'Warren's Third Case,' and brought it up-to-date, incorporating in it the lists which I had made of Uncle Hamilton's effects. I had just finished writing when my fountain-pen ran dry, and, somehow, this fact suggested to my mind Uncle Hamilton writing his draft letter to Cousin Bill, in bed at the Trepolpen. I felt irrationally convinced that Uncle Hamilton had written this letter while in bed. But to write in bed, if one uses ink, a fountain-pen is essential. And no fountain-pen had been found in any of Uncle Hamilton's pockets. So far as I remembered the handwriting of the letter, it looked as if a fountain-pen had been used, though I could not be sure of this. Did the Trepolpen Hotel provide pen and ink in the visitor's bedrooms? I should have been willing to bet quite heavily that it did not, at all events, in the cheap single bedroom which the economical Uncle Hamilton would have taken. Well then, the letter had probably been written in the lounge, before Uncle Hamilton went upstairs to bed. Why not? Why must I assume that it was written in Uncle Hamilton's bedroom? Because it was not written upon hotel note-paper, but on a sheet taken from a cheap writing-block. Hotels like the Trepolpen do not provide writing-blocks for their guests. They provide note-paper, with probably an elaborate picture of the facade of the hotel, occupying half the first page, so that you can mark your room with a cross—if you can afford to face the sea.

I was so pleased with this piece of reasoning that I got out of bed, found a pencil and added, in pencil, underneath my notes:

Query: Where is Uncle Hamilton's writing-block?*

Then I put down the notebook, switched out the light, and fell asleep.

*The reader should be able to add a much more pertinent query to these notes.

5.
Monday, June 14th

I HAD barely finished my early morning tea when Dick came into my room to make quite sure that I hadn't again been sick in the night, and was awake. He was fully dressed and seemed a little impatient to be up and doing.

'We've still two hours before ten o'clock,' I said. 'Don't bustle me. Like the philosopher, Descartes, I can't abide early rising. You know that he died in Sweden, through being forced to rise before twelve at Queen Christine's Court?'

'No, I didn't know that.'

'Ah, that comes of not having read Greats at Oxford,' I said.

'Well,' Dick replied, 'I'm not Queen Christine, and I won't bustle you. But I thought I might be allowed to do one little piece of detective work on my own, as a foil to your magnificent exploits. I propose to go to that shop—Jacka and Protheroe wasn't it?—where the porter at the Trepolpen—I never can remember his name—recommended Uncle Hamilton to buy his bathing suit. If he didn't buy one—I don't know why I say that, because obviously he must have bought one somewhere since he asked the Trepolpen porter where he could get one. But somehow, with your innuendoes, you've made me question everything. Anyhow, I'm going to Jacka and Protheroe to make inquiries. I suppose they open at eight. I'll meet you in the dining-room at breakfast.'

When he left me, I got up and went across the passage to the bathroom. As I lay back in the hot water and scrubbed my legs, I thought about Dick, and the change I seemed to have discerned in him since he first 'enlisted my services' as he would have put it. I suppose if one suddenly found that one's uncle was really dead, even an uncle whom one rather disliked, one was bound psychologically to have a shock. When my Aunt Catherine died at Macebury—but there was no need to go over that again. I was too prone, perhaps, to brood over my first two 'cases,' and read the experience they had given me into everything. It was my fault that Dick felt called upon to verify the fact that his uncle had bought a bathing suit at Jacka and Protheroe's. Why should we verify anything any more? We had found Uncle Hamilton's clothes unmistakably in Polgedswell Cove, and the only possible inference was that Uncle Hamilton had been drowned while bathing there.

As for Cousin Bill's visit to Falmouth when Uncle Hamilton was at the Trepolpen, and the letter which Uncle Hamilton had written—or drafted—to Cousin Bill, they were playing far too large a part in my imagination. And I had even infected Dick. I was sure that he suspected that I suspected something, and was somehow on his guard. We weren't any longer two Oxford friends on a holiday jaunt to Cornwall. We were two wary men of the world, and poor Dick had set out before breakfast on an utterly needless piece of investigation, just because I had set the example of being inquisitive. When I met him at breakfast, the least I could do was to soothe him, and bear with him if his nerves were on edge, as well they might be.

But when I did meet him at breakfast, half an hour later, he was in so triumphant a mood that soothing was out of the question.

'It all fits perfectly,' he said. 'I saw Mr. Protheroe, a very bright little salesman, and he remembered Uncle Hamilton calling at the shop on Saturday evening. Uncle Hamilton bought a black-and-white striped bathing suit with skirt—American model. He asked Protheroe if he knew of a quiet cove suitable for gentlemen who wore wigs to bathe in. Protheroe said he didn't. He was a family man, and when he did bathe, it was with the Missus on the town bathing beach. Uncle Hamilton also bought the largest hiker's knapsack they had in stock.'

'Why such a big one?' I asked.

'I don't know. If we ask "why, why, why" of everything, we shall end by making nonsense of the whole universe. One has to believe in absurdities sometimes. It was absurd of Uncle Hamilton to come to Cornwall for the week-end, absurd of him to bathe, and still more absurd of him to be drowned while bathing. But it just happened like that. We shall never know quite what happened in his poor old brain. Meanwhile, we've now really done all we can. I've telegraphed the sad news—I'm not saying that flippantly, it *is* sadder than I should have thought likely—to Cousin Bill, our family solicitor, and Mrs. Pressley. I shall ring up Cousin Bill to-night, when I get back to Tylecroft, and I shall also probably ring up Stroud then too, if I can get hold of him. Stroud, by the way, is the name of Uncle Hamilton's solicitor. I think you suggested that I ought to go and see him with Cousin Bill.'

I agreed, and he suddenly stopped talking and began to eat hungrily, while I, who had finished my breakfast, looked at the morning paper.

There was a touch of silent melancholy about our homeward journey. I felt a nostalgia for Cornwall, even for those sea-swept creeks which we had explored on Sunday, and Dick seemed preoccupied with the tasks that still confronted him. During our luncheon—sandwiches for the third day in succession—he said:

'Do you know, that Aldershot Tattoo starts to-day, and I imagine the traffic on the Staines road will be frightful. Would you mind very much if we went straight to South Mersley? We can leave the main road soon after Basingstoke. There'll be supper of sorts at Tylecroft, and I shall be very grateful if you'll share it with me. I can motor you to London after the meal.'

I said, of course, that I could easily get home by train, and that I shouldn't think of making him turn out again. In a way I was rather glad to pay a second visit to Tylecroft. Was it Dick's house now? And if it was, what would he do with it? How soon would he be allowed to take possession? For his sake, I wished that Uncle Hamilton's body could very soon be washed ashore.

We reached Tylecroft shortly before seven. For the previous hour I had been adjusting myself to the encroachments of semi-suburbia upon the real country. The journey had been almost too quick. Was that the flaw in this mechanical modern world? Has our conquest of space and time outstripped our powers of mental adaptation? It seemed absurd after the unbroken freedom of Bodmin Moor to be halting every hundred yards by traffic lights, and passing an endless display of privet hedges, rambler roses on trellis-work, and dusty laburnums. Perhaps Uncle Hamilton was fortunate to have died where he did, without the sanctity of a suburban funeral.

The gate at Tylecroft had been left open for us, and as we circled round the monkey-tree in the middle of the drive, I noticed that all the blinds in the front of the house had been pulled down, as if we were entering a house of death. Somehow those blinds gave me a clue to Mrs. Pressley, who appeared on the threshold while Dick was putting his key into the lock of the front door.

She was dressed in black, and mopped an eye with a

handkerchief. I heard her say, 'Oh, Mr. Richard!' while I waited on the front step and Dick went with her into the narrow hall. I was beginning to wish, selfishly, that I had insisted on going straight back to Central London, when I heard steps in the drive and saw a young woman approaching. She was, I suppose, between twenty-five and thirty, not very pretty, but, so far as I could judge, *chic* in appearance. When she saw me, her pace slackened, but she still advanced, as if making an effort of will, and almost joined me on the steps of the front door.

'Can I help you?' I said, as she gave a puzzled look at me and the open door.

'I have come to see Mr. Richard Findlay,' she said. 'Do you know if he's at home?'

The moment she spoke I realised that my late Aunt Catherine would have described her as 'ladylike, but by no means a lady.'

'He's just arrived,' I said. 'Can I give him any message?'

'Well, I should prefer—' she began to say, but at that moment Dick reappeared, and said:

'Good heavens, Olive!'

I was so embarrassed myself at this odd encounter on the threshold of Tylecroft that I didn't notice if Dick was embarrassed too. 'Olive' was clearly not very sure of her ground, for she blushed beneath her make-up as she said:

'Oh, Dick, I called yesterday, and two hours ago. I must speak to you.'

Dick said: 'Look here, let's all go into the garden for a moment,' and drove us down the steps into the drive and across the lawn to the loggia at the side of the house, where I remembered having coffee after my dinner with Uncle Hamilton. Then, as we sat down like automata in wicker chairs, he went on: 'Now, Olive, I've got very bad news. My Uncle Hamilton has been drowned in Cornwall. He was bathing in one of those dangerous coves. My friend here found the clothes. By the way, I must introduce you. This is Mr. Malcolm Warren, whom I've known since I was at Oxford. This is Miss Olive Crowne,* one of the officials of the South Mersley Garden City. You've heard of our Garden City, of course?'

The question was addressed to me, and I said: 'Oh, yes,' while Miss Crowne could not refrain from saying with a simper:

'A very minor official, I'm afraid.' Then apparently recalling the sad news, she went on: 'Drowned in *Cornwall*, did you say? Did he go to Cornwall?'

'Yes,' Dick answered. 'He told me and he told Mrs. Pressley he was going there. When he failed to turn up last Tuesday, we became rather anxious, and in the end I persuaded my friend here to join me in making a search. Now, I really think we all deserve a drink. I wonder if you'd be an angel, Malcolm, and go indoors and ask Mrs. Pressley for the whisky and the sherry? There won't be anything else, I'm afraid. I expect Olive will take sherry.'

'Well, that would be very nice,' she said, as I set out on my errand. I thought it rather cool of Dick to make me confront his gorgon of a housekeeper within ten minutes of our arrival, but remembered that Miss Olive Crowne had something private to say to him. What could that be, I wondered? And was she staying to supper?

Presumably not; for seeing the dining-room door open, I went into it, and found only two places laid for the evening meal. As I was going to ring the bell by the fireplace, Mrs. Pressley herself came in and, somewhat shamefacedly, I asked her for the drinks. I was glad to find that her sniff of disapproval was reserved for the sherry. When I said two tumblers and *one* sherry glass, she must have divined that the sherry was intended for Miss Crowne. She held up a decanter with three-quarters of an inch of muddy liquid at the bottom, and said:

'I suppose that will be more than enough, won't it, for

*A different aspect of Miss Crowne can be found in *Olive E.* (Constable, 1937). It is only fair, however, to warn the reader that *Olive E.* is not a detective story.—C. H. B. K.

one? But I think I'd better get another syphon for you two gentlemen. Luckily the whisky bottle is nearly full. If Mr. Richard wants anything else, you might remind him that Mr. Findlay always kept the cellar key.'

I said nothing till she had gone out and come back with a tray and glasses and the syphon, when I murmured how sorry I was to meet her in such sad circumstances. She seemed glad to talk, and said: 'Sad, yes, I should think so. I little thought when I went away with my daughter to my niece's wedding that I should come back to a funeral. But so far it's only the poor gentleman's clothes that have been found, isn't it? I mean, while there's life there's hope. His first visit to Cornwall too. What a pity he should have chosen a dangerous part!'

I asked her if she knew what induced him to go there, for such a short holiday, and she said she didn't. Mr. Findlay had simply told her he was going there, soon after she had asked permission for her own little holiday. 'Well, if you're going to Essex, Mrs. Pressley,' he had said, 'I think I'll go to Cornwall. It's somewhere I've never been to before.' Mrs. Pressley evidently read a tragic implication into this remark, for she took out her handkerchief and wiped her eyes with it.

'I'm afraid the news has been a sad blow to you,' I said.

She looked at me for a moment, as if wondering how far I was sincere, and then said, very simply: 'Yes, it is. You couldn't help getting fond of him after a while. I know just how he struck strangers, and how he struck Mr. Richard from time to time. But he had a sweet side to him, and he never put on airs, or pretended to be better than he was. I shall always miss him. . . .' Then she added, in a different voice: 'But I'm keeping you waiting far too long, Mr. Warren. Mr. Richard will be waiting for his drink, to say nothing of the young lady. Are you sure you can manage the tray?'

She watched me nervously as I went out with the drinks into the hall, and down the front steps. When I was half-way across the lawn, Dick ran out of the loggia and took the tray from me.

'That really was sweet of you, Malcolm,' he said. 'Miss Crowne won't be staying very long now.'

There was a trace of relief in this remark of his, and when we had rejoined Miss Crowne in the loggia, conversation seemed to flow fairly easily. Miss Crowne had once spent a holiday at Marthen and knew Polgedswell Cove.

'We were told never on any account to think of paddling in it, even,' she said. 'I can't think what possessed your uncle, Dick. However, he did go there, and that's all there is to it, I suppose.'

I found myself wondering if she had ever met Uncle Hamilton, but didn't like to ask a direct question. From the way she spoke I gathered that she knew a good deal about him, though I couldn't picture her as being a friend of the family. She drank two glasses of sherry rather quickly, undeterred by its muddiness. From time to time she gave me a quick look, as though she was trying to sum me up, just as I was trying to sum her up. But whenever Dick moved, she watched him possessively. At length, after a third glass of sherry, which emptied the decanter, she stood up and said she must go.

'Goodbye, Mr. Warren, and goodbye, Dick. I'm afraid you'll have all sorts of boring things to see to.'

Dick escorted her to the gate, and when I found that he was away longer than I had anticipated, I got up and strolled round the garden, examining the rose-trees which Cousin Bill used to supply to Uncle Hamilton at half price. They were just beginning to reach their prime.

The garden as a whole seemed better kept than when I had visited it three years before. There were more beds in the lawn, and, though there was no attempt at any landscape effect or beauty of design, there were several plants worth looking at. Uncle Hamilton had evidently been going in for intensive cultivation. Indeed, as I was approaching the big garage, I was met by an appalling smell from a shed nearby, which contained a sack of fertiliser. Holding my nose, I read the label: 'Ichthyomano. Rose Fertiliser prepared only by Garvice and Bagshaw, Ltd.'

Dick came up as I was beginning to retreat from the malodorous spot.

'Do you make that stuff?' I asked.

'Yes,' he said. 'It's a novelty of ours this season, and a very fine one, too, I'm told. Isn't it foul? There's another sack of it in the garage. If I weren't comparatively used to smells like that I could hardly drive the car in or out. But making smells is largely how I get my living. I don't suppose you've ever visualised me in the factory, have you?'

'It's quite impossible to do so,' I answered. 'Does everything smell like that?'

'Well, not quite so badly, perhaps. But we ought to go and get ready for supper now. Mrs. Pressley has hotted up something and will be annoyed if we're late. Then, after dinner, I must ring up Cousin Bill. I should like you to be there when I do.'

Supper was less bad than I had feared. Either Mrs. Pressley's cooking had improved since my first visit to Tylecroft, or my standard was lower. After all, on the first occasion I had been bidden to a dinner party and was justified in expecting something rather special. This was a scratch meal, served in a house of mourning, and one could not have complained however vile the fare. But Mrs. Pressley had made an effort. Perhaps I had ingratiated myself with her?

When we had finished our coffee, Dick said: 'Now, before I take you upstairs to my room, I think I'd better get this telephoning done. The only telephone in the house is on that desk. Writing-desks in dining-rooms always remind me of lodging-houses, don't they you? I think this ought to be a good time to catch Cousin Bill. He's so bucolic, he probably goes to bed at nine.'

When he had got his number, I heard the following half-conversation:

'Is that you, Bill? Yes, this is Dick speaking. . . . Oh, about seven. There was a good deal of traffic. We came round through Hurstley, to avoid the Tattoo rush. . . . Yes, it was a great shock. . . . Well, I'll tell you all about that when we meet. . . . Oh yes, we'd known for some weeks, both Mrs. Pressley and I. So far as I remember, he decided to go there as soon as Mrs. Pressley asked if she could be away. . . . You remember I mentioned it when you dined here. . . . It was her niece getting married, or something of the sort. . . . Yes, only for a long week-end. . . . What a very extra-ordinary coincidence! . . . Did you see him? . . . No, I don't think he did know. At least, he didn't say anything to me about expecting to see you. . . . No, I didn't even know that myself. . . . Oh yes, so you did, I remember! . . . Well, I suppose it isn't very surprising, as you arrived so late. And as you say, it's quite a big town. . . . *(Long pause.)* Well, obviously we must both go and see Stroud tomorrow. Stroud, spelt the same as the place. That's the name of Uncle Hamilton's solicitor. . . . Oh, I dare say, but I know he did most of his business with Stroud, and, as I've met him, I don't think we can do better. I'll ring him up first thing tomorrow to make an appointment, and then ring you. . . . I hope it hasn't been too much of a shock for Aunt Grace. . . . Oh, I am so sorry! It must be very worrying for you, though they say it's a perfectly safe operation nowadays—that's if the worst comes to the worst. Do give her my love, will you? And tell her how much I hope she'll soon be better. . . . Well, that's all we can do to-night, I think. . . . Yes, to-morrow morning, as soon as I've got hold of Stroud. . . . Goodbye.'

Dick put down the receiver and turned towards me.

'Cousin Bill says he didn't see anything of Uncle Hamilton in Falmouth. He didn't even know or remember that Uncle Hamilton was going to Falmouth. So their being there the same night was a pure coincidence.'

'Was he upset?' I asked.

'Oh yes—so far as one can judge over the telephone. As a matter of fact, he's a good deal more upset about his mother, my Aunt Grace. The doctors want her to have her appendix out.'

I suggested that Cousin Bill might be a little resentful that Dick had made the search in Cornwall without consulting him. Dick agreed.

'I dare say he does think it a bit odd,' he said. 'But there it is. I couldn't have faced a trip down there with Cousin Bill. Besides, suppose there had been nothing in it, Uncle Hamilton might have been annoyed at my chasing him across England, but he would have been outraged beyond words if I had made the chase a family affair, dragging in Cousin Bill and Aunt Grace. No, I still think I acted for the best. Now let's leave this ugly room and go upstairs to my flatlet. I should like to show it you, and Sibyl will be wanting to clear away.'

Dick's room on the second floor was a great contrast to the rest of the house. Apart from a *cabinet de toilette* skillfully made in one corner, it had all the air of a comfortable study. The furniture, though modern, was not shoddy. There were three attractive modern paintings on the glossy white walls, and the polished oak floor was covered with old Oriental rugs. There was a modern gas-fire in the grate, and the mantelpiece supported a chromium and glass clock, a chromium candlestick, and two Tang figures, which did not seem to clash.

Dick pointed to a big divan draped in green and silver damask, and said: 'Sit there, won't you? That turns into my bed. Don't you think I've been rather clever? You can imagine what this room used to be like. Of course, now that I'm older, I'm regretting that I didn't buy antiques instead of all this modern stuff. Still, it's a change from the rest of the house. I think Uncle Hamilton considered there was something immoral about it.'

He sat down himself in a writing-chair at an angle to a big flat-topped walnut desk in front of the window, which looked over the garden. Was that the window, I wondered, through which, as a romantic boy of sixteen, he had watched the spring rain beating endlessly upon the peach blossom? Again I asked myself if the house was now his, and what he would do with it. As if reading my thoughts he said suddenly, after a pause:

'Malcolm, I wonder if you'll do me another favour, a last favour, and let me make you executor of my will? I haven't bothered to make a will yet. I suppose, if I had died, my bits and pieces and the threepence I have in the bank would have gone to Uncle Hamilton and Aunt Grace—oh, and perhaps to my cousins on my mother's side of the family, too! I was forgetting them, Uncle George's children, but they seem so remote. Anyhow, it didn't matter a damn. There would have been so little to divide up. But now, well, I can't help thinking that Uncle Hamilton has left me something in his will. I feel I was 'nearer to him,' as they say, than Cousin Bill or Aunt Grace, who were his only other living relations. And he wasn't the type to leave everything to a cats' home. At any rate, it's quite time I did make a will, and I can't think of anybody I'd like to be my executor better than you. Will you take the job?'

I saw no reason to refuse. Apart from more amiable considerations, stockbrokers like being made executors, as the post usually brings them business—valuations, sales of securities for death duties, distribution of the estate among the legatees, and so on. My senior partner used to boast that he was executor of no less than thirty-seven wills. But in this instance such an *arrière pensée* was hardly relevant. Dick was younger than I, and more than likely to outlive me. So I said:

'Certainly, Dick, though I hope I shall do you many favours before this one—if I'm able to do it at all. But I expect you'll alter your will hundreds of times. It's only one's first will that one thinks so frightfully dramatic, as if one were already entering the tomb. One gets quite hardened later. My Aunt Catherine altered her will every three months, though perhaps she isn't a very happy example to choose. Besides, you'll not only want to alter your will, you'll want to alter your executor. For instance, when you marry you'll probably put your wife as sole executrix, if she's a sensible woman.'

To my surprise he blushed slightly at this remark, and at the same time his glance wandered momentarily to an expensive photograph of an amazingly beautiful girl which stood framed in chromium on the writing-desk. I could not help contrasting the poise of the head, the calm regularity of the features, the almost philosophic quality of the eyes and the obscure smile which seemed to lend them light, with the poor tawdry little charms of Miss Olive Crowne.

'Who is that very lovely lady?' I asked.

'Oh, that's Hilda Montaubyn,' he answered with deliberate carelessness. 'Haven't you met her?'

'I don't think so. I'm sure I should have remembered if I had. Is she on the stage?'

'Not exactly. She was in a repertory company for a time, but she's not doing anything now.'

'Does she come from South Mersley?'

'She has an aunt by marriage who lives in Mersley Park. I met her there. And she acted at the Garden City Theatre for a time. Now she lives with a girl friend in a flat in a converted house in Westbourne Terrace.'

'Westbourne Terrace,' I said. 'Why, that's where you—'

'Where I last saw Uncle Hamilton. Quite right. Do you think there's a fatality about that street?'

I felt rather ashamed of having drawn his attention to the coincidence—for surely it could be no more—that Miss Montaubyn lived in the street where Dick had bidden his uncle a last goodbye. My remark was in bad taste. To counteract it I made another, the taste of which was equally bad, if not worse.

'Is Miss Crowne a friend of Miss Montaubyn's?' I asked.

He looked at me in surprise, as well he might, but answered very calmly: 'Oh no! I don't suppose they have ever heard of one another. Olive's not a bad girl. She wasn't at her best to-night. She used to be quite pretty. I'm afraid she's a bit dissatisfied with life, like a good many people.'

'Her job didn't sound too bad,' I said. 'An official in the South Mersley Garden City.'

He smiled a little.

'Actually, that's a grandiose way of putting it.'

'You mean she's really a typist in the office?'

'No, though I believe she can type. No, she just works for her living in one of their semi-philanthropic institutions—a rather self-righteous atmosphere which must be trying to her. You know, all social endeavour and uplift. And Olive has always been a "good time" girl and fond of a little fun, as I dare say you diagnosed. However, as you said, there are many worse jobs. Now I'm going to fetch the whisky which we left downstairs.'

While he was out of the room I wandered round it, and spent a short time admiring Miss Montaubyn's photograph. It was odd to have come across two of Dick's 'affairs' in one evening; for I had little doubt that there had been something between him and Miss Crowne, and even less doubt that he would like there to be something between him and Miss Montaubyn. I wondered if Miss Montaubyn was her real name, or a stage name which she used in private life. I wondered, also, if Dick was quite 'off with the old love before getting on with the new.' I felt Miss Crowne would be a clinger. Dick had always been secretive with me about his love-life. Perhaps it was as well. For a time he had seemed to chase ladies of title or position in London. But that was when he was younger and nearer to his Oxford self. No doubt he had also had romances nearer home, which may well have been more satisfying, if less brilliant.

I was sitting innocently on the bed-sofa when Dick came back with the drinks.

'I suppose you haven't any idea,' he said, as he gave me

mine, 'how long the formalities take in a case like this? I don't want to hurry indecently, of course, but the bills have got to be paid. I can't keep Mrs. Pressley and Sibyl waiting years for their wages—or the tradesmen for that matter.'

'I'm afraid I can't help you there,' I answered. 'Your solicitor will know, or he'll soon find out. I dare say there will be quite a long delay.'

'Do you mean six years, or something like that?'

'Oh, no, but it might well be six months.'

'Well, I doubt if I could keep Tylecroft going for six months, even if—'

He paused for a moment.

'Even if what?' I asked.

'Oh, I meant even if I used all my capital. But perhaps the bank would come to the rescue.'

'I've no doubt it would,' I answered. 'Or your solicitor will find you the money. I shouldn't worry about that. Besides, in a few days the body will be washed ashore somewhere. They almost invariably are, I believe.'

'Are you sure of that—or are you saying it to comfort me?' he asked.

'I'm not sure, but I seem to have heard it, or read it somewhere—probably in a detective story. Now, oughtn't I to be thinking of going?'

'Your best train will be the 10.26. You've time for one more drink. Won't you have one?'

I refused, but he helped himself, and as we made desultory conversation for another quarter of an hour I reflected again that he must be suffering from considerable mental strain, if not emotional disturbance. I admired the grip he seemed to have on himself. In such a crisis I should have been much less admirable. I should have felt faint, or sick, or perhaps, in a moment of reaction, revealed myself as gloating over the future and unduly excited over the contents of Uncle Hamilton's will. I certainly shouldn't have been able to sleep that night, whereas Dick was yawning as if he were longing for bed. It seemed a shame to drag him to the station, but he insisted on driving me there, and waited politely on the platform till my train moved out. His last words to me were:

'Once more, Malcolm, I am most frightfully grateful to you for everything you've done.'

I have always had a fondness for the shabby, slow suburban trains which run in the late evening. To me there is something romantic about their tired homeward glide between rows of little houses with their lighted windows. On such journeys I find released in me a serenely contemplative quality—a hint of the Divine essence in man—which weaves innumerable fantasies round those drawn translucent curtains and the human beings shadowed against them by the lights within, or appearing for a second in the square of an uncurtained window; for few people are shy about being seen by a passing train. I have even wondered if the guards and engine drivers, who, no doubt, know the names of every little house, ever form contacts with their momentary neighbours, here wave a handkerchief or blow a kiss, or shudder here at some tragedy which they know is being enacted within those half-seen walls. and in the houses there are surely some who have made the train a real and personal thing—my realities are all personal—watch its coming with joy and its going with regret, like astronomers thrilled by the radiance of a predicted star.

But on this night my thoughts did not flow in this calm channel. They were still busy with the events of the day—a kaleidoscopic day—beginning with the Greenbank, Falmouth, and ending, after a long, swift motor-drive, with the evening at Tylecroft—a disjointed evening marked by the ill-timed arrival of Miss Crowne, my few words with Mrs. Pressley when I was sent to bring the drinks out to the loggia, Dick's telephone call to Cousin Bill, and my talk with Dick in his room under the philosophic gaze of Hilda Montaubyn. In particular, one little sentence spoken by Dick to Cousin Bill stuck in my mind and tickled my curiosity. The words were: 'No, I didn't even know that myself—Oh yes, so you did, I remember.' What was it Dick didn't even know himself? And what had Cousin Bill done that Dick remembered? Was it possible that Dick knew something of Cousin Bill's request to his uncle for financial help? When I had read Uncle Hamilton's draft letter to Cousin Bill, I had felt inclined to assume that there must have been a meeting between the two men in Falmouth, even though it seemed absurd for them to choose so distant a meeting-place, considering that they lived less than thirty miles away from one another. But Cousin Bill had declared to Dick he didn't know Uncle Hamilton was going to Falmouth, and further denied that they had met there even by accident. It seemed, then, that the request for financial assistance must have been made some time before Uncle Hamilton had left home. Probably Uncle Hamilton had said he would think over the matter and, during the solitude of his little holiday, had reached his decision not to give any help. And the same night he had written the draft letter on a sheet of paper torn from a writing-block.

Almost every phase of this little episode suggested a query to me. And other things, too, began to puzzle me. Why, for example, was Miss Crowne so eager to speak privately to Dick? Why had she called on him yesterday and twice to-day? Why all this urgency? Well, the affairs of the heart are urgent. The most reasonable explanation was that she had got wind of the beautiful Hilda Montaubyn, and longed desperately to be convinced by Dick that there was 'nothing in' his new friendship. Poor Olive Crowne! How could she hope to compete? There was nothing, nothing at all which she could say or do to alter the relentless future.

Then suddenly, as we were nearing London, my mood changed. Why all this questioning? Why try to probe these details? The broad facts were plain and simple. The truth was I had been so bustled by events—an experience I dislike—that I was thrown off my balance and was hunting for something which wasn't there. True, I had been involved in a drama, but there was no call to make it into a drama of mystery and detection. Once more my humdrum life had come into contact with violent death, but it was an accidental death this time that I had been investigating, and the impulse I found in myself to make something more out of it was a neurotic impulse which should be kept severely in check. Otherwise I should merely make myself and other people uncomfortable. Worse, if I persisted I should make myself appear a fool.

I took myself sternly to task, and continued my self-rebuke when I was in the taxi on my way to my flat, and while I was undressing for bed. My part in the drama, such as it was, was over, and the sooner it ceased to obsess me the better it would be for everyone.

As I turned out the light at my bedside, I said to myself decisively: 'So ends Warren's Third Case—which was really no case at all.'

6.
Tuesday, June 15th, to Thursday, July 1st

NEXT morning found me back in the office. My partners, whom I had warned that I might not return till the Wednesday, greeted my arrival with unusual delight, which can be explained by the fact that two of them felt at liberty to go to Ascot at once. As a rule, days of important races are slack on the Stock Exchange, but it happened that there was a good deal going on in my office, and so far from having time to moon over my week-end in Cornwall, I found myself exceedingly busy.

Towards the end of the day, as my labours lessened, I began to feel that Dick would probably ring up to report progress, but he didn't, and I went to bed that night thinking much less of my 'Third Case' than of various problems with which I had had to cope during the day.

On the Wednesday I was again hard pressed. Ascot continued to be a lure, and I found myself practically in charge of the office. Dick rang up about half-past three. His news was that his solicitor, Stroud, was making certain applications, and was hopeful that leave to presume death would be given within three months. Dick had been told, in confidence, the contents of Uncle Hamilton's will, which, after a few legacies (among them five hundred pounds to Mrs. Pressley, and a thousand to Dr. Fielding), divided the estate equally between him outright and Aunt Grace for life, with remainder to Cousin Bill. Dick and his cousin were the executors. Very roughly, the value of the estate was sixty thousand pounds. Tylecroft was left absolutely to Dick. 'Of course, I shall sell it,' he said. Meanwhile, there was no news from the police in Cornwall as to the finding of Uncle Hamilton's body. Stroud had made all necessary financial arrangements to tide the Tylecroft household over the interregnum. Perhaps I would care to come and dine some night, and meet Cousin Bill, who had shown some curiosity about me?

I said I should be delighted, and asked how Cousin Bill had taken our expedition to Cornwall. Did he feel that he had been kept in the dark?

'I dare say he did,' was the reply, 'but he's very uncommunicative. When I told him the whole story he said little except, "Humph!" Really, I find him rather hard to deal with. He's so utterly different from everything we used to stand for. However, he hasn't been obstructive, and was quite willing to let me take the lead in negotiating with Stroud, being the first named executor. He's still worried about his mother's appendix. He's devoted to her. I suppose big, fat men can feel devotion like other people. By the way, I ought to warn you that the police will soon be getting in touch with you, and asking you to make an appointment to give them your version of the affair. I hope you don't mind. I've had a long interview with them, and they sent someone down to question Mrs. Pressley and Sibyl.'

At this point I had to close the conversation rather abruptly, as the office-boy came in to tell me that one of our more important clients, a Mrs. Molyneux-Brown (whom actually I had introduced to the firm), was on another line and wanted to speak to me. When she came through, however, it was not to give me an order, but to ask if I would spend Saturday and Sunday, July 10th and 11th, with her and her husband in the country. My impulse is always to refuse invitations from people whom I don't know very well, but my loyalty to the firm made me master it, and I said I should be delighted to go. July 10th and 11th were still some way ahead, and I little knew how important that visit was to be.

The police-call of which Dick had warned me came over the telephone the following morning, before I had left my flat for the office. I was asked to go to my local police station at any time convenient to myself. I made an appointment for five o'clock, and when that hour came found myself repeating the statement which I had made to the police in Cornwall. Apart from the normal feeling of guilt which, I take it, most of us have when we enter police-stations, I had felt rather perturbed during the day lest I should be asked any searching question relating to Cousin Bill. By now, I thought, the authorities must have read Uncle Hamilton's draft letter to him, and they had probably heard of his visit to Falmouth. They might even have heard, through the garrulous waiter at the Radnor, that I knew of his visit to Falmouth. However, if they had, they showed no signs of it, and I was allowed to go away without being asked any question which could have caused me a moment's hesitation.

As I ate my solitary dinner that night, I said to myself yet again that my 'third case' was now finally closed.

Dick rang up the same evening, as I was going early to bed, to ask if I would care to dine with him the next night. I had to refuse, as I had arranged to spend the week-end in Somersetshire with my mother and step-father. He said he was sorry and hoped to see me soon, but he was planning to take a short holiday in France, and would probably be away for most of the next fort-night. I asked to what part he was going, but he said he hadn't decided. I presumed he must have managed to raise some money on the strength of his expectations. Then I told him about my call to the police-station, and he seemed glad that they were 'getting a move on.' There was still no news from Cornwall. Was there any other news? I asked. He said there wasn't, except that Cousin Bill's mother was rather better, and they hoped she wouldn't need to be operated on after all. Our conversation became desultory, and yet, somehow, neither of us could gracefully put the receiver down. For want of anything better to say I asked after Mrs. Pressley, and then, more impertinently still, after Miss Crowne. Had he seen her again since Monday?

'Why?' he said. 'Do you want to meet her? I can arrange it, if you like.'

I said defensively that I thought her an interesting character. I should have liked to ask about Miss Montaubyn, but was too crushed by Dick's counter-attack. Nor did I find out if he had seen Miss Crowne again.

At length he said abruptly, 'Well, I'm going to bed. Good-night, Malcolm,' and released me.

The following Tuesday morning, June 22nd, I received a small parcel addressed to me in Dick's handwriting. To my surprise it contained the notebook which I had entitled 'Warren's Third Case.' I had completely forgotten about it since my return from Cornwall. Accompanying it was this letter:

TYLECROFT,
SOUTH MERSLEY.
June 21st, 1937.

DEAR MALCOLM,

I imagine you will like to have the enclosed for your criminological museum. You mustn't blame me if your Third Case falls a little flat. I found the document inside a map in the pocket of the near-side door of my car. I suppose you had the map in your coat pocket, along with the precious volume, and in restoring the map to the car, made me an involuntary present of your 'case book.' Of course I have read it right through with great interest. Indeed, I have even shown it to Cousin Bill. Perhaps that was rather naughty of me.

I go abroad to-morrow. Still no news from Cornwall.

Yours rather hurriedly,

DICK F.

P.S. Stroud has made my will for me, and, taking you at your word, I have appointed you as my sole executor. You get £100. So, if you hear of my sudden death, you must get busy!

This unexpected return of my case book made me feel very foolish indeed—foolish in having lost it, foolish in having forgotten about it after losing it, and foolish in having written anything in it at all. During breakfast I read the meagre contents with anxiety, which was not relieved when I came to the passage describing my interview with the waiter at the Radnor who had shown me the visitors' book containing Cousin Bill's name. What must Cousin Bill have thought of me for ferreting that out? And I felt still more disturbed, later, when I came to the sentence of which I had been so proud:

Query: Where is Uncle Hamilton's writing-block?

This unfortunate sentence, in itself quite meaningless even to Dick, must have aroused the gravest suspicions both in Dick and his cousin that I was playing some extraordinary game of my own, and trying to turn their domestic tragedy into a melodrama. I wondered that Dick had not asked me what I meant by it. Perhaps he thought he had put himself in the wrong by reading my case book, and that the least he could do was to make no reference to its contents. When I next saw him, I should have to offer some explanation. This, however, would be difficult, as I did not want to confess to having read Uncle Hamilton's draft letter, especially as I had concealed my knowledge of it from Dick.

Then I went to the office, and quieted my misgivings by making a complex if inaccurate analysis of some company accounts. It was not the first time I found office work a sedative for my nerves.

The rest of the week passed without incident. So did the next, till Thursday, July 1st, when the fading memories of my 'Third Case' were again revived. While I was waiting for one of my partners to relieve me for luncheon, my eye was caught by the following paragraph in the *Financial Times:*

GARVICE AND BAGSHAW, LTD.

We understand that this old established private Company, whose business is the manufacture of chemicals and synthetic fertilisers, has been bought by the Universal Chemical Combine, Ltd. The capital of Garvice and Bagshaw consists of 80,000 five per cent. cumulative preference shares of £1 and 40,000 ordinary shares of £1. There are no debentures. The preference shareholders are receiving a share for share allotment of U.C.C. five-and-a-half per cent. cumulative preference shares, and the ordinary shareholders are receiving for each share held by them one U.C.C. ordinary share and a cash payment of thirty-two shillings. The present market price of U.C.C. ordinary shares is thirty-six shillings. The directors of Garvice and Bagshaw are Mr. David Bagshaw (Chairman) and Mr. Paul Bagshaw (Managing Director). We understand that Mr. David Bagshaw will retire from business, while his son, Mr. Paul Bagshaw, will join the board of U.C.C.

Garvice and Bagshaw, Ltd., have had a long and successful career, a dividend of seventeen-and-a-half per cent.

having been paid on the ordinary capital since 1921, while in the year 1935 a bonus of——

At this point my partner came in and I went out to luncheon. I was not interested in Garvice and Bagshaw's fine financial record, but I wondered very much how the merger would affect Dick. Would he be taken on by the new company, or would he find some more congenial work? With his legacy in prospect he could afford to pick and choose. He could even afford to do nothing. I knew that his work with Garvice and Bagshaw had always fretted him, though latterly he had been fairly well paid. But even if his salary were to be raised by a good deal, I could hardly see him becoming a cog in the huge machinery of the Universal Chemical Combine. With Garvice and Bagshaw he had been a member of the family, even though they might have treated him as a poor relation. He had always seemed able to take holidays when he wished, and his hours were not too inflexible. I wondered how long he had known of the amalgamation. That would depend, I supposed, on how far he enjoyed the confidence of his directors. Perhaps since his Uncle George's death in the previous December, he had been treated more as an outsider. I felt I ought to get in touch with him, and after my meal, I rang up Tylecroft to find out if by any chance he had come back from abroad. I was answered by Sibyl, Mrs. Pressley's daughter, who said that Mr. Richard wasn't expected home till the middle of next week at the earliest. I took the opportunity of asking her if there was any news from Cornwall, but she said she hadn't heard of any.

That evening I dined in the house near Paddington, to which I had been for a cocktail party when I first started to investigate Uncle Hamilton's disappearance, and discovered that he had spent the first night of his absence from Tylecroft at the Strafford Royal Hotel. It was only natural that, when dinner and bridge were over, I should make a slight *détour* from my direct homeward route, and walk down Westbourne Terrace, once more trying to guess the spot where Dick had bidden his uncle a last goodbye. I was the more interested in Westbourne Terrace because I now knew that it contained the abode of Hilda Montaubyn. Was it possible that Dick, after depositing his uncle, paid her a visit? Well, if he had, it was quite irrelevant. But having seen her splendid photograph on Dick's writing-desk, I could not help feeling curious about her, and hoping that by some chance she would pop her glorious head out of one of the upper windows as I passed. Late as it was, I should have almost been tempted to call upon her, if I had known her address. But she was not in the telephone directory. I had searched there the morning after I had first learnt of her existence. So I had to content myself with looking upwards at the windows, out of which no head popped, and wondering vainly which of them belonged to her. And, I reflected, if that broad, innocent street held some romance for me, how much more must it hold for Dick—in view of everything; for I had come to the conclusion that he hoped to marry Miss Montaubyn as soon as he came into his inheritance. I could tell from Dick's manner when he spoke of her that she was no passing affair, such as Miss Crowne had probably been to him. Nor was her face the type to encourage only a random flicker of desire.

But these maudlin thoughts, which persisted till I had reached my flat, were rudely put to flight when I had read my evening post. One letter only, lying face downwards on the little mat just inside my front door. The envelope was 'commercial' in shape and my address was correctly type-written.

I opened the letter with that vague distress which one feels when one thinks one is about to open a tradesman's bill, and this is what I read:

Dear Sir,

I understand that you have been investigating the death of Mr. Hamilton Findlay in Cornwall. Do you think you have finished your investigations? I think not. Why do you suppose Mr. Findlay went to Cornwall? This is just to make you sit up and take a little more notice.

Yours,

X.

The stamp, which I examined carefully, bore the postmark of my own postal district. In fact the letter might have been posted in the pillar-box at the end of my own street.

7.

Friday, July 2nd, to Sunday, July 4th

AFTER a disturbed night, during which my thoughts were so agitated that there is little point in my trying to recall them now, I awoke with one decision firmly made. I would ask my senior partner's advice about the anonymous letter.

My senior partner has a fine character, and I knew that his judgment, however whimsical and impulsive it might sometimes seem to be, would be based upon a remarkable spirit of fairness, and an appreciation of nuances which could find no place in any purely legal code.

It was during a lazy period about twelve, when we were sitting alone together in our little office room, that I had my opportunity.

'Jack,' I said. 'I want to consult you about something rather serious.'

He looked up from newly printed photographs of his yacht, and surveyed me with consternation. No doubt I had spoken in my special voice which, he says, always makes him afraid I am going to suggest moving to a larger office, closing one of our most important accounts, or investigating a scandal in the half-commission department.

'What is it this time, Malcolm?' he asked.

'Well, Jack,' I began diffidently, 'I've been involved in a rather extraordinary affair—at least, I don't know yet whether it is extraordinary or not, that's the trouble. If it's quite normal, I oughtn't to hint in any way that it seems to have some unusual aspects. I might easily cause embarrassment and distress to a number of people by doing so. On the other hand, if it isn't quite as straightforward as I should like to think, I ought to do a good deal. It might even be my duty to go to the police.'

'Good heavens, Malcolm, you're not mixed up in another murder case, are you?'

'In the strictest confidence, Jack, there is just the possibility that I am.'

He whistled.

'I'm not asking you to tell me what it's all about,' he said. 'You evidently feel you can't do that. But I would suggest this to you. By an extraordinary coincidence you've been involved in two murder cases already. It's really too much to suppose that you're going to get involved in another. On the other hand, your past experience must predispose you to think you are. What I mean is, if you came across a case of accidental death, the possibility of murder would leap to your mind at once—you couldn't help it. You'd worry yourself into thinking so, just as the hypochondriac worries himself into thinking he has appendicitis at the smallest sign of a tummy-ache, and goes on imagining the tummy-ache long after it has ceased to exist. I do urge you, if the chances seem about evenly balanced in your mind, to give yourself and this case—whatever it is—the benefit of the doubt, and put it right out of your mind.'

We paused for a moment in our talk while a typist came in and collected some letters from my partner's desk. When she had gone out of the room I said:

'If you'd given me this advice yesterday morning, Jack, I should have completely agreed with you. In fact, I had put the affair out of my mind. But since then—last night to be exact—I had an anonymous letter, the object of which is quite unmistakably to arouse my suspicions.'

Jack whistled again. He prides himself on this accomplishment.

'Do you recommend that I should be influenced by the anonymous letter, or not?' I asked. 'That's the one definite point on which I can ask you to advise me, at this stage.'

'In the ordinary way,' Jack answered judicially, 'the best course is to take no notice of them at all. I've had two during my life. One I knew to be spiteful rubbish, and it was easy to throw it into the fire with disgust. The other one contained some information I suspected might be true. I thought about it for a long time, and in the end I decided not to let myself be influenced by it. In other words, I deliberately didn't take some steps which I might perhaps have taken of my own accord. I don't know whether I was foolish or not. I felt very uncomfortable for a time, but luckily in the end the guilty party—I mean the party on whom the letter had thrown suspicion—confessed voluntarily and everything ended well. But your case is rather different. Have you any idea at all who wrote the letter?'

'So far as I can see,' I answered, 'it might be one of the four people, or even more.'

'Do you think you can trace the writer?'

'I'm not at all sure that I can, but I could try. That is if you're not going to tell me to throw the letter into the fire with disgust.'

'No,' he said, 'I'm not going to tell you to do that. The fact that you've had an anonymous letter shows that somebody's not playing the game. I see you smile at the old-fashioned phrase, but you know what I mean. To use a modernism which I detest, there's some funny business going on somewhere. Not necessarily on the writer's part. For once the writer may be comparatively innocent—a little uneasy in mind, as you are, or even afraid to speak openly. No, Malcolm, I'm afraid you can't let the matter rest now. You must try to track the writer down, and I suppose you ought to probe anything else in the affair which you may have thought suspicious or unusual. And at the first sign of there being anything really wrong, you must go straight to the police. I'm not sure that I oughtn't to tell you to go to the police at once, with the letter. I don't like to think of your putting your head into a hornets' nest.'

'I certainly don't feel justified in going to the police yet,' I said. 'I think it's probably four to one that the letter was just a piece of malice, and if I don't keep my own counsel I shall be playing into the writer's hands. In some moods, I think the whole business quite absurd.'

'You don't think,' he asked, 'that somebody may be playing a joke on you? "Here's Malcolm Warren, that busybody, who imagines he's such a clever detective. Let's make him look silly for once." Does that fit at all?'

'Yes, it might,' I said. 'Another reason for treading daintily. I don't want to appear a public fool. But if it is a practical joke, it's rather a grim one.'

Then the telephone bell rang, and our conversation had to stop for a while. When we were able to resume it, it was time for my partner to go out for luncheon, and he said little beyond telling me to run no personal risks, and not to hesitate to come to him if I wanted any help.

I left the office earlier than usual that afternoon, went to the post-office nearest to my flat, and posted an envelope there, addressed to myself. I noticed that the next collection was at 5.15. The collection after that was at 6.15. I then went to the pillar-box at the end of my street, hoping that it was a fair sample of all the pillar-boxes in my neighbourhood, and posted another envelope there, which I had marked '2'. The next collection there was at 4.45, and the one following was at 5.45. I was eager to find out, if I could, how late in the day a letter could be posted, so as to reach me the same night. Looking back now upon this little scheme, I realise that it would have been simpler and more accurate to make inquiries at the post-office—though, perhaps, even here I should not have been given a definite reply. But I felt secretive, and the idea of having to worm my way past the haughty ladies behind the counter to some responsible official was distasteful to me. My methods usually tend to be furtive and a little odd.

Soon after 5.15 I went out again, carrying two more envelopes. Going first to my pillar-box, I noted with satisfaction that the 4.45 collection had been made. When I had posted an envelope marked '4,' I walked on towards the post-office where I had posted my first envelope, repeating to the rhythm of my stride, 'odd numbers from post-office, even numbers from pillar-box . . . odd numbers from post-office, even numbers from pillar-box.' Soon I got mixed between odd and even, and wished I had written the numbers down in a notebook, so as to leave no room for doubt. But it was easy to remember that I had posted my first envelope from the post-office, which was near my tube station.

On reaching the post-office I posted Envelope No. 3. The 5.15 collection had been made, and my letter would presumably catch the next one at 6.15. I felt fairly sure that the person who posted the anonymous letter had set no special store by my receiving it the same evening. On the other hand, the fact that I had received it the same evening showed that it had been posted during the afternoon. How late in the afternoon it could have been posted I hoped to discover through my little manoeuvres. It is probably unnecessary for me to say that I was almost convinced that the person who posted the letter was not, normally, a resident in the London area. Hence, if I could find that any of my suspects had paid an afternoon visit to London on Thursday, July 1st, I should be on the track. I could rule out the possibility of the letter having been posted in the morning, since, in that event, I should have received it before I set out for my dinner-party.

I spent a good deal of time that evening not only trying to decide what steps I would take if I did discover the sender of the anonymous letter, but also weighing up what I may call the moral aspects of the case. Again I asked myself how far I was justified in 'interfering' or playing a game of my own. While wishing to keep clear of the law myself, I have never had any desire to entangle others in it. I have no passion for justice in the abstract, and, except for certain crimes which rouse a sensational distaste in me, my sympathies are always vaguely on the side of the criminal. At the same time, as I know from my first two 'cases,' the knowledge or suspicion of another person's guilt can make me feel most uncomfortable. I had hoped very much that, when I had made my statement at the local police station, I could put aside any qualms or questions which suggested themselves to me regarding Hamilton Findlay's death. There had been, it is true, certain features in the whole episode which seemed rather 'out of character'—to use a phrase which occurred a good deal in my first long talk with Dick. And as we made our joint investigation in Falmouth, such features, instead of explaining themselves away, seemed to recur like bouts of a fever which cannot shake off. There was no doubt there was something a little wrong about the whole affair. But I had argued, isn't there something a little wrong about every affair? Does normal life really exist at all? Is there not a waywardness in every event, a conflict of impulse behind every action? Suppose I had to give a full account of myself for a single day, would not a skilled questioner be able to drag out of me a whole mass of foibles, inhibitions, and illogicalities which would give my most innocent actions a background of fantasy? And events, even in the inanimate world, seem to me to have the same capriciousness. When one thinks, for example, of the scope of coincidences which exist throughout the whole range of life, isn't it rather amazing that one doesn't notice more of them? Jack himself had said that very morning that my experiences inclined me to be suspicious.

But at that moment the evening post arrived, reminding me that the anonymous letter I had received was, at least, no creature of my imagination.

I went to the door and found two envelopes addressed in my own handwriting, the unnumbered envelope which I had posted at the post-office to catch the 5.15 collection, and Envelope No. 2 which I had posted in the pillar-box before 4.45. The other two envelopes presumably would arrive next morning. On the basis of this slender research I felt myself entitled to conclude that the poster, not necessarily the writer, of the anonymous letter had been in South Kensington before 5.15 on Thursday, July 1st.

I decided to ring up Tylecroft before going to bed. As I had hoped, the telephone was answered by Mrs. Pressley.

'Oh, Mrs. Pressley!' I said; 'I'm so sorry to bother you at this rather late hour, but I felt I should like to know if there was any more news from Cornwall. I tried to catch you yesterday afternoon, when I saw you, and your daughter—wasn't it?—in South Kensington? But you moved too quickly for me.'

'Me in South Kensington yesterday?' she said, in great surprise; 'you must have been mistaken, Mr. Warren. We were both here in South Mersley. Actually we spent the afternoon at St. Giles' garden fête. Sibyl was helping at the embroidery stall. But fancy you remembering me well enough to think you recognised me!'

So far as I could judge there was nothing but innocent pleasure in her voice at the thought that her appearance had impressed itself upon me.

'Well, I could have sworn it was you,' I said, blushing at the lie. 'However, we all have doubles, haven't we? I was sure I saw you and your daughter turning down Sussex Place—that's just by South Kensington Station, you know. What a good thing I didn't run after the two ladies! Well, I mustn't waste your time over my silly mistake. I really rang up to know if you could give me any news from Cornwall, and could tell me when you're expecting Mr. Richard home.'

'News from Cornwall! There's none that I know of,' she answered. 'Mr. Richard sent a postcard saying he would be arriving on Wednesday evening of next week. I'll tell him you rang up.'

'That's very kind of you. He'll probably let me know soon after he gets back. Meanwhile, I'm so sorry for all your sakes that you haven't any definite news. You must find the suspense very tiring.'

'It is that, sir,' she said. 'But I'm afraid we can't have any hope now. It wouldn't be like Mr. Findlay to stay so long away from home without letting anyone know. And, of course, those clothes which you and Mr. Richard found in Cornwall make it only too plain what happened.'

'Yes,' I said, 'I'm afraid they do. Well, good-night, Mrs. Pressley. Next time I think I see you, I'll make quite sure it is you, before I go saying "How d'you do?" '

She laughed, and her voice once more showed a gentle satisfaction when she wished me good-night.

Poor Mrs. Pressley! As if she hadn't thousands of drab doubles in this drab world of ours. I should have felt more shame in deceiving her if she hadn't reacted to the deception precisely as I had hoped she would. Unless she were a brilliant actress—and there was no need to suppose she was anything of an actress at all—she could never have feigned that suppressed gratification. I felt that I could almost hear her thoughts over the telephone: 'Fancy Mr. Warren thinking he recognised me in South Kensington, when he's only seen me twice in his life. There must be something striking about me, even at my age—and in quite a smart neighbourhood, too!'

No, it couldn't have been she or her daughter who had posted the anonymous letter yesterday afternoon. Apart from the alibi, which I didn't intend to test, the psychological evidence against it was too strong. And, less justifiably, perhaps, I felt equally sure that Mrs. Pressley had not written the letter and given it to a friend to post. If she had, she would have been much more emphatic in her denial that she had been in London, and she would have produced her alibi with fear or indignation, instead of a girlish complacency.

There remained Sibyl. I felt it needless to doubt her alibi for the Thursday afternoon, but I could not altogether ignore the possibility that, unknown to her mother, she had written, or dictated, the anonymous letter and given it to a friend to post. To some extent I had summed up Mrs. Pressley's position in the household at Tylecroft, but I knew nothing of Sibyl's. Had there ever been anything between her and Dick, or between her and Uncle Hamilton? I hardly thought so, because she was so very plain. When I had seen her she struck me as the type to be very much under her mother's thumb, and not likely to have any secret life of her own. But one never knows. These mousy little people are capable of strong passions, which lead them sometimes into the most inappropriate antics.

Still, of all those I suspected Sibyl was last on the list, and I resolved I would only reconsider her if I made no progress in other quarters.

My immediate difficulty was how to make any progress at all. I spent Saturday afternoon and Sunday with my married sister and her military husband who is stationed near Gloucester. A dull visit. I felt that they had only asked me out of politeness, and they may well have thought, from my abstracted air, that I had only gone to them out of politeness, and to please my mother, who liked to see the family 'keeping together.'

The conversation ranged ceaselessly through topics which I found repulsive, and it was even worse when my hosts tried to talk of 'my subjects,' by which they meant books such as I would never dream of reading, and the wrong kind of concert full of trills and palpitations.

It was with relief that I got into the London train on Sunday night, and could settle down without interruption to devise my plan of campaign.

8.

Monday, July 5th: 2.30 to 5.30 p.m.

Luckily we were idle in the office on Monday, and I was able to leave my work almost immediately after luncheon without inconveniencing anyone. As I put on my hat my senior partner said, with a solemn wink:

'Sleuthing?' and I nodded solemnly in reply. It made me feel that my errand was a little unreal.

My intention was to go to South Mersley Garden City, and try to see Miss Crowne.

I knew little of the Garden City beyond the random information which Dick had given me about it. Apparently it had been conceived as a social experiment on an ambitious scale by a certain Lady Petter-Bury, who endowed it munificently with her late husband's fortune. It was intended to be a microcosm of the ideal state, a prosperous ant-hill, with a cult, however, of liberalism rather than communism. While its inhabitants had to conform to a strict code, they were supposed to retain sufficient freedom of thought and action to be able to develop their 'legitimate' aspirations. The emphasis was on the adjective 'legitimate,' which presumably meant 'acceptable to the governing body.'

In as much as the 'City' was a voluntary settlement, there is no wonder that the 'citizens' tended to be those people to whom the ant is a pattern of virtue, and not those like myself who regard it as a detestable and valueless insect. None the less, even this community was bound to contain some misfits, and I suspected that Miss Crowne was one of these. She would, I felt, prefer the Casino at Nice, or a day at Goodwood, to the Communal Lecture Room and physical training before breakfast.

I began to wonder, as my train approached the station, what treats, if any, came her way. Had Dick been her chief provider of good things? Or had she other young gentlemen friends? At all events, she had not seemed greatly contented with life when I saw her in the garden of Dick's home.

I made my way to the Garden City by bus. The buildings were less forbidding than I had expected, and I felt that it might be possible to live there fairly happily, if one were allowed to live privately—but this, probably, was exactly what one was not allowed to do.

The bus stopped in a kind of square which, with its aggressive cleanliness—but how much less 'character'—might have put many a fashionable West End square to shame, and when I got out, I found myself outside a modern red-brick house bearing the inscription 'S.M.G.C. Community Centre.'

I went in by a door marked 'Public Entrance,' and then through an inner door marked 'Inquiries.' The Inquiries Department was occupied to two young women of athletic build. One seemed to be showing the other some photographs, and neither paid any attention to me for two minutes. Then, when the larger one had given me leave to state my business by uttering the word 'Well?' I said, 'Do you happen to know a Miss Crowne, who I believe works somewhere here?'

I thought for a moment that I was going to be asked what right I had to be inquiring after Miss Crowne, but the young lady replied, with curiosity rather than animosity in her voice:

'Miss Crowne? Yes, we know Miss Crowne very well, don't we, Daphne? You'll find her in the Arts and Crafts Shop.'

Then Daphne said to her companion, 'But isn't it her half-day out, Ellen?'

My heart sank. Had I made the journey for nothing?

'But it's Monday,' I said weakly.

'Here,' answered Ellen, reprovingly, 'we all have two free half-days a week. One of Miss Crowne's half-days might quite easily be Monday. But you're wrong, Daphne, Miss Crowne's days were altered in the spring. She has Thursdays now, not Mondays.'

Thursdays, I thought, and almost said the word aloud. 'Then I shall find her all right,' I asked, 'in the Arts and Crafts Shop?'

'Oh, yes, you'll find her, and her assistant, too, for that matter. I suppose you know where the shop is?'

I confessed that I didn't, and she directed me with veiled amazement at my ignorance.

After this little interview, I proceeded towards the more formidable interview which was the object of my visit to South Mersley. I had, even then, as I walked across the main square and up an avenue, very little idea of how I hoped to conduct my investigation. I had not even planned what I would say to Miss Crowne when I saw her. I relied on my sensitiveness to 'atmosphere' rather than on question and answer. If I could see Miss Crowne in her daily setting, and watch her reactions to my unexpected coming, I felt I should go away far better informed than any policeman with a notebook. Perhaps my preference for psychological deduction is a form of self-praise; for I was born with a distrust of cold facts, and no presentation of life without an emotional tinge has ever interested me. People like me are beginning to be attacked by the adjective—or is it a noun?—'escapist.' I suppose our temperaments don't fit in with some political system or other.

Absorbed with reflections on these lines, I reached my destination, and for a moment paused outside the two windows of the Arts and Crafts Shop, surveying the wares which they displayed.

I was quite ready to pay for my footing inside by buying something, but try as I would, I could see nothing which I should not immediately have to send to one of my mother's parochial jumble sales. I must look round inside, I thought. I could do with a blotter if they have one made of old leather. But alas! though the Arts and Crafts Shop stocked several blotters there was none to suit my taste. As I went through the door I saw my quarry, if I may so call her, showing handkerchiefs to a lady at the back of the shop. I was, however, pounced upon at once by another and younger lady, presumably Miss Crowne's assistant, who tried in vain to satisfy my requirements. I judged her to be under twenty. Her hair was artificially silvered, and her face was so carefully made up that it was hard to see any expression behind the mask. But the set of the eyes and the mouth seemed to me to hint a kind of sophisticated naughtiness—I might almost say viciousness—which, in one so young, made me feel uncomfortable. I marvelled at finding such a person in the Garden City and wondered what patronage enabled her to keep her job, or why she wanted to keep it. Compared with her, Miss Crowne, whose blowsy charms were presented to me in profile, looked the picture of moral health.

When about ten blotters had been produced for me and rejected, the sales-lady said, politely, but with infinite lassitude, 'I'm afraid there's nothing at all to suit you here.'

'Perhaps,' I suggested, 'I could look round a little.'

As I spoke, I took another glance at Miss Crowne, who seemed as busy as ever with her customer. My companion must have noticed the glance, for she said at once, 'Have you really come to see *her?*'

I answered, 'Partly. I have had the pleasure of meeting

Miss Crowne before. But I also wanted to see your shop, which I've heard a good deal of.'

'Well,' she said, 'this is it all right, and the prices are all marked in plain figures. You'll call me if you want anything, won't you? But I don't expect Miss Crowne will be very long now.'

At this she left me to my own devices, and retired, effectively out of range, through a door in the back of the shop. Meanwhile, Miss Crowne, who had evidently recognised me, looked up to make sure that I was still there. I had the feeling that she was deliberately dallying with her customer. Did she shrink from meeting me again? Or was she preparing her behaviour? However, I ambled round the shop with as much unconcern as I could muster, and surveyed an assortment of embroidered napkins, painted wastepaper baskets and lamp-shades adorned with crude wood-cuts. A clumsily made bottle of greenish glass seemed one of the least unattractive objects in the shop, and I thought of buying it till I saw the price was twelve and sixpence. As I was putting it back gingerly on its shelf, Miss Crowne came up behind me and showed her customer out. There was nothing for it but a rapturous greeting on both sides.

'Why, Mr. Warren, fancy seeing you here! I'm terribly sorry I had to be so long.'

'I'm delighted to find *you* here,' I said. 'I happened to be in South Mersley this afternoon and thought I'd pay you a call.'

Her next remark might well have been, 'Have you seen Dick lately?' But she didn't make it. Perhaps she knew he was abroad. Instead, she said: 'Are you really trying to buy any of this stuff?'

'Well,' I answered, 'shops like this have a way of being useful for Christmas.'

'But it's July.'

'Exactly, I always begin my Christmas shopping in July.'

'I suppose you have such heaps of presents to give.' She

laughed, and I had the momentary impression that her remark implied that she thought me very rich and that she was, even then, in some remote corner of her mind, wondering whether I might not be, as they say on the Stock Exchange, a 'commercial proposition.' The phrase is really too crude and too unkind to use in connection with Miss Crowne's thoughts, which were probably of the most indefinite order, but I am convinced that the part of her which was 'on the make' did whisper faintly to her 'better self,' 'Why not vamp him if you can?' After all, Dick had probably told her a little about me. He was always ready, conversationally, to exaggerate my resources, and the public are only too willing to believe that all stockbrokers are millionaires. Actually, I suppose, the average stockbroker makes about as much money as the average doctor—more in booms and less in slumps.

But for the time being I had small leisure to wonder what I should do if I found Miss Crowne becoming too friendly. I had decided on the spur of the moment to employ the same manoeuvres on her as I had, the previous Friday night, employed over the telephone on Mrs. Pressley.

After we had made a little more conversation, I said suddenly:

'Why did you refuse to recognise me last Thursday afternoon?'

'Last Thursday, where?'

She paused for a minute as if pulling herself together.

'Near South Kensington Station,' I said. 'I was on a bus and waved. I think I even shouted at you, but you walked on, and by the time I got off I couldn't see you anywhere.'

'Did you say near South Kensington?' she asked. 'In the West End?'

'Yes.'

'Why—' she hesitated such a long time that in my own mind suspicion almost became certainty. 'Why, I wasn't anywhere near there.'

'But I am sure I saw you.'

'You've only seen me once before,' she said defensively.

'Yes, but once is enough.'

My remark puzzled her, and I could see her blushing very slowly.

'Do you mean to say,' I went on, 'you weren't in the West End at all last Thursday?'

Again a hesitation. Should she lie, or tell a half-truth? She lied.

'Of course I wasn't. You don't suppose I can afford jaunts like that, do you? I was here. I don't mean in the shop, but in this ruddy suburb, if you want to know.'

Her tone had become frankly hostile. It would not have been hostile if she had not found it necessary to lie. So it was she who had written the anonymous letter, and posted it almost on my own doorstep.

'Well, it just shows how I must have been thinking of you,' I said with triumphant gallantry. 'But it was silly of me to make a mistake. Don't you ever manage to get up to the West End?'

I was appealing shamelessly to her worser nature by this remark, but it couldn't be helped.

'Only when I'm asked,' she answered, in the same sordid strain, and I was forced to reply that this must happen pretty often.

After this, having gained my point, I might have gone away, but I was eager to see a little more of Miss Crowne while I had the chance. Indeed, if I was right in supposing that she had written the anonymous letter it was essential that I should see more of her.

'I suppose you couldn't come out to tea with me,' I suggested. 'Can't your assistant, who seems to have disappeared behind that door, look after the shop for you for half-an-hour? You don't seem exactly swamped with customers.'

'Of course we're not,' she said. 'We run at a loss, but it doesn't matter, as we're subsidised. Still, I'm supposed to be on duty. I could give you some tea and a bit of cake in there, if you like.'

She pointed to the door at the back.

'That would be delightful,' I said, 'but what about the other young lady? She rather frightens me.'

'Oh, I can send *her* out. She doesn't generally stay after four. She's only here to get experience. They don't pay her.'

'Well, send her out,' I begged.

'All right, I'll try,' she answered, and went through into the recess. A moment later she came out again and said, 'She's gone away—by the back door. Come in, won't you, and see how the poor live?'

I followed her through the inner door into a small room which was half kitchenette and half office. While Miss Crowne heated some water on a gas-ring, I had leisure to notice a typewriter standing on a table, largely covered with books and papers. The typewriter filled me with curiosity. I had learnt from my detective-story reading that, to the expert, all typewriters have individual characteristics. Was that the machine on which the anonymous letter had been typed? I longed desperately to have a sample from it, and thought bitterly that if I had been Inspector French, I could at once have asked for one, without arousing any suspicion. But, being Malcolm Warren, I could think of no pretext whatsoever for doing so. Indeed, I was so frightened of betraying my inquisitiveness that I started to talk about Miss Crowne's assistant.

'She's a Miss Fillyan—with a y,' Miss Crowne said. 'She lives with her uncle, who is an elderly clergyman in the Garden City. He's connected somehow with the nobs who run this place, though he hasn't any money to speak of. Jane—you wouldn't think that was her Christian name, would you?—is rather a mystery woman. She doesn't care a damn for anybody, least of all her uncle.'

'You think Jane gets up to mischief?' I asked.

'Well, don't you?'

'I haven't the least idea. I must say she struck me as being a little—formidable.'

'She's a bad hat.'

'I was a bit surprised to find her here,' I said.

'Well, you know, she's the type who can get away with anything. The authorities haven't summed her up yet, and the Reverend has a good deal of influence.'

'How long has she been here?' I asked.

'About six months. She came just after the new year.'

'And do you think she hopes to get a permanent job here?'

'I don't know. I can't make her out at all, but she seems to interest you a good deal, Mr. Warren.'

'She's so peculiar.'

'Yes, you're quite right. She is peculiar. Now, here's your tea, and let's talk of something pleasant.'

But this was just what I found it difficult to do. I hadn't come to South Mersley Garden City to talk of something pleasant, but to try to find out who had written the anonymous letter, and why it had been sent to me. As I watched Miss Crowne doing the fussy honours of our little tea, I became more and more convinced that she was the writer. She suspected that I suspected her, though she was still hoping for the best. She was watching me, too, much as I was watching her. Perhaps I had an advantage over her, in that I was attacking and she was defending, and I think she feared, in a muddle-headed way, that anything she said might be used in evidence against her. She even seemed diffident in talking about Miss Fillyan, though surely Miss Fillyan was an innocent subject of conversation. Or wasn't she? I resolved to learn a little more about her if I could, before going away.

Then, while by way of temporary truce, we were discussing a tennis tournament, I suddenly decided to adopt still further measures. After all, there was no need for any secrecy on my part.

'I've been wondering,' I said, with assumed hesitation, 'if you've been wondering why I'm really here in South Mersley this afternoon. I'm sure you'll never guess.'

She bridled unconvincingly and said, 'Well, I had hoped it was to see me, but I suppose that's flattering myself. Was it to see Miss Fillyan?'

I laughed and said, 'Oh, no. I didn't know of her existence till half-an-hour ago. No, there's quite a different reason—I mean, apart from my wishing to see you again.' I didn't care how forced the compliment sounded, and went on, 'I was hoping you might be able to help me. The fact is, I've had an anonymous letter—'

She interrupted me with a show of violent indignation. 'And you think I wrote it, I suppose. Well, you're a nice one—'

'That clinches it,' I thought.

Aloud I said, 'I haven't even told you what it was about yet.'

This sobered her at once, and she blushed painfully as she realised how foolish her tactics had been.

'Well, you can hardly expect me to be excited about what was in it, can you, if you've come here thinking I wrote it? Is that why you came here?'

'I came here because I thought you might be able to help me,' I answered. 'The letter had to do with old Mr. Findlay's death—suggesting it wasn't the accident it seemed. I should have consulted Dick, of course, if he'd been here, but as he isn't, I thought I'd better get in touch with a friend of his. Can you conceive anyone writing such a letter to me? I don't know many of Dick's friends, least of all friends who might be interested in his uncle's death.'

She gazed into her tea-cup for a long time, dabbing at the tea-leaves with her tea-spoon. Then she said doubtfully, 'It is a most extraordinary thing. Could it be that old cat, Mrs. Pressley, do you think? She might have got some extraordinary idea into her head.'

'I did think of her,' I admitted, 'but I set a little trap for her, and it didn't catch her.'

'Have you been setting a little trap for me?' she asked, with a nervous laugh.

I laughed nervously, too, feeling unable to tell a lie. Do real detectives ever have such scruples?

'I want you to suggest someone else on whom I can try the trap,' I said. 'You know much more of the situation down here than I do. I feel sure the letter must have been written by someone down here. Apart from me, Dick's London friends—at all events those whom I know—hardly know he had an uncle. It must be someone with a grievance, somebody who wanted to make mischief. Can't you think of anyone who might fit in?'

Again she considered the situation, while I wondered if she was going to confess. But she had evidently decided not to do so.

'Well, of course, there's Dick's cousin, Mr. Hicks,' she said, at length.

'I hardly think it would be like him, though,' I answered. 'Mind you, I've only met him once, but from Dick's description he doesn't sound like an anonymous letter-writer.'

'Perhaps not,' she said doubtfully. 'I've only met him once or twice myself. Still, it's hard to think of anybody else. Who could there be, now? Let me see—'

'Some lady friend of Dick's?' I suggested.

She shook her head vigorously.

'Oh, no. At least I don't know of one. I wish I could help you. Of course, I don't know many of Dick's family friends. I mean the people he knows more through his uncle than because he likes them. As a matter of fact I don't think there were very many. Tylecroft wasn't a house where they entertained. Mr. Findlay wasn't what you'd call in society.'

Her volubility reached a halt, then she added, with a

touch of pride in her voice, 'How about Dr. Fielding? Have you thought of him?'

I hadn't, and it was my turn to ponder over what I was going to say next. Meanwhile, my puzzled silence gave her courage, and she went on.

'He may be disgruntled about Mr. Findlay's will. Dick said that Dr. Fielding only got a small legacy. After all, he was Mr. Findlay's great friend, almost like a lady-companion. He probably expected a great deal more.'

'Is he very badly off?' I asked.

'Yes, compared with Mr. Findlay. He lives in a very small house in a row in Kashmir Road, and only has a half-daily charwoman to look after him. I imagine he sponged on Mr. Findlay a good deal.'

'Do you think he is the type to write an anonymous letter?'

'Oh, I don't know him well enough to say that. I gathered from Dick that he's the type of man it takes years to get to know—a real recluse.'

'You have met him, then?'

'Yes, once or twice. He's even called at this shop with Mr. Findlay, and bought two picture postcards.'

'I wish I'd met him,' I said. 'I wonder if I could manage it.'

'You can manage it easily enough, when Dick comes home,' she said sensibly. 'After all, this is really Dick's business, isn't it? I don't think either of us is called upon to do anything without consulting him, do you?'

I was on the point of agreeing with her heartily, when there were steps in the shop, and my hostess, murmuring that she would be as quick as she could, jumped from her chair and went through the door.

As soon as she had gone, my thoughts turned again to the typewriter. If only I could secure an example of its work! I dared not use the machine myself, for fear of being overheard, but was it impossible to find some specimen already typed, which I could purloin? What I wanted was a typed envelope, or something of the sort which would not be missed if I took it. But search as I would among the accounting books and papers littering the typing-table, I could find no typing by Miss Crowne. I concluded that she probably did her typing late in the day, and would not begin till I was safely off the premises. I was, however, able to note the make of her machine, an 'Ipsofacto,' Model 19B, serial number D/3875. It would be something, I thought, if I could prove that the typescript of the anonymous letter corresponded with the ordinary typing of an Ipsofacto.

But even while I decided to consult one of my office typists on the subject, I assured myself that such proof was really superfluous. Miss Crowne had already betrayed herself to me.

Through the door, which she had left slightly ajar, I could hear her talking to her customer, a lady named Mrs. Heavens, I gathered, who wished to buy some hand-painted menu cards such as she had had before. I had begun to feel that all the inhabitants of the South Mersley Garden City were in some way connected with my problem, and I even had the curiosity to wish I might make the acquaintance of Mrs. Heavens, whom I could hear but not see. Then my thoughts reverted to Miss Fillyan. Dick, who presumably visited the shop from time to time, must surely have met her. Was she a flame of his, too? If so, there would be no love lost between her and Miss Crowne. But I felt sure that neither of them could compete in that respect with Hilda Montaubyn, whose lovely photograph I had seen on Dick's writing-table at Tylecroft. When I had embarked on the case, if it was a case, I had been sure that at least there were no ladies in it. Now there were three—Miss Crowne, Miss Fillyan and Miss Montaubyn—not to mention Mrs. Pressley and her daughter Sibyl.

Needless to say, the 'case' now seemed to centre round the anonymous letter rather than Uncle Hamilton's death.

At that moment Mrs. Heavens twittered a farewell, and Miss Crowne rejoined me. I resolved to go, as soon as I could, after one more reference to Miss Fillyan.

'Sorry I was so long,' Miss Crowne said.

'It's rough luck on you being single-handed,' I replied. 'Miss Fillyan hasn't bothered to come back yet.'

'Oh, she won't come back this afternoon. Didn't I tell you that? You seem remarkably interested in her, don't you?'

'I don't know,' I said non-committally.

'Well, you'll find her here most mornings, but I shouldn't hope for very much if I were you.'

'Why?'

'Because she hasn't any use for people your or Dick's age.'

'What do you mean? Does she like boys in their teens?'

'No, She prefers rich old men.'

'To rich young ones?'

'Well, there aren't many of those about nowadays, are there? It must have been lovely to live when the stage-door was besieged with wealthy young men-about-town.'

She paused, speculating perhaps on what her destiny might have been in a different age, and I paused, recalling a passage from my French translation of the 'Arabian Nights,' in which two women discuss very frankly the respective charms of young and elderly lovers—and somewhat surprisingly the joint vote favours the elderly. I recollected, too, a brilliant woman of my acquaintance who said she always preferred an old lover to a young one, because old men were *plus cochons*. But I could hardly credit Miss Crowne being versed in such psychology. Probably she was simply trying to assure herself that Jane Fillyan and Dick Findlay meant nothing to one another. Well, that might, or might not be. Meanwhile, it was high time for me to go.

'You know,' I said, 'I think you've given me frightfully good advice this afternoon. You can imagine that getting this anonymous letter made me feel jittery. But I'm sure you're right in saying that I've no call to do anything about it till Dick comes home. And I don't think I will. Now I must say goodbye, and thank you very, very much for being so good to me this afternoon.'

I held out my hand and she took it, pressing it very slightly with her fingers.

'Goodbye,' she said. 'I am so glad you don't think I wrote that letter. I'm sure the best thing you can do *is* to wait.'

We continued to say goodbye as I walked with her, back into the shop, and through the shop to the main door. I said it once more—mingled with a 'Hope to see you again very soon'—while I opened the main door and passed through it into the Garden City. Then I waved, and with no little relief walked rapidly away.

9.

Monday, July 5th: 5.30 to 9 p.m.

IN my first flush of excitement after seeing Miss Crowne, my pace almost increased to a run. Then it slowed down, as my thoughts became more reflective. The result of the interview had been to bring home to me still more that I was really involved in a mystery. Even if Uncle Hamilton's death had been as natural as it seemed, Miss Crowne at all events had her doubts—or pretended to have doubts. Quite wantonly she had thrown a stone into a tranquil pool. Was it just for the fun of seeing the ripples spread outwards over the calm surface? Or was there some purpose or necessity in her stone-throwing? I tried hard to think of an adequate motive, but, beyond the vague suspicion that unrequited affection might be playing a part somewhere, I could find none to satisfy me.

And why had she sent the letter to me, and not to Dick? Perhaps she had written to Dick, too—and to other people as well. Was it a mean attempt to make trouble where no trouble was due—to delay Dick's receipt of his inheritance? Or was it a first essay in blackmail—a threat to someone, not necessarily Dick, that she would make more trouble if something or other were not done? 'You see,' she could say to the unknown victim, 'I've sent off that letter. Mr. Warren came over himself to talk to me about it. You thought I wasn't in earnest, didn't you? But I haven't done yet.'

Then, having walked a long way past the bus-stop in the Garden City Square, I called a halt to these thoughts. I would have betted heavily against Miss Crowne's being a deliberate and systematic blackmailer. Thoughtless and impulsive, yes. Spiteful, perhaps. But villainous, no.

Then yet another possibility occurred to me. Had she written the letter in the hope that I should fasten its authorship on the wrong person? In other words, might her purpose in writing the letter have been not to make me suspicious about Uncle Hamilton's death, but to make me suspect someone other than herself of having written it—presumably with unfortunate consequences for the supposed writer? It may make the problem clearer if I illustrate it by an example taken from another sort of crime. Let us suppose that A sends some slightly poisoned chocolates to B, with the intention not that B should be poisoned, but that B should suspect C of having sent them, and take measures to C's detriment. I must admit that this theory seemed, at the time, somewhat far-fetched, but I felt glad that I had asked Miss Crowne directly who, in her opinion, might have written the letter. Her first answer was Mrs. Pressley, whom she had called an old cat. (Perhaps Mrs. Pressley had sniffed when Miss Crowne visited Tylecroft.) When I said I was convinced of Mrs. Pressley's innocence, she suggested Mr. Hicks—Dick's Cousin Bill. This suggestion struck me as far more significant than the mention of Mrs. Pressley, and the fact that it was not her first suggestion confirmed my view of its importance on psychological grounds. I began to wonder very much whether there was any relationship between Miss Crowne and Mr. Hicks. Had he met her at Tylecroft and pursued her? Or had he tried to put a spoke in her affair with Dick? Had he, perhaps, denounced the affair to Uncle Hamilton?

If so, I felt sure, Miss Crowne would bear him no good will. Then, when I had suggested that Cousin Bill was not the type to write anonymous letters, she mentioned the name of Dr. Fielding—Dr. Fielding, who lived in a small way in Kashmir Road, South Mersley.

In my walk towards the station, I had now passed beyond the confines of the ant-hill, as I dubbed the Garden City, and reached the fringe of the real South Mersley, which was still inhabited somewhat decayingly by those who believe that man's justification lies in himself as an entity, and not merely as a cell in the social organism or as a minute link in the chain of evolution. Unlike the gardens in the Garden City, these gardens were fenced or walled. The old trees grew in them haphazardly, instead of being young and regimented for a communal effect. Here privacy was more important than the general view. Even the houses were painted according to the caprices of the owner. In the Garden City the paintwork was uniform and standardised. Here one could imagine each little owner saying, 'Let the colours clash. I don't care. Why should I look beyond the limits of my own land? Nobody asked you to look here at all. Go away to your own home and don't criticise mine!' The spiritual implications of that change of scene were enormous, and as I entered it I felt free. I not only felt free. I felt resolved to visit Dr. Fielding, before I went home that night. The impulse came upon me quite suddenly, and I decided to execute it before the voice of caution or my own timidity could stop me.

Miss Crowne had said that Dr. Fielding lived in a small way in Kashmir Road, and I remembered Dick's having told me that Dr. Fielding's house was not very far from Tylecroft. This gave me the general direction in which to walk, but I still did not know the full address. Coming to a telephone kiosk I went inside and looked at the Directory, but though there were several Fieldings in it, even Dr. Fieldings, there was none who lived in Kashmir Road,

South Mersley. No doubt, I reflected, my Dr. Fielding lived in too small a way to afford a telephone. There was nothing for it but to go to the Public Library, which I had seen in the High Street that afternoon, and look up the address in the Post Office Directory. I could, of course, have asked Mrs. Pressley, but thought it wiser not to stir her imagination by doing so.

Luckily the Public Library was still open, and I found the address I wanted without difficulty. Dr. Oscar Thomas Fielding lived at 58, Kashmir Road, South Mersley. Reference to a map of the district showed me that Kashmir Road was little more than a quarter of a mile from Tylecroft, and I made my way there with all speed. Indeed, for the time being, I concentrated on walking as quickly as I could, fearing that once I stopped to think, my resolution would fail me. A scriptural text echoed in my head to the effect that one should take no heed of what one would say, for the words would be put in one's mouth.

When I reached Kashmir Road itself I was breathless. 'It really won't do to arrive panting,' I told myself, and tried to saunter. Kashmir Road was long and narrow. The houses were small and semi-detached with small and mostly neglected gardens. It was a road in which no one could live in anything but a small way.

No. 58 was half-way down, on the right-hand side. I opened the creosoted wooden gate nervously, walked up the few feet of brick path and pressed the bell in the jamb of the peeling door, listening for the sound of a ring inside. (A friend of mine says I have 'positively microphonic' ears. Indeed all my senses are acute, but in self-defence I have become introspective and observe as little as I can of the external world. What a mental make-up for a detective!)

There was no sound of a ring inside. Was the bell out of order? I waited for a long time and pressed the button again. Still no sound, and no one came to the door. Then, with increasing decision, I used the knocker. After a short interval I heard steps, and, when they had reached me, the door was opened furtively, as one imagines doors are opened in times of civil disturbance, and I found myself face to face with—I can only call him an 'old buffer' with a beard, in shirt-sleeves and baggy tweed trousers.

Almost falsetto, he said, 'Yes?'

I had much ado not to say, 'Dr. Fielding, I presume.'

Instead I said, 'Could I see Dr. Fielding?'

The door opened more widely, and the old buffer said, 'I am Dr. Fielding—though, perhaps I should tell you at once, I am not a doctor of medicine.'

I smiled as ingratiatingly as I could, and said, 'Oh, I haven't come here to find a doctor of medicine! I've come to see you, if I may. My name is Malcolm Warren. I am a friend of Richard Findlay, the nephew of your friend Mr. Hamilton Findlay, who—as, of course, you know—'

He opened the door to its fullest extent, and his voice became deep bass, as he said, 'Come inside, please.'

He preceded me through a narrow hall—linoleum and a piece of imitation old oak—and led me into a small room which had access to the back-garden—an oblong stretch of lawn planted with narrow uninteresting borders. The room contained an untidy table, an untidy desk, two arm-chairs and three disproportionately big book-cases. I felt that if I were allowed to browse among those books I could discover Dr. Fielding's secret—if he had one. The titles were mostly scientific, and the word 'electro-magnetic' occurred in them often. For the most part the volumes were old and shabby, and I judged that, however vast a store of learning was before me, it was probably the outmoded learning of a past generation. What is more piti-able than an antiquated scientific textbook? The dullest letter of Pliny, the most tedious mediæval chronicle is by comparison full of life.

Dr. Fielding removed a shabby tweed coat, counterpart of the trousers he was wearing, from the more comfort-able of the two arm-chairs, and asked me to sit down.

Then he was interrogatively silent.

'I don't know if you've heard,' I began, 'that it was I who went with Dick to Cornwall, to look for—'

Then I paused and blamed myself for not having arrived with a proper exordium prepared. Who was I to go blurting out the details of our trip to Cornwall before this old man? It was Dick's story, not mine. But, after all, Dr. Fielding must know.

I went on: 'It was I, you know, who found Mr. Findlay's clothes.'

He nodded very gravely. I wished he would talk. I had come to hear him talk, but there was nothing for it except to talk myself. A shaft of sunlight through the window struck his enormous beard. 'Always beware of beards,' I thought foolishly; 'they lend themselves so easily to disguises. I wonder what sort of a chin he has?'

His hair was thick and grizzled, his eyebrows were thick and untidy. The eyes, which were wide apart, were distorted by spectacles. The nose was bulbous—and all the rest was beard.

'I heard,' I said, 'that you were to dine at Tylecroft on that Tuesday—June the 8th, I think it was—when Mr. Findlay was first missed. I know that you were very much in his confidence—'

This stilted phrase gained me a little nod of approval.

'And for this reason,' I continued, 'I felt I could turn to you—in the absence of Dick, who is abroad—to help me with a problem which is worrying me.'

'What may that problem be?' he asked, again with a touch of falsetto in his voice. For a minute I wanted to laugh. Then I said, with as much gravity as I could:

'Last Thursday I had an anonymous letter—postmarked S.W.7, my own postal district. It was a short letter, and I know it by heart. This is what it said: "Dear Sir, I understand that you have been investigating the death of Mr. Hamilton Findlay in Cornwall. Do you think you have finished your investigations? I think not. Why do you suppose Mr. Findlay went to Cornwall? This is just to make you sit up and take a little more notice. Yours, X."'

'Have you brought the letter with you?'

I blushed, and my respect for the old man increased.

'I'm afraid I carelessly left it at home,' I answered. 'But those are exactly the words it contained. It was typewritten.'

At this my eyes were drawn, as if by a magnet, to the table in the middle of the room. On it, between two dusty piles of books, was something in a case. A small sewing-machine? Or a typewriter? Obviously a typewriter.

The fact that I only noticed it at the very moment when I referred to the letter as being typewritten—still more the fact that my eyes were fastened to it with such horrified curiosity—was disgraceful in a would-be detective, and, amateur though I am, I still feel ashamed of myself. Yet, at the time, I could not be sure if Dr. Fielding had noticed my incautious glance; for he kept his eyes turned to the arm of my chair as he replied: 'It is always distressing to receive an anonymous letter.'

'Yes,' I said, trying to disguise the shock of my discovery, 'and particularly when the letter has such very grave implications.'

There was a pause, and I felt increasingly uncomfortable. Indeed, I began to wish very much that I had never set foot in Kashmir Road. I had come to catechise Dr. Fielding, and now it seemed likely that he was going to catechise me. I shuddered as I thought of the questions he might be going to ask me. 'Have you any idea who wrote the letter?' Or, 'Are you quite satisfied that my friend Hamilton Findlay's death was entirely accidental?' At all costs I must try to dominate the conversation, even if I had to keep up a running soliloquy.

'Of course,' I went on, 'one is always tempted to regard an anonymous letter as a nasty attempt to make mischief. I mean, one tends to wonder more about the writer than about the actual letter. Why should anybody write to me in this strain—and anonymously? Suppose for the moment that you, Dr. Fielding, had felt uneasy about what has happened, you would have gone to Dick, or perhaps to your solicitor. You might even have gone to the police, but you would certainly never have written to me under a pseudonym. It would have been so foolish.'

'Perhaps the letter was written by a foolish person,' he said calmly.

'I think it probably was,' I replied. 'Well, subject to your views, I think there are two courses open to me. I can either wait till Dick comes home, and let him deal with the letter, or, if one oughtn't to lose any time, I can take the letter straight to the solicitor who is handling the case. By the way, I'm not quite sure of his name. Could you help me there?'

Without answering me, he got up and went to his desk, where he fumbled for a while among some papers. Then he said, 'Yes; here it is. Can you take it down? E. J. Stroud and Co., 9, Outer Temple Yard, W.C.2. I may say I heard from these people to the effect that Mr. Findlay had left me a legacy. They add in their letter, "You will no doubt appreciate that in the special circumstances a considerable time may elapse before the usual application for probate can be made." I have myself no legal knowledge.'

'Nor have I,' I said, when I had written down the address. 'But I suppose—'

Dr. Fielding appeared so little interested in my supposition that he looked at his watch, while making his way back to the chair.

'I'm afraid I'm keeping you,' I said.

'Oh, no,' he replied. 'I have, as a matter of fact, nothing to do this evening. I was only wondering if the hour was suitable for me to offer you a glass of sherry. Do you drink sherry, Mr. Warren?'

I told him diffidently that I did, and, while I was urging him not to put himself to any trouble, he went out of the room to fetch the drink. As the door shut behind him, I stood up and walked across to the table. Yes, it was a typewriter—a bulky old-fashioned model, it seemed to be. I doubted whether any of my office typists would know the make—'Gower and Windley, Series B.' Then suddenly, as I reached the window, and looked through it mechanically on to the plot of garden, I remembered my previous certainty that Miss Crowne, and no one else, was the writer of the anonymous letter. What a fool I was to let the sight of a typewriter on Dr. Fielding's table disturb me so. Thousands of people had typewriters. Was I going to suspect them all? Really, I thought, it was time I pulled myself together. So far I had misconducted the interview disgracefully. I had learnt nothing, and three or four times I had been on the verge of blurting things out which were better kept to myself. Why let the old buffer nonplus me? Thenceforward I would be bolder, even at the risk of seeming odd or domineering. If he asked me questions, I would refuse pointblank to answer them. If I asked him questions—and there were several which I wanted to ask—I would insist on his answering. Why couldn't I behave like a man of the world—a middle-aged man of the world—instead of like a nervous schoolboy in the presence of a headmaster?

Then the door opened, and Dr. Fielding came in with a bottle and two glasses. The sherry was bad—like a mixture of port and Madeira—but it gave me courage. When I had praised the drink, and settled down in my chair, I said, with unnecessary firmness: 'Now, Dr. Fielding, I should be delighted to hear your views.'

'*My* views?' he twittered.

'Yes; yours. I've told you the contents of this letter, and I'm sure you know all the main details of Mr. Findlay's death. I want to know what you really think about it all.'

He didn't seem altogether surprised at my change of tone. It was as if, while he was searching for the sherry and I had been looking out into the garden, we had been talking telepathically together, and our new conversation proceeded quite naturally from that unspoken conversation.

As he meditated his reply, I went on, so that there should be no further beating about the bush: 'Were you surprised when Mr. Findlay decided to go to Falmouth?'

'Surprised—well—of course, Cornwall is a distant county and the railway-fare is expensive. By the way—but this is irrelevant—'

'Yes?' I said peremptorily.

'You talk of Falmouth, and I understand that Mr. Findlay did, in fact, stay in an hotel there, but the first I heard of Falmouth was when Dick—er—told me the sad news.'

'But—you knew—'

'I knew that Mr. Findlay had decided to go to Cornwall. I did not know that he had decided to go to Falmouth. I asked him where he would stay, and he said he hadn't made up his mind, but that he supposed it would be Newquay or St. Ives. I told him that my married sister sometimes stayed at the Atlantic Towers Hotel, St. Ives, and found it excellent. He replied that he would bear it in mind, but that he did not wish to incur too much expense.'

'If that were so, didn't you express surprise that he chose Cornwall for his week-end?'

'I did—lightly.'

'And what did he say?'

'He said, "All the more reason for my not being too extravagant when I get to Cornwall."'

'But why Cornwall at all?'

'I asked that, too. But Mr. Findlay was, under the surface, a decided character, and I had the impression that his mind was quite made up.'

'It seems so inconsistent,' I said meditatively.

'It seemed to me inconsistent at the time.'

'Can you remember when you had this conversation?' I asked.

'Yes,' he said, pausing for a moment of emotion—the first I had seen him betray. 'It was the last time I saw

Hamilton. The Tuesday before he went away.'

I looked at my pocket-diary and said, 'That would be June 1st, wouldn't it? Just a week before you came to dine at Tylecroft and found only Dick there.'

'Yes. It was just a week before that day.'

'Was it a long conversation?' I asked.

'No. It was at our Chess Club. We were having our summer tournament. That explains why I didn't see Hamilton on the Wednesday, Thursday or Friday before he went away. I was competing and he wasn't. He looked in on the Tuesday to see how I was getting on, though, as a rule, he wasn't interested in the game unless he was playing himself.'

'He didn't enter for this tournament, then?'

'No. He was hardly up to tournament form.'

'Could he give you a game?'

'In practice, I'm rather ashamed to say he could. He knew nothing of the science of the game, but he never made a mistake—according to his lights, that is. I used to tell him that he played chess like an animal—by instinct rather than by reason. My own game is just the opposite. I know the theory well, and I conceive the most abstruse developments of my position, and then—I forget to make the key-move, or I run into some elementary trap which a jog of the elbow would remind me to parry. He used to beat me as often as I beat him. But against serious players, whose wits don't go wool-gathering like mine, he stood no chance, and he knew it. So he didn't play in our tournament—'

I judged it only decent to be silent for a minute or two at this point, while Dr. Fielding was probably tasting the full bitterness of his loss. A strange link—chess. Yet doubtless there are stranger.

When, at length, I realised that he was not going to speak till I spoke, I said, 'Was this conversation of Tuesday, June 1st, the first time he told you he was going to Cornwall?'

'As for Cornwall, I can't be sure. I'd known for quite a long time that he was going away somewhere or other. He told me so, soon after Mrs. Pressley—his housekeeper—asked for her holiday. I think he suggested that I should go with him—that was certainly before he ever mentioned Cornwall, as he would have known that I could not afford the fare there for so short a visit. But I reminded him that I hoped to play in the tournament here, which includes the Saturday. So naturally he made his own plans. But as to when he first declared his intention of going to Cornwall, I can't be sure. Now, Mr. Warren, will you not let me fill your glass?'

Little as I cared for Dr. Fielding's sherry, I felt I was, for once, drinking in a good cause. One glass had certainly loosened the old man's tongue, and I felt bound to see what effect a second glass would have. Accordingly I accepted his offer on the understanding that he would not let me drink alone. He demurred a little, pleading that he was unused to alcohol, but I insisted as firmly as I dared. On the whole, I think he was glad of the excuse.

'I'm now coming to some rather delicate ground,' I said, after I had paid the sherry one or two fulsome compliments. 'Do you think by any chance that there might be a lady in the case?'

At this I thought I saw his eyes flicker behind the thick lenses of his spectacles.

'Well, really, Mr. Warren—' he began, with a slight show of indignation. But I interrupted him, and said:

'I don't want you to betray any confidences, Dr. Fielding, though I'm sure you are a man to take a broad-minded view of these things—'

'Broad-minded, yes,' he said airily. 'I flatter myself that I have always been that. I used to esteem myself a leader of thought in my generation. We prided ourselves on tolerance and a belief in personal freedom. Nowadays I believe the opposite view is coming into fashion, and the individual is being increasingly subjected to what I may call a code of farcical taboos which will soon reduce him to the level of a prize animal. It is odd how quickly the wheel can turn full circle. However, I must not weary you with this. You asked me if I thought there might possibly be a lady in the case. I reply—I reply—"Well, yes, that is a possibility."'

He looked at me almost triumphantly, and went on, 'Mr. Findlay was of course a careful and conventional man—far more conventional than I should have been, if I had had his means and inclinations.'

'Inclinations?' I said, tentatively.

'Please do not think I am implying that my very good friend was a libertine or debauchee. In the main his interests were quiet and domestic, like mine—though of course he could not meet me in the realm of science. But there were occasions, to my knowledge, when he took a discreet but by no means lukewarm interest in the fair sex. I did not solicit his confidence over these—er—episodes, and he rarely gave it to me. At the same time, one cannot always turn the blind eye, you know.'

'I take it,' I said, 'that you are not suggesting some old-established friendship, or liaison, say, with a lady already married—'

'No,' he answered decisively, 'that is not my suggestion at all. There was nothing very romantic or permanent in my friend's attachments. He was not one to give himself up to a hopeless passion.'

I was amused at the way in which we both seemed to employ the language of Jane Austen in order to describe occurrences which Jane Austen would have thought unworthy of her pen. I wondered, too, whether our euphemisms would allow Dr. Fielding to come down to details.

'Was there, to your knowledge,' I asked, 'one of these episodic attachments in progress at the time of Mr. Findlay's death?'

He finished his drink at a gulp and put the glass unsteadily on the floor.

'I thought our conversation would lead to this question,'

he said. 'And I have been wondering how far I should be justified in answering it. I must be quite firm over this point. I will not disclose the name of the lady. Mind, I am not quite sure myself of her identity—well, that is a prevarication. I am reasonably sure, though I have no proof, Mr. Findlay has been, this summer, interested in a certain young lady, and it did occur to me that he might be planning to spend his holiday week-end in her company. In my view that was why he selected Cornwall—a county so distant from here. I have already told you that Mr. Findlay paid a scrupulous regard to the conventions. I believe, however, it is a fact that the pressure of convention diminishes in proportion to one's remoteness from home. I have, just once or twice, known Mr. Findlay to commit indiscretions on holiday which he would never have committed here in South Mersley.'

'But—' I said, recalling my conversation with Ormerod, the porter at the Trepolpen, 'no lady was seen in Mr. Findlay's company in Falmouth. He stayed at an hotel of rigid respectability.'

'In that event,' suggested Dr. Fielding, 'he must have decided to go alone. There may have been some hitch. Or he might have fixed his rendezvous somewhere outside the town. I take it he didn't spend the whole day sitting in the hotel lounge.'

'No. He went for some long walks, according to the porter. Was Mr. Findlay fond of walking, by the way?'

'Yes. On our holidays he would often walk me off my legs. His appearance was rather deceptive, and concealed a good deal of stamina.'

'And swimming?' I asked. 'Was he fond of swimming?'

'I believe he thought himself an accomplished swimmer, on the strength of a swimming prize he had won at school. On the other hand, the fact that he wore a wig made him reluctant to bathe in public. A foolish foible, perhaps. No doubt, in the seclusion of Cornwall, he felt able to gratify his taste.'

He would hardly have bathed, wig and all, I thought, if

there had been a lady with him. But perhaps she was only there on the Sunday—if she was there at all. Dr. Fielding seemed very sure that there was a lady in the programme. If only he would tell me her name! But I judged that it would be unwise to press him any further that afternoon. Besides, I was eager to make my escape before the effect of his potations wore off. When they did, he would soon realise that he had been unguarded, and would probably retaliate on me. So I closed the conversation abruptly by looking at my watch and murmuring about an appointment in London, which I would miss if I did not go at once. Dr. Fielding followed me a trifle unsteadily to the front door, while I thanked him over my shoulder for his kind hospitality. I left him waving weakly with his left hand and urging me to visit him again.

When I reached South Mersley Station I felt very tired—too tired even to think over my experiences of the afternoon. It was about half-past eight when my train arrived in London, and after eating a few sandwiches in the buffet, I went straight home to bed.

10.
Tuesday, July 6th, to Thursday, July 8th

NEXT morning on my way to the office, I said to myself, 'Look here, Malcolm, there's still somebody whom you've got to go and see. Mr. William Hicks—Dick's nursery-gardener cousin. We can't be sure if there was any young lady with Uncle Hamilton in Falmouth, but we do know William Hicks was there, staying at the Radnor. There seems every reason to suppose that Uncle Hamilton wrote him a letter—or the draft of a letter—during the Falmouth visit. It's too much of a coincidence to suppose they didn't meet. You must pay Mr. Hicks a call, even if he sets the dogs on you.'

But how was I to pay a call on Mr. Hicks? I considered the matter for some time, and then decided that if I could borrow a motor from a friend I could visit Cantervale Nurseries on my way to the house of Mrs. Molyneux-Brown, whose party, it may be remembered, I had promised to join for Saturday and Sunday. The nearer the date of the party came, the less I relished the prospect of going. It was like a visit to the dentist, in my imagination—perhaps worse; for the agony would be more protracted. Still, I had promised, and it was a duty to my firm to keep the promise.

My duty to the firm, as it happened, kept me very busy all day, and I had little leisure in which to marshal the impressions of my visit to South Mersley. During luncheon, I reflected that Dr. Fielding's evidence seemed to confirm the existence of those traits in Uncle Hamilton which I had regarded as being too much 'out of character' to be credible. Apparently Uncle Hamilton was both a walker and a swimmer. What an irony that his winning a swimming prize at school should have brought him to his death! Suppose a voice from heaven had cried out, during the prize-giving, 'This is your death-warrant, Hamilton Findlay,' at the very moment when the beaming headmaster was presenting the cup, or whatever it was, to his proud pupil! What *would* they all have done? The applauding parents, too?

The fantasy was so charming that I spent ten minutes embroidering it over my coffee.

During the afternoon my senior partner told me that he was taking his wife to Paris for the week-end. They were going by air, and I felt bold enough to ask if I could borrow his car while he was away. Luckily I had acted as chauffeur for him once or twice when he had an injured arm, and he knew that I was not altogether irresponsible.

'Do you want it for sleuthing?' he asked, with one of his winks.

'Yes,' I said. 'By the way, I think I know who wrote me that anonymous letter. I'm inclined to think it was just a sudden burst of malice. But I hope to be able to tell you the whole story some day.'

Jack mastered his curiosity in fine fashion, and gave me instructions how to collect his car.

Then I turned once more to my work.

In the evening a friend came to dine at my flat—a good little meal, though I say it as shouldn't. I felt thankful that

Mrs. Rhodes was my housekeeper and not poor Mrs. Pressley of Tylecroft.

After dinner we played backgammon and talked gloomily of the future of the world.

At breakfast on Wednesday, July 7th, I had a letter from Dick—the first since he had gone abroad:

HÔTEL DE VENISE,
BLAIREAU-SUR-MER,
CALVADOS,
FRANCE.
Sunday, July 4th.

DEAR MALCOLM,

Of course I should have written before. 'Not even a picture postcard,' you will say. No, not even that. But you know how it is when one goes abroad. No time for social obligations.

I have been here for rather more than a week. A charming slightly sophisticated fishing village, with a few Anglo-American villas in the background. I have friends staying in one of the biggest and best, and I consider myself a 'boarded-out' member of the house-party. We're early for the season, such as it is.

We bathe—warmish water, and *safe* (poor Uncle Hamilton!) and play tennis. On Saturday nights the Casino goes all gala, and one gambles. I wish you could see it—such decayed plush and, oh, the *croupes arrondies* of the frescoed nymphs on the walls. But you know what I mean—you've seen the casinos of old-fashioned French watering-places. They are the counterparts of thatched summer-houses in Victorian English gardens. Nostalgia!

As a matter of fact, the Casino has altered my plans a little. I sat down at chemmy on Saturday night, clutching a few francs in my hot hand—and I left the table at 4.15 a.m. with one hundred and eighty pounds! Play was a good deal higher than usual, owing to the arrival of a yachtful of rich Americans. Lucky Dick!

After my win, I feel it would be stupid to come to South Mersley, home and beauty, on Wednesday, as I had arranged, and I have decided to stay on here for a day or two. I may finish up in Paris, but it depends rather on the movements of my friends. At any rate, I don't expect to see Tylecroft till Friday afternoon, July 9th.

We must meet as soon as I get back. I'd ask you during the week-end, but I'm sure you will be fixed up. So shall we say Tuesday week, July 13th? (Are they the Ides of July, by any chance?* A pleasant change from the Ides of March.) *Aux Trois Pommes*, eight o'clock and don't dress. And don't say it's your turn, because I can well afford to get a little of my own back, entertaining you.

I take it you have no news. The law, I suppose, is taking its usual leisurely course, and it will be years before we can deal with Uncle Hamilton's estate. With one hundred and eighty pounds in my pocket, I feel it hardly matters. Let me know about Tuesday week—to Tylecroft.

Yours ever,

DICK.

The gaiety of this letter persisted in my head throughout my day in the office, and formed a strong contrast to my work, which was more than usually unexciting. Yet, when, in the evening, I came to reply, I could not escape a feeling of annoyance with Dick for running away and enjoying himself, while I, whom he had dragged into the affair, was left at home to face the music of an anonymous letter. Indeed, the first draft of my letter was so censorious in its tone that I tore it up, and wrote the following:

July 7th.

DEAR DICK,

I was delighted to get your letter this morning, though I agree with you that you might have written sooner!

*No. They are not. The Ides of July, like those of March, are on the 15th.

Events here have been less quiescent than you might have supposed, and at the risk of disturbing your villegiatura—though you won't get this till you come back to England—I feel bound to tell you that I've had an anonymous letter—typewritten and posted in this postal district, S.W.7. Short, but not sweet. This is what is says:

'Dear Sir, I understand that you have been investigating the death of Mr. Hamilton Findlay in Cornwall. Do you think you have finished your investigations? I think not. Why do you suppose Mr. Findlay went to Cornwall? This is just to make you sit up and take a little more notice—Yours, X.'

The letter reached me last Thursday night. Perhaps I ought to have taken it straight to your solicitor. Perhaps I ought to have thrown it into the fire. I did neither, but on Monday I did pay a visit to South Mersley, where I saw Miss Crowne and Dr. Fielding, in the hope that one or other of them would shed some light on the problem. Neither of them did—directly, that is to say. But Dr. Fielding indicated that your uncle was less of a Puritan than you seemed inclined to suppose. He suggested that there was a lady in the case, and I feel that if we track down this lady-business, we shall be able to explain a good deal that appears eccentric in your uncle's behaviour.

I think, by the way, you have underrated Dr. Fielding's intelligence. You have probably been prejudiced against him because he was a friend of your uncle's.

I shall be delighted to accept your invitation *Aux Trois Pommes* for Tuesday night. But I think we ought to get in touch with one another before that. I suppose you will get this on Friday. I am playing bridge with the Seymours that night, but you may have time to ring me up while I'm dressing. On Saturday morning, too, I shall be here, till, anyhow, 11. I am spending Saturday night and Sunday with 'business friends'—motoring there and back in a borrowed car. I expect to get back here late on Sunday night, though it may be one of those houses where they won't let you leave till early on Monday morning—which I loathe. Then Monday in the office, and Monday evening a blank so far.

I am glad you have had such a happy and prosperous time, but you must now devote all your energies to unravelling the mystery of the anonymous letter. I am keeping the document as an exhibit in what you call my criminological museum!

Yours ever,
MALCOLM.

P.S.—A paragraph in the *Financial Times* of July 1st about Garvice and Bagshaw, and their absorption by the Universal Chemical Combine. I suppose you have known about it for some time. What are your own prospects?

M. W.

Even this revised version of my letter was ungracious, especially in comparison with Dick's letter to me. But, though I re-read it two or three times, I saw no reason to try to match his sprightliness. The sooner he came back to earth the better. And if it gave him the impression that I was 'a bit peevish,' I didn't mind. I was peevish—and rather more. So I put it in an envelope addressed to Dick at Tylecroft, and marked 'To await arrival,' and posted it before going to bed.

The next day, Thursday, July 8th, our head typist, who had been away from the office for three days, returned to us, and I had my first chance of making inquiries about the typescript of the anonymous letter.

Finding her alone in the typing office about lunch-time, I showed her the envelope, and asked her if she could suggest what make of machine could have typed it. I told her that it had contained an anonymous letter, but asked her to say nothing about it to the rest of the staff. It was, I said, only a stupid and offensive practical joke, and I had a fair idea of its author. Meanwhile, it would help me a lot if I could identify the machine which had been used.

As soon as she had studied the envelope, she said, 'Well, it looks to me, Mr. Warren, as if it had been done on an Ipsofacto. We have one, you know. Miss Danby uses it for the half-commissioners' letters. Let me produce a specimen for you.'

At that she went across the room to Miss Danby's vacant desk and typed out a facsimile of the envelope I had shown her. I compared the lettering of the two envelopes, and could see no difference between them, except that one or two of the letters produced by the office machine were a little faint.

'Would that faintness be accounted for by a different technique on the part of the operator?' I asked her.

'Oh, I don't think so, Mr. Warren,' she answered. 'We've had our machine quite a long time, and it's very slightly worn out. I believe no two typewriters write exactly alike. At least, that's what you always read in detective stories, isn't it?'

I agreed, and examined the machine she had been using. It was described as Model 17, serial number B/2720. Turning up my pocket-book, I saw that Miss Crowne's machine was Model 19B, serial number D/3875—presumably a more recent creation.

'Well, I really think that settles things,' I said. 'As a matter of fact I've been suspecting that my envelope was typed on an Ipsofacto. I'd no idea we had one in the office. Do you happen to know anything about a machine called Gower and Windley?'

'Gower and Windley? That's a very old make, isn't it? I don't think they're made any longer. I seem to remember one at the typing school I went to. But I'm sure that a Gower and Windley couldn't have written your envelope—unless they've produced an entirely new model.

I'm sure they haven't, though. I think they've gone out of business altogether. I can make inquiries if you like.'

'Oh no, thank you very much,' I said; 'it suits my theory perfectly to suppose that this envelope was written on an Ipsofacto—a rather newer Ipsofacto than ours.'

'May I look at the envelope again?' she asked. 'You know, I should be inclined to say that the person who produced this wasn't frightfully experienced. I don't mean he's a complete amateur, but I should say he isn't a whole-time typist.'

'I can't think how you diagnose that,' I said, 'though it all fits in perfectly.'

'Well,' she said, 'look at the alignment, to begin with. Of course, if I saw the whole letter and not only the envelope——'

I had been waiting for such an outburst of curiosity, and had decided to nip it in the bud.

'No, I can't possibly show you the whole letter,' I answered. 'But you've been splendidly helpful over the envelope. I'm now quite certain who the writer was. By the way, I thought that in modern machines the type was interchangeable. Couldn't this have been typed, say, on a Remington?'

'I don't think so, Mr. Warren. It's quite true that all the important makers offer you several choices of type, but they're never quite the same. This type is what we call a "No. 3." It's a very favourite office type. We have a No. 3 on Miss Danby's Ipsofacto, and a No. 3 on my Remington over there, but you couldn't really mistake the two. If I typed a copy of your envelope on my machine, you couldn't confuse it with the envelope I typed on Miss Danby's, or your own envelope—though, if you weren't careful, you could easily confuse your own envelope with Miss Danby's, because they're both typed with Ipsofacto No. 3.'

'It's very complicated,' I said, 'but I see what you mean. Of course, I suppose there is the possibility of a deliberate cheat. For instance, Miss Danby could fix her Ipsofacto type to your Remington, couldn't she?'

'Oh, I dare say she could, but that would be almost forgery, wouldn't it?'

'Yes,' I said, 'you're quite right. It would be almost forgery, and there's no need for me to suspect anything of the kind. As I said to begin with, it's just an offensive practical joke, and, thanks to you, I'm now quite sure who the joker was. I'm most grateful to you. And now I must go and have my horrible midday meal.'

'One thousand pounds to a penny it was Miss Crowne!'

My horrible midday meal became almost festive at this thought. I was particularly pleased to have spotted her as the writer of the letter on psychological grounds, long before I began to think of analysing her typescript. I have always loathed the 'cigarette-end' aspect of detection. 'Antimony and cobalt in certain proportions produce such and such a poison and a slight discoloration of the thorax.' Well, they may. But it oughtn't to be necessary to know that kind of thing. A blush, a verbal hesitation, a twitching finger, a laugh, a philosophical idea—these are your real clues. The ingredients of crime lie in the amalgam of character and circumstance. One must find out who the criminal is, but it isn't always necessary to hound him or her to justice. *Her?* I nearly laughed aloud into my plate of liver and bacon—liver a mesh of rejected sinews, and bacon a piece of flaccid and clammy green fat. *Her?* No, it wasn't Miss Crowne who had killed Uncle Hamilton, if he was killed at all.

But he had been killed. During prunes I admitted that to myself for the first time—but finally.

We are still dealing with Thursday, July 8th, and I should like to say that when my day's task was over and I returned to my flat, the joys of *The Times* Crossword Puzzle, and my gloomy book about the European situation, I was hardly surprised to find a letter by the evening post in an envelope similar to that which my head typist had scrutinised so carefully during the morning. I should like to say I was not in any way surprised. But I was. I was shocked.

DEAR SIR,

Please take no notice of a letter I wrote you a week ago about the death of Mr. Hamilton Findlay. It was a stupid practical joke, of which I am very ashamed. I know nothing about Mr. Findlay's death.

You may guess who writes this. Well, if you do, it's my own fault, but please don't bully me about it, or follow it up. Throw the first letter in the fire, and this one too. I feel too ashamed to sign my proper name.

Yours,

X.

Postmark S.W.7. Date, Thursday, July 8th. (Miss Crowne was free on Thursday afternoons.) And the type—a newish Ipsofacto No. 3.

11.

Friday, July 9th, to Saturday, July 10th

FRIDAY, a blank day till I left the office. A day of hard work, which I felt would probably lead to nothing. A tedious day.

On my way home in the tube I wondered what I should say to Dick when he telephoned—and surely he would telephone—about the second anonymous letter. Should I let him know that I suspected his hand in it—or at least his influence? 'Well, of course, I told her to write it,' he would reply. To which my answer would be 'Why bother? Why practise these little deceptions upon me? You called me in to this case.'

'But, my dear fellow, you know there isn't a case. This anonymous letter doesn't make one.'

'Perhaps not, Dick, but none the less . . .'

This imaginary conversation developed itself till I was in my bath. I had felt sure Dick would ring up while I was in my bath. I can force people to telephone to me merely by having a bath. But this time my powers failed. The telephone bell did not ring, though I lay for a long time in the hot water, waiting.

At length, when I feared that I should be late for my bridge party with the Seymours, I got out, dried myself and returned to my bedroom to dress. But to my ears, which were all agog for the telephone bell, my flat had never seemed so still.

Should I give him five minutes, ten minutes, a quarter of an hour? Even at the risk of being late? Who were the Seymours, anyhow? This rude rhetorical question was prompted by my excitement. Then, as the silence of the telephone bell became almost loud, I suddenly asked myself why I counted on Dick's keeping to the programme in his letter. Dick, with a hundred and eighty pounds in his pocket—Dick returning via Paris—it would have been utterly 'out of character' if he didn't delay his return by a day or two. No. I must possess my soul in patience till we met *Aux Trois Pommes* on Tuesday. And even then he might telegraph and postpone our meeting. Almost certainly he would postpone our meeting.

I went to the Seymours. A party of twelve. Dinner followed by bridge. During dinner I heard a young woman say, 'But Sir Horace told me himself that gas-masks will have to be issued in September.' I shuddered and then reflected that I might bring out the remark with a knowing air at the dinner-table of Mrs. Molyneux-Brown the following night. 'My dear lady,' I would say, 'I happen to know that Sir Horace said we shall all have gas-masks in September. There *will* be an Autumn Crisis.'

They would all think me so well-informed and send me their Stock Exchange business.

I lost two pounds at bridge, and left about midnight. When I got back to my flat, I looked reproachfully at my telephone. Why couldn't it tell me if Dick had rung up or not? But it couldn't. My fault, for not having a resident housekeeper. I fell asleep wondering if I should ever have a house with a proper staff—butler, footman, parlour-maid, a couple of housemaids, cook, kitchen-maid and vegetable-maid. To have a vegetable-maid, I felt, I would do anything.

Saturday morning, July the 10th. Mrs. Rhodes with my not very early tea. Shave, bath, breakfast. Kidneys and stuffed tomatoes. Was Mrs. Rhodes in love with me? I didn't deserve them, but I enjoyed them very much. Why didn't Dick telephone? Had he reached home or not?

I rang up Tylecroft and was answered by Mrs. Pressley. Yes, Mr. Richard had arrived the previous evening. No, he wasn't in. He had gone out already. But he had left a message in case I rang up. He'd gone to see his solicitor. He would probably ring me up on Monday, but in any case he was looking forward to seeing me for dinner on Tuesday.

She ended up with, 'I hope you're quite well, sir.'

'Oh, yes,' I said, touching the wooden table, 'I think so. And I hope you are.'

'I can't complain,' she said. 'I'll tell Mr. Richard you rang. Goodbye.'

So—he was back and he hadn't rung me up, but he had expected me to ring him up and had left a message for me, and had gone to his solicitor about the anonymous letter, instead of talking to me first. Perhaps he thought it was an invention of mine. Perhaps he thought I—with my mania for mysteries—had actually written it myself. Perhaps, on the other hand, he knew it was Miss Crowne, and was going to have that erratic young woman brought to her senses by a solicitor's letter. But Miss Crowne had already recanted to me. Did he know that? Perhaps his thoughts were quite different.

Well, I thought, the climax of all this will be reached if I meet Dick on Tuesday night in the restaurant of the *Trois Pommes*, but in the meanwhile I, Malcolm Warren, have still my little part to play. I stole a march on Dick once when I discovered the hotel—the Strafford Royal—at which Uncle Hamilton had stayed the night before he went to Cornwall. I will steal a march on him again by visiting Cousin Bill at Cantervale Nurseries this very afternoon. If there's anything to be nosed out there, I will nose it out. And there must be something. There is always that draft letter, written by Uncle Hamilton and dated the day before he was drowned—if he was drowned—on a sheet of paper torn from a cheap writing-block, which we never found—either in his knapsack or in his luggage.

Of course Uncle Hamilton might have left the writing-block behind in the hotel accidentally. He would never have done so on purpose, unless he had used the last sheet, or the last sheet but one. Why hadn't I pursued this 'clue' before, and wired to Ormerod, the porter, asking if the remains of a writing-block had been found in Uncle Hamilton's waste-paper basket? I hadn't. Had the police? And suppose they had, and the answer came back, 'No writing-block was found, either in Mr. Findlay's bedroom or anywhere in the hotel.' What then? To what conclusion was I being driven?

I spent the morning buying a pair of evening socks—I had gone in shreds to the Seymours—and collecting my senior partner's motor from his house in St. John's Wood. I reached my flat with my borrowed car at about one o'clock, consumed the dressed crab and cheese which Mrs. Rhodes had put out for me, and packed. While I packed I thought of Uncle Hamilton packing for his Cornish trip, and the luggage which we had examined in the police station at Polpenford.

One pair of patent leather shoes, and so on.

Patent leather shoes—for Cornwall? With no evening-dress to justify them. What did he wear at Tylecroft as a rule? Probably carpet slippers.

At two I set out on my journey. Sedcombe, as I knew from the map, is in the south-west corner of Surrey. Mrs.

Molyneux-Brown, my hostess, lived fifteen miles further on, inside the Hampshire border. The village of Sedcombe was apparently on a loop from my direct road—a *dêtour* of barely four miles.

I had decided that the pretext for my call at the nursery was to be the purchase of a plant for Mrs. Molyneux-Brown. She had told me, I was glad to remember, that she was not at all satisfied with the garden, which had been neglected by her impoverished predecessors, and was having it thoroughly remodelled by experts. I may not have mentioned that the Molyneux-Browns had only moved to the country the previous year. Before that they had lived in Wimbledon. I knew Mrs. Molyneux-Brown to be both resolute and impatient, and was convinced that she would see that her husband became a complete country gentleman with as little delay as possible. My contribution to his metamorphosis from City gent. to country gentleman should be a plant from Cousin Bill's nursery. As to what plant, Cousin bill himself should advise me. At least, I hoped he would.

It was half-past three when I turned off the main road and reached the village of Sedcombe. I learned, on inquiry, that Cantervale Nursery lay in a lane which itself made a loop to the looproad on which I was travelling. If I took the first turning to the right and went straight on I should not only pass the entrance to the nursery but in due course rejoin the Sedcombe road, and the main road.

I was glad the directions were so simple, for the lane in which I found myself was so narrow that it might easily have been a cul-de-sac, or one of those farm tracks which, on a winter's night, lead you into a pool of sticky mud, where your wheels spin hopelessly and for ever. Luckily this was a hot summer afternoon, and though we had been having our usual English abundance of rain, there was little fear that I should be caught in a morass.

Meanwhile the lane twisted this way and that, and

bumped me unpleasantly from side to side, as I tried to keep my wheels in a pair of ruts which I surmised were made by Cousin Bill's lorry. So intent was I on my steering, that I overshot the entrance to the nursery, and only realised I had done so when I saw a noticeboard with the legend, 'Cantervale Nursery-Garden: Proprietor, William Hicks: Open every weekday till six o'clock'—and a white hand pointing in the direction from which I had come. It was silly of me to have missed the entrance, I thought, and perhaps sillier still of me to have expected the nursery to be open on Saturday afternoon. However, in this instance, silliness was rewarded, and I was just deciding to get out of the car and explore the entrance to see if I could reasonably back into it, when I saw another notice, half covered by two mop-head acacias, which said, 'To South Entrance,' and another white hand enjoined me to continue. I was glad not to have to reverse in an unfamiliar car, and continued slowly on my way till I came to a dilapidated oak gate. I opened the gate, drove in, and found myself on a track which went very steeply up a little hill—a hill sloping both towards the lane and towards my left. The right-hand side of the track was thickly screened with conifers. The left-hand side was open and one could look over the grass verge of the hillock on to a small lake, which I should have thought would have made an admirable aquatic garden. Perhaps Cousin Bill had hoped that Uncle Hamilton would lend him enough capital to develop it. Perhaps he was actually going to develop it, when his half-share of Uncle Hamilton's estate was realised. Then the track, still going steeply uphill, took a sudden twist to the right, and, after running parallel to the lane for about a hundred yards, led me to a flat weedy expanse in front of a ramshackle building which had once probably been a farmhouse.

I stopped the car and got out. Should I ring the front-door bell? My knowledge of nursery-gardens was restricted to the rare visits I had paid to one near my mother's home in Somerset, when she said she must have a few plants 'to brighten up the front.' Then I saw a wooden shed on the right labelled 'Office' and surrounded by greenhouses. I was making my way there, when a middle-aged gardener came out of one of the greenhouses and approached me.

We said 'Good-afternoon' to one another and I asked if Mr. Hicks was at home.

The reply was, 'I'm sorry, he isn't, sir. Did you wish to see him specially about anything?'

I explained that I was personally acquainted with Mr. Hicks and had hoped he would show me round the nursery and give me some advice as to the plants I wished to buy.

'I'm sorry, sir,' he answered, 'but I can't say when Mr. Hicks will be back. His mother was taken very ill this morning, and the doctor said she was to be operated upon at once. Mr. Hicks has gone with her to the nursing-home. Is there anything I can do for you, sir?'

'Well,' I said, 'I thought I should like to buy a few plants as a present for a lady with whom I'm spending the weekend. But I'm terribly sorry to hear such bad news of Mrs. Hicks. I do hope the operation will be successful.' Then I paused for a moment and went on, 'I should be very grateful if you could suggest something for me to buy.'

'Certainly, sir, I'll do my best, though it isn't an easy time of year to move stuff. It'll have to be something in a pot, I'm thinking. Perhaps you'd like me to show you round, in any case.'

I said I should be delighted if he would. Like nearly all gardeners he was a very pleasant fellow, and his conversation would have interested me in any event. But it also occurred to me that as I had come to 'nose things out' at Cantervale Nurseries, I might do some good 'nosing' while the owner was away. Accordingly I encouraged my guide to talk as much as he would. Luckily, he was fond of talking, and though his speech was eked out with phrases such as 'If I may say so, sir' (with which a slow brain tries to disguise its slowness), I learned quite a lot.

I learned, for instance, that Mrs. Molyneux-Brown did not go to Mr. Hicks for her plants. Mr. Hicks had supplied Sir Derek Grosjean, her predecessor at Neetham Priory, but she herself went to Howards. Who were Howards, I asked? Howards were one of the grandest horticultural firms in the country. They didn't advertise in the cheap papers, but you always saw them at the Chelsea Show, where they won important prizes. They specialised in laying out whole gardens, and gave you an oil-painting to show you what your place would look like when they had finished with it. Of course, they were terribly expensive. People said they charged you half a guinea for a common Michaelmas Daisy—and as for shrubs and such-like, you could pay the earth if you wanted to. Naturally, they could afford to give you good stuff, and replace it, if it died. If it was Mrs. Molyneux-Brown I wanted the plants for, it wouldn't be too easy to please her. He had heard that the gardens at Neetham Priory had been entirely altered since Sir Derek left.

Mr. Hicks, I gathered, catered for a different class—or had been forced to cater for it, since his father's experiments in the production of new roses hadn't been too successful. A big villa population was beginning to invade the district from the outer suburbs of London—people who wanted a dozen geraniums, a box or two of annuals, and a nice little macrocarpa hedge—and Mr. Hicks thought he ought to adapt himself to their needs. Not but what it went against the grain. Mr. Hicks would have loved to specialise in something and to produce a new flower. But you wanted money for that. Now how about some rambler roses for Mrs. Molyneux-Brown?

We had reached the rose-garden and my companion pointed to some tall plants in pots, with the long stems tied round bamboo canes.

'These would travel,' he said.

'But I'm afraid not in my car,' I answered. 'I'm sure they would scratch the paint or the cushions. I have to be careful, as I've borrowed it from a friend.'

'No,' he said disconsolately, 'they're not easy to carry. And I don't suppose the lady would want them, either. They say she has a pergola a quarter of a mile long, built and planted by Howards.'

'How about something for the rockery?' I suggested.

'For the rock-garden? Well, it's hardly the season to transplant things in the rock-garden—though we have a few heaths in pots. They might do. Mr. Hicks has been thinking of specialising in heaths. They're a popular plant nowadays—don't require much looking after once they're established, and are suitable for small gardens. There's plenty of peaty lime-free soil, too, in this part of the country, which they like. . . . Here we are, sir. Mr. Hicks brought these back from Cornwall with him at the beginning of last month.'

'Why!' I said hurriedly, before the subject could be changed, 'I was in Cornwall about a month ago—at Falmouth.'

'Mr. Hicks went to Falmouth too, sir. There's a nursery thereabouts which was selling off its stock, and I think Mr. Hicks thought he might do a deal with them. At all events, he took a nursery-van with him. But he didn't bring back much. I think he was disappointed with the prices they were asking and with the quality of their goods, which weren't up to what they set out to be in the catalogue. He bought five dozen of these tree-heaths (*Erica Arborea** is the name of them), but little else besides. Still, they've sold well. We've only got those four left.'

'Well, let me take those four,' I said. 'You've done rather well, haven't you, to get rid of all the others in a month.

*The plants which Warren was shown were Erica Arborea Alpina. The true Erica Arborea is scarce.

It's funny to think I might have seen your van about the town.'

It was a clumsy remark, but it had an undeserved success.

'Oh, it's a plain van, sir. Besides, Mr. Hicks wasn't away long. He left here very early on a Sunday morning and was back again late on the Monday night—or perhaps I should say, in the small hours of Tuesday morning. He didn't like to be away long while his mother wasn't well. Besides, he's kept pretty busy here. Now sir, I don't think these should dirty your car, if I put a good layer of paper round them.'

'No,' I said, 'I think they'll go in the "boot." Do you mind if I take a little walk round the rest of the place while you're wrapping them up?'

'Not at all, sir. I'll put the plants in a barrow and meet you by your car.'

In the gardener's company, I had covered about two-thirds of the nursery. The remaining third, which was largely given over to fruit-trees, lay behind the house, and, as I found on continuing my walk, joined the embankment overhanging the pond. It was a pretty little stretch of water, fringed on the far side, where another hillock rose, with willows—to my mind, one of the loveliest of trees. Though I couldn't see the bottom, the water seemed clean and wholesome.

I thought again how easily, given capital, the site could have been made into a water-garden, with Japanese irises and spiræas at the edge, and water-lilies in the middle. Then, when I had passed the side of the house, I looked over my left shoulder and saw the gardener putting the heaths into the back of my car.

'You've got the makings of a splendid water-garden down there,' I said.

'Yes, sir. Mr. Hicks would have liked to develop it, but

he didn't think it would pay. It isn't many people nowadays who have a piece of ornamental water like that. Four feet by six in the middle of crazy paving is all most people rise to. They wouldn't understand anything on this scale.'

'How deep is it?' I asked.

'I should say it averages, at this time of the year, about five feet, except in the middle, by the spring, where it's much deeper. In the winter it rises a good deal, and almost floods the drive you came in by.'

'Don't Mr. Hicks' customers ever ask if they can have a bathe?'

'I don't know about the customers. Mr. Hicks has a dip himself every morning before breakfast. And some of the village boys come round and try to bathe of an evening. But we try to keep people from bathing without permission.'

'Why?'

'Well, they often do damage in other ways. They even take plants from the nursery, and in the fruit season we have a lot to do to stop them from robbing the trees. Mr. Hicks is thinking of closing the entrance you came in by, sir. There's plenty of room for cars to turn in front of the house.'

'Yes,' I said, 'that's all right if you don't miss the main entrance, as I did. If you do, you'd either have to turn round in the lane, or go on till you come to the Sedcombe road again and turn back there. But I'm wasting your time, and I ought to be getting on. How much do I owe you?'

'Eight shillings, sir.'

I gave him a ten-shilling note, asked him to have a drink with the change, got into the car and drove off—by the main drive this time. Then I reached the gate, turned to the right into the lane, and passed the second gate through which I had driven into the nursery. Noticing that I had left it open, I got out and shut it. (Suppose a herd of cows strayed in, and Hicks sued me for damage?) Then I soon reached the Sedcombe road, and after another mile and a half the main road, where I found a road-house and had tea. And an hour later—at about half-past five—I reached the stately entrance gates of Neetham Priory, the residence of Mrs. Molyneux-Brown.

12.

Saturday, July 10th (continued), and Sunday, July 11th

I HAVE sometimes been asked, when telling this story, why I give so much prominence to my week-end with Mrs. Molyneux-Brown. Why not say simply, 'After leaving Hicks' nursery-garden I spent Saturday night and most of Sunday at Neetham Priory, *and then* . . .'?

My answer is that I *feel* this visit to be an integral part of my story. In the first place, it preceded the climax so closely in point of time as to appear linked up with the climax—just as people remember with peculiar vividness what they had for dinner the night before some disaster or delightful surprise, and feel afterwards that the dinner was part of the next day's drama. A superstitious feeling, if you like—yet who are we, with our limited knowledge of the law of cause and effect, to be too dogmatic about the foolishness of superstition?

But the visit had another, more logical, function, which it exercised through its psychological effect on me. I am convinced that without this visit—if, say, I had spent the week-end quietly in my flat in London, or with my mother in Somerset—I should not have acted afterwards as I did. Nor should I have been stimulated to make certain deductions—or guesses—which enabled me to stumble on the truth.

As to *why* the visit provided such a stimulus, it is more difficult to answer.

I had first met Mrs. Molyneux-Brown when she and her husband lived in Wimbledon. At a cocktail party I was able to introduce to her a poet in whom she was interested. This made her interested in me, and when she found out that I was on the Stock Exchange, her interest increased. She was fond of a flutter, and though she warned me at once that her husband had several brokers and that there was no hope of my being given any business by him, she was good enough to give me some of her own. She was too hard a woman to like very much—too practical, too eager to get on. Whether her interest in art was entirely spurious or not, I can't say. She never gushed or made a fool of herself about it. At the same time, she could never say, 'That—is—lovely,' and convince you that she felt it. Her interest in money, and what money can buy, on the other hand, was certainly not spurious. She was a shrewd buyer of pictures and antiques.

The house in Wimbledon, at which I dined twice, was a rich man's house, but not very remarkable. When the Molyneux-Browns moved to the country I assumed that they had bought an ordinary country house. Instead, as I found out, they had bought a real 'show-place.' Either Mr. Molyneux-Brown had somehow acquired much more money or he had decided to spend much more. Mrs. Molyneux-Brown never boasted, and when she had talked to me about Neetham Priory at a theatre party in London, I never for one moment suspected the scale of its magnificence. In fact, the first hint of it came to me from the gardener at Cantervale Nursery, when he referred to her pergola as being a quarter of a mile long. At the time I had thought this a monstrous exaggeration, but when I had passed a second pair of entrance gates, and the house and gardens came into view, I had for a moment the reverential sensations of Elizabeth in *Pride and Prejudice*, when she saw Mr. Darcy's majestic abode for the first time.

The house-party, or such members of it as had arrived, was by the tennis courts and I was shown the way there by a footman. Mrs. Molyneux-Brown rose from a bevy of brilliant sports costumes, welcomed me and introduced me to three people, none of whose names I caught. I was asked if I would like a game, and said that I had purposely not brought my tennis things as I played too badly. I caught a gleam in my hostess's eye, as if she were wondering what she could do with such an awkward man. Meanwhile I was wondering what had induced me to come. I was then told off to play bowls with two elderly ladies and a middle-aged man who looked like a tutor. I was no worse than any of them, and we had a pleasant game. Then, lured by drinks, I rejoined the main party, and found a chance of mentioning the absurd little present of four heaths which I had brought. Even while I spoke, I realised that it would have been much more tactful to say nothing about them, though the footman who had taken my luggage had seen them and would probably take them to my bedroom, if I didn't dispose of them.

'Oh, that is too kind of you,' my hostess exclaimed. 'I will ask Henry to give them to Higgins. He will know exactly where to put them. I do wonder if they're a kind we haven't got.'

'No earthly hope of that,' I thought ruefully, 'unless they're too common for you.'

Another lady—Mrs. Molyneux-Brown's secretary, as it happened—was then asked to show me the rock-garden, and I was glad to see it. I had always thought before that rockeries and rock-gardens were much the same thing. Now I was enlightened. This one was hollowed deeply into the earth and looked like a natural ravine, presenting on its sides a miniature alpine landscape. Two streams leapt over boulders and converged in a pool at the bottom. I was told that the pool and its surroundings were a miracle of beauty in the spring. In the drier parts grew every plant which should grow in rocky surroundings, and I was ashamed to notice a tract of three or four hundred heaths like those I had brought, but bigger and better. I understood now why Mrs. Molyneux-Brown went to Howards rather than to William Hicks—poor William Hicks who was so short of capital.

While we made our way back to the house I paid the garden a few compliments.

'Can it really be true,' I asked, 'that none of this was here when Mrs. Molyneux-Brown took the house?'

'It's absolutely true,' the secretary answered. 'There was nothing here at all except some badly kept lawns and a few old-fashioned flower-beds where they didn't even bed out geraniums and cannas. There were the trees, of course. The garden would be nothing without them still. But I wonder sometimes whether all this modern gardening wouldn't have looked more in keeping with a modern house. As it was, the garden was quite charming without flowers. Now it makes you feel that the house can't really be old. Of course it's unfair to judge the effect by the first year.'

I liked the secretary from that moment, and decided to cling to her skirts, if I could, throughout my visit.

My bedroom, though doubtless one of the meaner apartments, was nearly the size of my flat. My things had been unpacked for me—always a questionable blessing. In my *bourgeois* way, I like to feel that I am living in the lap of luxury, but if one puts things away oneself, it is easier to find them again. A notice in a gold-filigree frame told me that dinner was at half-past eight—half an hour later than it had been in the Wimbledon house—half an hour higher in the social scale.

I dressed in leisured fashion, dreading the time when I should have to go downstairs. A small decanter of sherry stood on a Regency *étagère*. I helped myself. The sherry was very good—how different from the sherry which Dr. Fielding had offered me in Kashmir Road, South Mersley. And, for that matter, how different was Neetham Priory and its whole setting from the whole setting of my own life, my London flat, my mother's home in Somerset, my office and my senior partner's muscular Christianity, South Mersley, where my thoughts had been straying so frequently of late—South Mersley, where Dr. Fielding lived and Uncle Hamilton had lived and Dick still lived—and the other South Mersley of the Garden City, where poor, blowsy Miss Crowne had her work, and that little gad-fly Miss Fillyan with the artificially silvered hair—I fell into a reverie. In my view reveries are never entirely without profit.

Then came the time, when like a snail I crept unwillingly downstairs. More introductions—cocktails or sherry? I took sherry, having already drunk some in my bedroom. All the younger people took cocktails. I thought to myself, 'This means I'm middle-aged.'

At dinner I sat between an American Princess and a grey-haired woman whose name I seemed to know—Dame Catherine Burns. For the first two courses I had to keep my head rigidly turned to the right, listening to the Princess's experiences in Bali, which were manifold. After that I was free to talk to Dame Catherine, who pretended to be interested in me, and thus made the time pass quite agreeably. I resolved to see more of Dame Catherine, if I could, in default of the lady-secretary who was not dining with us.

It was like the parody of a smart dinner-party, but real. You heard sentences such as: 'But, my dear man, Mussolini himself told me last year,' and 'The whole European crisis first arose in the island of Sumatra.' I produced my little story of gas-masks in the Autumn as gleaned at the Seymours' table the night before, but it provoked little comment, and was quickly capped by something much more terrifying.

When the women had left, a hawk-faced middle-aged man, who, since the exit of the American Princess, was sitting on my right, suddenly said to me, 'Don't you think this party is exactly like the opening of a detective story, and that somebody ought to be found murdered to-morrow morning?'

The remark struck me in a sore place, and, trying to hide my confusion, I said, 'Whom would you choose for the victim?'

'Why, our host, of course,' was the reply. At this Mr. Molyneux-Brown, who had the air of a guest and clearly disliked most of his wife's friends, leaned forward and boomed out, 'Eh? What's that about me?'

'I said you ought to be murdered in the night!' was the reply.

'What do you mean? Murdered? Me?'

It would be just my luck, I thought, if he was found murdered. However, he wasn't, and if anyone was, it never reached my ears.

After dinner—bridge. Again I lost two pounds, and my cards weren't particularly bad either. 'I must be playing badly,' I thought, 'because my wits are elsewhere. They're in Cornwall, at Polgedswell Cove. They're in South Mersley. They're in William Hicks' nursery-garden, by the edge of that pretty little lake with the willows on the far side. By the edge of that pretty little lake—'

I was putting soda in my whisky and splashed it all over the tray. The house-party at Neetham Priory was not, as my hawk-faced neighbour had said at dinner, like the opening of a detective story. It was like the end of one.

Cousin Bill took a dip in the pretty little lake every

morning before breakfast. Would he do so if there were a body in the lake? And the village boys weren't allowed to bathe there of an evening. . . . I felt confused, almost ill, and went upstairs to my room without saying good-night to anyone.

But when I had got in bed, the 'clue' of the draft letter from Uncle Hamilton to Hicks presented itself once more to my attention, and occupied it for some time. Why had the letter been found in Uncle Hamilton's note-case? Why had it been left there? Was it mere carelessness? If so, it was gross and wanton carelessness. It was the date of the letter, of course, which was crucially incriminating—June 6th. I retained a visual memory of it, as it was written—6 vi. 37—a neat, methodically written date, the day and the year in Arabic numerals and the month in Roman numerals. It was just how Uncle Hamilton would have written dates. . . .

Then there was the clue of the patent-leather shoes. There were other clues also—too many of them, and they buzzed in my brain like bees, till they reduced it to such confusion that sleep came to me. But it was at the very moment of my falling asleep—a moment which often fills itself for me with a tragic intensity of vision—that I asked myself a question which the reader has been waiting for me to ask for a long time: *Where was Uncle Hamilton's mackintosh?*

Ormerod, the porter at the Trepolpen, had described him as arriving with a brown mackintosh over his arm. No one would go to Cornwall without a mackintosh or coat of some kind. And yet we had found no mackintosh or coat, either in the heap of clothing in Polgedswell Cove or in the suitcase at Truro. What had become of it?

I put this question to myself, as I say, in the twinkling of an eye, and fell asleep upon it, just as I have often fallen asleep after other vivid moments, imagining that an aerial torpedo is bursting through my bedroom ceiling or that someone is running me through with a sword—moments of nightmarish clairvoyance, of death-in-life, which are quite likely the preludes to sweet dreams.

When I reached the breakfast table next morning, I found the 'younger set' in possession. They all seemed to know one another, and the room resounded with cries of 'Bert, Bill, Pamela and Pauline.' I was asked again if I didn't feel like a game of tennis, and again said 'No.'

It was a bright hot day, and I went out and sat for a while with a book by the tennis courts, half reading and half watching the incessant games. Then, when I feared that I was going to be pressed into making up a four—there were three eager would-be players standing around me—I got up unsociably and wandered slowly round the remoter parts of the garden. Hardly had I begun to congratulate myself that I was secure from public scrutiny, when Dame Catherine Burns, my left-hand neighbour at last night's dinner table, met me from the opposite direction and joined forces with me. Since talking to her at dinner I had been able to 'place' her. She was a well-known figure connected with the stage, and had sponsored many theatrical movements, including repertory companies. She had been good enough to seem interested in me the previous evening, and I thought it only fair that I should now seem interested in her and in her work.

I knew enough about the highbrow stage to ask a few appropriate questions, and she was soon telling me some of her experiences with actors, playwrights and theatrical managers. One of her stories ended with the words: 'That was when we were at Harrow—no, it wasn't, it was at South Mersley.'

'South Mersley?' I asked. 'Did you ever have a company there?'

'Oh, yes,' she replied. 'We came to an arrangement with the Garden City authorities and thought we were almost going to be a permanent fixture. Unfortunately, we quarrelled with them—or rather, they quarrelled with us. They wanted me to do nothing but poetic drama and Greek tragedies in Professor Murray's translation, while we wanted to extend our range a good deal further. They still regarded Ibsen as improper, and made themselves such nuisances that we had to go. A pity, as they have an excellent little theatre, and a big potential audience.'

'I know South Mersley a little,' I said. 'In fact, I know two girls who work in the Garden City—a Miss Crowne and a Miss Fillyan. But I don't suppose you ever came across them.'

'I can't remember either of their names.'

'Or Hilda Montaubyn?' I said, suddenly remembering that Dick had told me that she had done some repertory work. 'Does her name convey anything to you?'

'Oh, rather!' was the reply. 'She was in our company for about six months. And I still hear of her quite a lot through a cousin of mine. Do you know her well?'

'I've never met her myself,' I confessed, 'though I've seen her photograph and thought it very impressive. And I think a friend of mine is in love with her. I wish you'd tell me about her.'

'All right, I will, though I hope I shan't disappoint you if I don't sing her praises too highly. Hilda Montaubyn was a General's daughter and, to my mind, her tragedy is that she can never forget it. She has a kind of cold statuesqueness which makes you think at first that there must be something tremendous inside it. Then you find there's nothing inside it—only the General's daughter. Of course, she was quite good technically, or we shouldn't have employed her. She never gave any trouble, was never late, never made scenes, always knew her words and so on, but I used to feel we were putting a shop-window figure on the stage. She was certainly very lovely, as I gather you think she was from her photograph. I dare say she was even lovelier in the photograph than in real life. She had the type of beauty which lends itself to photographs, while in real life—well, it would be unfair to call her wooden or expressionless—'

'But those eyes,' I said.

'Yes, very remarkable, but a fraud. I've heard her called an expensive frame without a picture in it. But I oughtn't to talk like this. I may be hurting your feelings.'

'Oh, no, you're not, Dame Catherine! Do go on and say anything. Did she leave the stage because you said she wasn't much good? Perhaps I oughtn't to ask?'

'No, I don't think it was that, though it may have had something to do with it. I think she really left because she was so unpopular with most of the company.'

'Unpopular? I should have thought all the men would have been running after her.'

'One or two did, at first. But she hadn't the temperament to attract the average actor. And she exasperated the women, quite unconsciously. Little superior ways, probably, which came out in spite of herself. She never made scenes, but *they* did. It was really a relief when she left us. If she'd been first-rate, or dependent on acting for her living, I should have tried to keep her, but as she was neither, I didn't put any obstacles in the way of her going.'

'She has money, then?'

'Not very much, but enough to live on.'

'Is she mercenary?'

'No, you could never apply that word to her. At the same time, I think she would like to be a lady of substance and position. I hope I'm not being too hard on her. You see, she irritated even me a little, perhaps because there was never anything about her which you could catch hold of, either good or bad. By the way, you said a friend of yours was in love with her. Is it a recent affair?'

'I should say it's going very strong at this moment. Why?'

'Then I'm sorry for him, because I've an idea she's nearly engaged. Of course, your friend may be the man. What is his name?'

'Richard Findlay.'

'No, this was an army officer—heir to a baronetcy, I believe. He sounds in every way suitable for her.'

'When did you hear of this semi-engagement?' I asked.

'Oh, in a letter, only a day or two ago. On Friday, I think, or it might have been Thursday. Of course, it mayn't be quite true, as my cousin is an ardent match-maker. She and her husband have a grand villa at a place on the north coast of France called Blaireau-sur-mer, and love entertaining rather indiscriminately. In fact, they're not unlike our good hostess here, though they haven't her intellectual aspirations. Hilda got to know them some time ago, and my cousin seems very fond of her. The letter, which came from my cousin in France, simply mentioned that 'dear Hilda' had been there about ten days, during which the young man—I can't remember his name, but my cousin described him as heir to a baronetcy, and it wasn't Richard Findlay—had been paying her great attentions, and Hilda herself seemed so happy that my cousin was sure they'd reached an understanding. My cousin puts things in a very Victorian way.'

'Do you think Hilda may have been so happy because she had two admirers at once?' I asked. 'They tell me some women are like that. Would it be like Hilda to play them off against each other?'

'Not nastily, or deliberately,' Dame Catherine replied. 'To do her justice, I don't think she's a coquette. But she might certainly enjoy being slow to make up her mind, and in the end I'm sure the future baronet will win.'

'And now,' she added, as we emerged suddenly upon the house-party, 'don't you repeat anything I've said. And don't you go falling in love with her yourself. That would never do. If you married her, you'd both be miserable, and she'd be the more miserable of the two.'

I should have liked to analyse this last remark almost as much as anything Dame Catherine had said, but we were immediately surrounded and forced to join in a mass-migration to the swimming-pool, which lay at the far end of the 'quarter-of-a-mile' pergola. Actually the pergola was nearly this distance in length.

When we reached the pool, which was a magnificent work in marble mosaics, Bill, Bert, Pamela and Pauline and three or four others at once went to the disrobing rooms, and I was inevitably asked if I didn't wish to join them and offered a costume. I refused, and was glad I did so, for in a few minutes the bathers came out of their cubicles, superbly arrayed, and performed such dazzling feats in the water that I felt my shabby way of bathing would have dishonoured the party. Then came cocktails, and much animated talk. The American Princess warned us to beware of Puritanism, the curse of the new generation.

'All Puritans are cruel,' she said, 'and I'd rather have free-love than cruelty any day. And beware of excessive readiness for self-sacrifice. It rapidly leads to mass-hysteria.'

The conversation became political, and we all gave vent to our feelings.

'This is the kind of life,' I thought, 'which is denounced from many a social pulpit—but at least it's better than—' I became introspective, tilting inwardly against those social theories which I most dislike.

After luncheon I went to my bedroom and unashamedly had a nap. I never have a moment of clairvoyance before falling asleep in the afternoon.

Then came tea, by the tennis courts, as on Saturday, and after tea I again played bowls—a game which one is told is excellent for the liver. Instead of becoming cooler, the temperature seemed to rise as the shadows lengthened. I had come in thin clothes, but they were not thin enough, and when my game was over I should have liked to have the bathing-pool to myself, just as poor Uncle Hamilton liked a whole beach to himself on account of his wig. My trouble wasn't a wig. It was that I can't dive, and all the men in the party were diving up to exhibition standard. So even at the risk of being thought senile, I didn't join in the evening performance at the pool, but handed round cocktails instead. While doing so, I had another conversation with Dame Catherine, but thought it wise not to pursue the subject of Hilda Montaubyn. The whole problem of the murder of Hamilton Findlay—I now called it this to myself—was seething in my mind below the surface, and seemed likely to boil over as soon as I left Neetham Priory.

Then came dinner, for which we had to dress—an inconvenience for me, as I was set upon going home soon after the meal was over. I sat between Pamela, who ignored me, and a peeress who told me how I could economise in my household shopping.

The meal broke up earlier than the night before, and I found that I was the only one to be leaving that night. Fortunately I was not asked to give anyone a lift. As soon as I could, I said goodbye to my host, who seemed startled to see me there at all, and my hostess, who didn't press me to come again.

Then as I was on my way to my bedroom to change into my day-clothes, I was caught by some of the 'younger set,' who were playing 'Drunken Sailor,'* and asked me to join in, only for one round. I did, and an hour passed in a flash. (I won eight shillings.) It was nearer midnight than eleven when I slipped out of the house to my car like a traveling salesman, leaving surreptitious tips on the dressing table.

I had a horror that I should find the garage locked, but though it may have been, my car was standing outside in the yard—presumably forethought on the part of Mrs. Molyneux-Brown's secretary. I put my bag inside, and looked to see if the four heaths had duly been taken out by Henry and given to Higgins. They had, and Mrs. Molyneux-Brown rose in my good opinion.

But what a relief I felt when I passed the lodge gates!

* An elegant little game of chance, played with poker dice.

13.
Sunday Night, July 11th

THE night was beautiful but sultry, and there were flashes of summer lightning in the distance. I drove quickly, hoping to get home before the storm. Meanwhile I was asking myself, 'What are you going to do when you do get home?' and an awful feeling of moral responsibility began to weigh upon me, especially as despite my feeling of certainty, there were still some clues which did not fit in with my theory. At all costs I must see William Hicks.

This thought intensified itself as I reached the borders of Surrey and realised that, with but a slight *dêtour*, I could revisit his nursery-garden.

Then suddenly, as the heat of the engine—was it running badly?—and the heat of the night, seemed to grow more oppressive, I thought, 'Why not bathe in his pond? His pond which attracts you like a magnet. If he does catch you, what matter? There are more unconventional things than trespassing in search of a dip.' I had been baulked of my bathe at Neetham Priory, owing to the brilliance of the bathing-party. Now I would have a whole lake to myself—a lake bordered with willows and illumined by a tropical moon; for, in my ignorance of the calendar, I assumed that the moon would rise. The idea exercised an irresistible fascination upon me, and when I reached the Sedcombe turning, I took it without hesitation, and I was equally determined when I came to the turning which led to Hicks' lane.

Somewhat to my surprise, the gate leading to the secondary drive was open. I had been careful to close it behind me the previous day. Had another customer been in that way, after me, or had the owner of the nursery-gardens himself left it open? As it was, it seemed like an invitation to 'come in,' and I did so, stopping the car about thirty yards inside the entrance. I don't think it occurred to me, in that moment of elation, to wonder if I could back the car out into the narrow lane, or whether I should be forced to go right up the drive and turn it impertinently in front of the house. I was quite content to leave it where I stopped, and to get out and walk over the grass embankment to the water's edge.

There was still no moon and the warm darkness was so perfect a substitute for a bathing-costume, that it never struck me that I hadn't one available. I didn't think, either, that I might need a towel after my swim. After all, I had a shirt to dry myself with, and a spare shirt in the car. I was drunk with excitement. Having been repressed for twenty-four hours at Neetham Priory I was resolved to give full rein to the caprices of my 'ego.'

I deposited my clothes in a little heap by a stone, which may have been used for mooring small boats, darted three yards down the grassy slope and plunged in. As I did so, a big drop of rain struck me on the forehead. I disregarded the warning and swam out into the middle of the pool. By the bank, where I had entered, the water was about three feet deep. In the middle, I could only touch bottom intermittently.

Except for the cry of a startled night-bird, there was no sound, and I enjoyed a moment of timeless ecstasy, feeling as if I were wearing the whole pool with its grasses and willows and even the mud beneath, as my garment, while the leisurely rhythm of the Satie *Gymnopédie* No. 1 seemed to blend with my deliberate strokes. It was an experience of pantheistic satisfaction—of a beneficent if sombre earth-magic—to which I should never have thought I could respond. When I realised that I was responding to it—at the very instant when I said to myself, 'Why don't you do this kind of thing more often, Malcolm Warren?'—half the spell vanished, and the spell vanished completely a few seconds later, when two most untoward things happened—one a terrific downpour of thundery rain, and the other the ominous barking of a dog.

I was at the further side of the pool, when I was thus rudely recalled to my everyday senses, and I began to swim across to my clothes as quickly as I could, without any further thought of the *Gymnopédie*. But I still had to pay for my folly, and before I arrived at the bank there was a great increase of barking, and an unpleasantly large dog ran down the bank and defied me to reach my clothes. The scene must have been like a comic picture postcard, but I found little to laugh at. After a moment's indecision, I made my way towards the corner of the pool nearest the lane, where the bank became steeper and, to my surprise, the water a little deeper. In fact, it now reached my shoulders. The dog didn't follow me, but stayed near my clothes, still barking and growling. My plan was to nip up the bank and gain the shelter of my car, where I could consider the situation and dress myself after a fashion. I had my evening things to put on, a spare dayshirt, a pullover and pair of trousers, but, alas, no spare underclothes or day-coat. Still, if I had been able to carry out my manoeuvre, I should at least have been able to reach London in fairly respectable condition, and write the next day to William Hicks asking him to send on my other garments which, incidentally, contained my latch-key and all my money. It would have been an amusing letter to compose. But I was not destined to try; for the sagacious animal (as a

Latin prose book would put it) divined my intention as soon as I began to emerge from the water, and came bounding along the bank with such a menacing bark that I flopped back into the pond through sheer fright. As I did so I grazed my toe on something hard under the water, and with my other foot trod on something soft and clammy.

What with the dog, the downpour, and the pain in my right foot, I now felt utterly dejected and cursed the idiocy of my escapade. There seemed nothing for it but to cross the lake again and try to reach the lane circuitously, after which I should have to regain possession of my car from the rear.

Meanwhile, the temperature fell with my spirits, and I began to wonder if I was destined to die of exposure.

I was on the point of swimming disconsolately to the willows, when it occurred to me that it would be just as well to see if I couldn't make friends with the dog first. Accordingly I went back to the corner of the pond and, in as firm a tone as I could achieve, uttered foolish phrases like, 'Hello, old boy! What's wrong now? Friend, friend!'

At first I thought I had succeeded. The barking died down to an intermittent growl and I was allowed to get a foothold on the bank. Then slowly the animal came down the bank towards me. We both paused. It was a contest of wills, and I lost. I jumped back into the water, and once more had a nasty blow on the foot.

'Damn!' I shouted, with exasperation. 'Damn everything!'

Then, just as I was about to swim wearily away, the dog, with renewed barking, suddenly turned tail and rushed up the bank and along the drive. For a few moments I paused irresolutely, hardly believing my senses. Then I swam along to the place where my sodden clothes were lying, got on to the bank and picked them up in a bundle. At the same time my fingers closed on something else which felt like a small piece of thin cardboard, with a straight edge.

They retained it mechanically in their grip while I walked along the bank towards the car. But this haven of refuge was not yet destined to be mine; for with a still more savage barking, the odious dog suddenly appeared out of the darkness and drove me back to the water. In my agitation, I dropped my clothes on the grass and leapt in, my fingers still clutching the bit of cardboard, or whatever it was.

However, the last act of the tragi-comedy was at hand. I saw the light of an electric-torch flickering in the direction from which the dog had come, and soon heard steps sounding in the drive. Evidently, Mr. William Hicks, the dog's owner, had been roused at last. Three parts covered by water, I composed myself as best I could for the encounter. I had been eager for some time to renew acquaintance with him, but these were hardly the circumstances I should have chosen.

Two minutes went by, and a big form penetrated the darkness. Then the torch played dazzlingly over my head and shoulders, and a voice said gruffly, 'Come out!'

'Mr. Hicks,' I said feebly. But either he didn't hear or he was so set on humiliating me that he took no notice of the fact that I addressed him by name, because once more he repeated his command, 'Come out! Come out of that at once, or I'll come in and get you!'

I obeyed like a worm, and felt like a worm as he surveyed me in the light of his torch.

'What's your name?' he asked curtly.

'Malcolm Warren,' I said. 'I'm a friend of your cousin, Dick Findlay, and a customer of yours. And I've a good deal to talk over with you!'

This unexpected reply made him silent for a second. Then he said:

'What on earth were you doing in there? It's all right, my dog won't hurt you.'

My teeth began to chatter.

'I called here yesterday and bought four heaths,' I said.

'I was hoping to see you, but you were away. By the way, I do hope you have good news of your mother?'

This polite question, uttered in such strange circumstances, might well have made any ordinary person laugh, but William Hicks took it quite seriously. (After all, his mother was very ill and he was very fond of her.)

'Thank God she's out of danger,' he said. 'I've been at the nursing-home till half-past eleven this evening. How did you know about that?'

'Your man told me yesterday,' I replied, 'and I heard from Dick some time ago that she wasn't well. Now, do you mind if I fetch my clothes—they're just over there—and go to my car and put something on? I'm feeling both chilly and silly.'

'The best thing you can do,' he said, 'is to drive up to the front door and come in. I can give you a towel, and some hot soup out of a tin. Your clothes must be pretty wet now. We can dry them by the boiler fire.'

'Yes,' I answered. 'Your dog kept them in the rain longer than I bargained for. I should like to dry myself, if I may.'

'All right,' he said. 'I'll be by the front door when you arrive'—and as if to obtain a guarantee that I should follow, he picked up my heap of clothes and walked off with them towards the house, while my enemy the dog ran quietly by his side.

And now, at last, I was able to gain the shelter of my car. I wondered for a moment whether I should undo my suitcase and rummage for something, however fragmentary, to wear, but the thought of a real towel and a fire and hot soup decided me to go straight to the front door, and to experience, for once in my life, the doubtful pleasure of driving a motor-car completely naked. However, before I was able to realise what the clutch pedal feels like to a bare foot—in fact as soon as I had switched on my dashboard lights, I realised that I was holding a visiting-card in the fingers of my left hand, and on examining it saw this amazing name:

MR. E. HAMILTON FINDLAY,
Tylecroft,
South Mersley.

'Let him warm the towel,' I thought. 'Let him heat the soup. I must think this out first.'

There was a torch in the cubby-hole of the car. I had tried it at the start of my journey, out of curiosity, little dreaming that I should ever need to use it. But it was now essential. 'If there's one card,' I thought, 'there'll be a great many more. One might have been missed and blown away. I must find the others.' And I jumped out of the car and scoured the bank with my light. One, two, three—at almost methodical intervals. I collected the cards and drove up to the house in fine style, and got out with the self-assurance I should have felt if I had been dressed for Ascot.

Hicks was waiting testily by the door. No doubt, during his walk up the drive, he had had time to recover from the surprise of our meeting and had begun to wonder why he should bother with me at all, or even whether I wasn't an impostor or a lunatic. He might well have thought the latter.

I contented myself with uttering bland apologies while he showed me into a large old-fashioned kitchen and through it into a kind of scullery and boiler-house.

'That heats my orchid-house,' he explained, 'and gives us hot water. You'll have to dry your things there as best you can, while I heat up the soup. Here's that towel I promised you.'

He went into the kitchen, and after rubbing myself down, I put on my dry pair of flannel trousers, my evening socks, a day shirt, a pullover and a dinner-coat. My foot was rather painfully bruised, but I managed to get my shoes on. I put my collection of the four visiting-cards bearing Hamilton Findlay's name into my pocket. I had been in half a mind to offer one of them to Hicks on a tray, but judged that the shock might be too much for his slow wits. He would merely get it into his head that I was a practical joker, or worse, and it would take me the remaining hours of the night—it was now half-past one according to the kitchen clock—to put him on the right lines again.

I was wondering how best to tackle him, when he put his head round the door and asked if I would come into the kitchen. I did so, and we sat down to a meal of tinned tomato soup, into which he put a little cream, and bread and cheese. I thought it best to delay coming to the point for a while, and induced him to talk about his mother. He told me that she had been ill for two or three months, and the doctors had wanted to operate but she was afraid, and grudged the expense, and had struggled on till Saturday, when she had had an acute attack, and there was nothing for it but to take her to hospital at once. They removed her appendix successfully, but they were doubtful whether she would survive, and he had been advised to spend Sunday within call. At about eight o'clock that evening she began to show real signs of improvement, and there was now every hope that she would recover. He had reached home at half-past twelve, feeling worn out with the strain, and went straight to bed, where he slept till the dog roused him. They sometimes had plants stolen at night, and he had come out intent on catching the thief. The dog slept in a kennel in an outhouse, and had the run of the place.

'I've put him back there now,' he added, 'as I expect you've seen enough of him for to-night. Tony's a bull mastiff, but I think his bark is worse than his bite.'

'How about your customers?' I asked. 'Doesn't he frighten them away?'

'Oh, he knows a customer at once. They generally like him. He goes everywhere with me.'

'I didn't see him yesterday,' I said.

'No, I'd taken him with me for company. I took him to-day, too.'

So, I thought, Tony was off the premises till after mid-night.

'Did you drive in by your south entrance?' I asked. 'I mean the one that leads past the pond?'

'No, I hardly ever go that way. The other drive is the proper way. The bends aren't so sharp, and the surface is better. Why?'

'I found the gate open.'

'It shouldn't have been.'

'It was shut yesterday afternoon,' I said. 'I shut it my-self.'

'Well, I suppose Mrs. Timmins—she's the wife of one of my men and looks after us—must have gone out that way, though heaven knows where she'd be going to. She always takes a field-path which is bang opposite the other en-trance. But are you hinting at anything?'

'I'm not quite sure,' I said. 'But I rather think you had a visitor here before me to-night.'

'A visitor? What exactly do you mean?'

Then, yielding to the impulse, which I had determined to resist, I took one of the cards from my pocket and gave it to him.

'A visitor who left this card,' I said.

A foolish gesture, perhaps, but not ineffective as a means of introducing the subject we had to discuss.

When Hicks had read the inscription on the card two or three times, he became so inarticulate with unuttered questions, that I had to speak for him.

I said, 'Let me talk for a bit. First, I swear this isn't a practical joke. I found this card and these three others like it on the bank of the pond. I picked up the first one when Tony allowed me to get at my clothes for a moment, as you were coming out of the house to look for the plant thief. I read it by the light of my car, and I had the idea that as I had found one card, there would probably be others lying about the place. I had a quick look round with my torch, and found the other three. I dare say there are more. You can search to-morrow.

'Now look at the card. It's wet, of course, owing to the rain, though it has begun to dry in my pocket. But I shouldn't say it's spent many nights in the open, would you? Before this little heat-wave we've had a good deal of rain. It might have been out last night, and perhaps the night before, but I should say no longer than that. My theory is that it was dropped by the pond to-night, before you got back to the house. I admired your pond yesterday in broad sunlight, and I didn't notice any cards lying about as I came up the drive. I admit that if I had seen them, I should probably not have realised that they were visiting-cards, but I should have noted that you had litter about the place and carried away a bad impression. For I've got to confess that I did come here to form impressions.'

At this, he moved irritably in his chair, and said: 'But I don't understand——'

I interrupted him quickly.

'Please don't ask me any questions yet. The whole business, of course, turns on your uncle's death. You know that I went with your cousin, Dick Findlay, to Falmouth, to look for your uncle, and that, instead of finding your uncle, we, or rather I, found his clothes among the rocks of Polgedswell Cove. Now I want to ask *you* some questions. What did you think about your uncle's trip to Falmouth?'

'How do you mean?'

'Well, were you surprised that he decided to go there for a week-end?'

'I don't know that I was, particularly.'

'Did he ever tell you he was going to Falmouth?'

'No, now that I come to think of it, I'm not sure he did. In fact, I think he didn't. He may have mentioned Cornwall vaguely, but not Falmouth. I'd arranged to go to Falmouth myself on business early in June, and I'm not sure

I'd have gone if it had really dawned on me that he was going to be there in the same town just at the same time. We weren't on very good terms, I'm afraid.'

'So it was rather a shock when you met him there?'

'I never met him there. It never entered my head that he was there. What are you getting at, Warren?'

'Don't worry,' I said. 'I only thought you must have met, because a half-finished letter to you was found in your uncle's wallet. It was dated the 6th of June.'

'That's the first I've ever heard of a letter from him in June. What was it about?'

'He was refusing to lend you money for your business.'

'But he'd already done that.'

'Done that?' I exclaimed. 'When?'

'Oh, some weeks before, at the beginning of May. I had dinner at Tylecroft and made him a business proposition. Incidentally, that was the last time I ever saw him. He said he'd think over what I'd said, but a day or two later I had a beastly letter from him, running down my father, as he often did, and saying that I wasn't any better, and that it would be a waste of good money to lend me any. I've still got the letter. I can show it to you if you like.'

'I'd be devoutly thankful if you would.'

He got up, went out of the room, and after two minutes came back and gave me a folded letter without comment. The letter was written on note-paper stamped 'Tylecroft, South Mersley,' in fancy black lettering. It was dated 6 v. 37, the month being represented by a Roman numeral. The handwriting was, so far as I could tell, identical with that of the draft letter, though it was more carefully formed. The letter read as follows:

DEAR WILLIAM,

I have been thinking over your suggestion, but can find no justification whatever for entertaining it. When your mother married your father, she had quite a fair income of her own, and the present state of your finances is entirely due to your late father's improvidence. I admit you seem to be a better man of business than he was, but I am far from being convinced that you have the will to run your establishment on sound commercial lines. In fact, I fear that if you found yourself in funds, you would at once waste your resources on some elaborate experiments such as your father used to undertake, to the detriment of his legitimate business.

It is true that you may have the will and the ability to create a name for yourself amongst a few horticulturists, and possibly even to win a high award at the Chelsea Show—but that won't pay off the mortgage on your nursery, and it certainly isn't an inducement to me to part with my savings. No, as I've said before, you must either run your establishment as a commercial proposition, leaving the fancy side to those more amply provided with this world's goods than you are—or you must give up your business, lock, stock and barrel, and get a job in some institution where your scientific interests might find scope for themselves. You may know someone at Kew who could help you, or at one of the agricultural colleges. I believe Dick once met the Professor of Botany at Oxford, but I don't suppose he could give you an introduction. But I am quite aware that it isn't *advice* that you were applying to me for, and as I'm not disposed to give you any other commodity, I may as well conclude by signing myself,

Your affectionate
UNCLE HAMILTON.

I read it slowly, comparing its contents in my mind with those of the draft letter, as I remembered them. Though I was unwilling to trust my memory too far in this respect, I had little doubt that, except for one or two small differences of phrasing, the letter which I was reading was a copy of the draft. For practical purposes, one could say an exact copy, with one great exception—the date. The draft had been dated June, and this letter—the finished product—was dated May. An Alice in Wonderland situation.

'This is tremendously interesting,' I said, at length. 'In fact, I've really seen this letter before. Do you know, by the way, if your uncle was in the habit of writing out drafts of his letters?'

'I can't tell you,' Hicks replied. 'You must remember I never saw very much of him. I didn't live in his pocket, like Dick.'

'No, you didn't,' I said. 'Would you mind very much if I keep this letter for a day or two?'

'I don't see any harm in it, though I don't know why *you* should have it. Isn't it time you stopped beating about the bush, and came out into the open with me? Why are you ferreting all this business out, anyway?'

'You must remember,' I answered, 'that your cousin called me into this case. Having been called in, I have a right to make my own investigations. Tell me honestly, what did you really think about your uncle's supposed bathing accident in Cornwall?'

He paused and then asked, 'Why do you say "supposed"?'

'Because there are too many things against its having been a real accident. Of course, you probably don't know half of them. Still, there are one or two facts which might have occurred to you. First, I come back to the fact that this was an extraordinary holiday for your uncle to take. Did that never strike you?'

'I can't say it did. I've never been very keen on my uncle, and when I heard he'd gone to Cornwall and been drowned there, I just thought, "That's that." It may seem beastly cold-blooded of me, but I can't help it.'

'When days went by, and the body failed to turn up, didn't you become a little uneasy? The bodies of people who are drowned bathing nearly always do turn up, you know.'

'I can't say that worried me, except for the delay in getting probate. There's no use pretending that the money he left my mother wasn't damned useful to both of us. Without it, I might have had to close down here. But are you seriously suggesting that my uncle wasn't drowned?'

'I am.'

'Then where is he?'

'I think very probably his body is in your pond—at the corner nearest the lane, where I found those visiting-cards. I think I trod on his body, and quite likely I grazed my foot on a weight holding it down. Unless, of course, there are rocks or stones in that corner. The bottom was perfectly smooth everywhere else.'

'I've always kept it clear for bathing,' he said, and then, as he took in the import of the earlier part of what I had just said, he scowled at me suddenly, and went on, 'I'd very much like to know what on earth you mean by all this. Are you suggesting I murdered my uncle, and put him in the pond?'

'I should like to warn you,' I answered, 'that this idea may be held in some quarters. You were in Falmouth when your uncle was. You had a meeting with him and asked him to lend you money—'

'But I didn't have a meeting with him,' he roared.

'I'm only saying it may be suggested that you did. You had your nursery-van with you. You left Falmouth the day your uncle left his hotel there. You arrived here in the small hours of the Tuesday morning. You had every opportunity of putting the body in your pond there and then. You, or rather your mother, got the full share under your uncle's will, and you admit the money was damned useful.'

'Are you from the police?' he asked huskily.

'No. I was simply an old friend of your cousin's. But I'm afraid I shall have a good deal to do with the police during the next few days. And so will you, for that matter. By the way, two or three little questions I forgot to ask you earlier. Do you know a Miss Fillyan of South Mersley?'

'No, never heard of her.'

'Or a Miss Crowne?'

'Was that the painted bit Dick used to trail around with?'

'Yes, you might describe her like that.'

'I think I met her once, at Tylecroft. I wasn't much impressed.'

'And Dr. Fielding—your uncle's friend?'

'I've met him, of course, over a number of years.'

'How did he strike you?'

'I don't think the old man struck me at all. He seemed decent enough in his way. I talked to him once about the use of electricity in plant-growing, but he was hopelessly unpractical. Now am I, or am I not, going to be told why you're asking me all these questions?'

'These questions have simply filled in little gaps for me. What you've got to decide is, what will you do when the police arrive to-morrow—or rather to-day, in a few hours' time?'

'Have you sent for the police?'

'No, but I think they will come. If they don't, I shall have to send for them.'

'Why?'

'Because I'm as certain as I can be that your uncle's body is in your pond. You can't know a fact like that and do nothing about it.'

'And what about me?'

'It's you I'm thinking of. On the whole, it would be much wiser if you don't get up with the lark and start examining the grass bank and the corner of the pond. Leave things just as they are for the police to find. Tell them where to look, if you like. Tell them where my car was, if they examine the place for tracks. Tell them anything you like about me. Give them my name and address, though they know it already. And now, go to bed. I'm going.'

'But look here, are they going to arrest me?'

'No, I don't think so for a moment. If they show any

signs of doing that, call your solicitor and tell him to get hold of me at once. This is my address and telephone number. I shall be there all the morning, and probably all day.'

I went across to the stove, got a pencil out of my coat which was still drying there, and wrote my address and telephone number on a piece of paper covering a dresser. Then I picked up my half-dry garments, gave him the piece of paper, and went to the door.

'I ought to apologise to you for being a frightful nuisance,' I said. 'I'll do that later, when we meet again. You must let me go now. I'm too sleepy to talk any longer. I'll only say one thing, to give you pleasant dreams. You'll probably come into a good deal more money than you think. And your mother's getting better. If that doesn't cheer you up, I don't know what will. Good-night.'

'But, Warren, look here—'

14.

Monday, July 12th

EXTRACT FROM A LETTER WRITTEN BY MALCOLM WARREN TO DETECTIVE-INSPECTOR PARRIS OF SCOTLAND YARD.

[*The reader can fill in the first part of this letter for himself, with a résumé of the events described in the first thirteen chapters of this book.*]

. . . and you can imagine how difficult I found it to get away. However, I'd so startled him that I had the upper hand, and though he had the physical strength to keep me there, he lacked the necessary nervous force.

I got back to my flat about four. Day was just breaking. I left the car outside, and tumbled into bed exhausted. But my sleep was poor, and I kept thinking of the letter I should have to write to you. In fact, I had started to write it before Mrs. Rhodes, my housekeeper, brought me my early tea.

I hope this letter isn't a terrible breach of Scotland Yard etiquette. You are the only policeman I know, and your handling of the case in Hampstead was so sympathetic to me, that I felt I must drag you in to protect me from your colleagues' crudity. I must apologise, too, for my novelistic style, but I warned you that I was going to tell you my story in my own fashion. If I condensed the facts to postcard size, you would, in your professional way, never be able to forgive me for not having called in you, or one of your cruder colleagues, before.

None the less, you will ask me when I first realised the truth, and I shall have to infuriate you by saying, 'I don't know.' You see I didn't approach the problem as you would approach it. I had my work and my pleasures—and the international situation—to think about. There were moments when enlightenment seemed to approach, and moments when it withdrew. And there was the moral question. I know the law is the law, but one has instincts which sometimes conflict with it. . . . However, I must get on with my analysis.

The first thing that struck me as odd about the whole affair, was the extraordinarily complicated nature of Hamilton Findlay's holiday arrangements, coupled with an air of vagueness in his plans when you would have expected them to be precise. This vagueness communicated itself to Dick, who in our first talk referred to his uncle's visit to Cornwall, not to Falmouth. Falmouth only dropped out as an afterthought. Why should Uncle Hamilton mention the county—and, for him, such an unlikely county—to which he was going, but not the town, unless he wished to leave his exact whereabouts as vague as possible? And why should he wish to leave them vague?

This uncertainty with which he veiled his movements was emphasised in my talk with Dr. Fielding. To Dr. Fielding he had suggested Newquay or St. Ives. No mention of Falmouth, so far as I could learn, to anyone but Dick. Why mention Falmouth to Dick, by the way? Why not be vague consistently?

But, assuming that this vagueness was deliberate, what was the reason for it? Clearly the reason was discreditable. Mr. Findlay was going away on an unofficial honeymoon, and didn't wish anyone to know. Dick said he didn't think it likely. Well, one doesn't suspect one's parents or relations of that sort of thing. Dr. Fielding, on the other hand, did think it quite likely. He knew the lady.

Now, if I had been the lady, and had been asked where I should like to go for such an expedition, what town would at once have suggested itself to me? Should I have voted for St. Ives, or Newquay, or Falmouth? No, I should have voted for Paris, and the Southern Railway time-table of the Channel services to Paris was found in the hip-pocket of Mr. Findlay's trousers, when we unpacked them in Truro police station. Mr. Findlay had, at all events, toyed with the idea of taking his lady friend to Paris—on the face of it a more likely destination than Cornwall.

This brings us to the question of Uncle Hamilton's luggage. We can picture him as a shabby little man, who rarely dressed for anything but the suburbs. Still, his luggage needn't have been so hopelessly un-Cornish. And remember those patent-leather shoes. Whether they ought to have been accompanied by a dinner-suit, we shall never know. Personally, I think a dinner-suit was included in the *first version of his luggage*.

At this point, I can almost hear you thumping your desk and saying, 'For the Lord's sake tell me who the lady was!' Very well, I will. It was Miss Fillyan. Evidence, Dick's statement that he had seen his uncle's eyes brighten at the sight of a pretty shop assistant. More evidence, Miss Crowne's statement that Miss Fillyan was drawn to rich gentlemen of middle age. Dr. Fielding, too, had met Miss Fillyan in the Arts and Crafts Shop. To make quite sure, I rang her up this morning. The conversation went as follows:

M. W. (*in a disguised, authoritative tone*). Miss Fillyan?

Miss F. Yes?

M. W. This is the police. We are investigating the disappearance of Mr. Hamilton Findlay. There is no need for you to be alarmed. We are not charging you with anything. In due course you will be asked to make a formal statement, but to save time, I want you to answer one or two questions here and now. Did Mr. Findlay arrange to take you to Paris for the week-end of June the 5th?

MISS F. Yes.

M. W. Did you go to Paris with him?

MISS F. No.

M. W. Why not?

MISS F. He never came to the station.

M. W. Which station was it?

MISS F. Victoria. We were to meet there on Saturday morning to catch the boat train. He never turned up. I hung about for hours. I heard afterwards that he had given me 'the bird' and gone to Cornwall where he was drowned.

M. W. How did you hear that?

MISS F. Miss Crowne told me.

M. W. (*pompously*). We know all about Miss Crowne. Did you tell Miss Crowne that you were going to Paris with Mr. Findlay?

MISS F. I told her in the end.

M. W. What do you mean by 'the end'?

MISS F. I told her a week later—on the Saturday, I think it was. I'd been feeling so worried and bottled up. It was awful waiting about in that station. Then I had to go home and explain to my uncle that the friends I was going to stay with couldn't have me after all. I spent a wretched week—

M. W. (*nearly giving himself away.*) It must have been most trying. But tell me, Miss Fillyan, what did Miss Crowne say when you told her your story?

MISS F. She wouldn't believe me at first. Then I think she did half-believe me, but she said if it was true it was very disgraceful and that I'd better never mention it to anyone. I liked that, coming from her! She went on to say that it must have been a joke on Mr. Findlay's part, but I know it wasn't.

M. W. Had you a passport?

MISS F. Yes. I got one last year when I spent a week with friends in Belgium.

M. W. Did Miss Crowne refer to the subject again?

MISS F. Yes. She kept on nagging me about it, saying how ashamed I ought to be and how I must never tell anyone, and at the same time wanting to know all the details.

M. W. Had she suspected your friendship with Mr. Findlay before?

MISS F. No, I shouldn't say so. He came to our shop with Mr. Richard, his nephew, once, and he came once with Dr. Fielding. But he was always very careful.

M. W. How did you first meet him?

MISS F. One evening when I was leaving the shop.

M. W. And where did your later meetings usually take place?

MISS F. Oh, different places. He took me to tea at Dr. Fielding's house sometimes, and Dr. Fielding used to go to the chess club and leave us alone.

M. W. There was no servant at Dr. Fielding's?

MISS F. Not in the afternoon or evening.

M. W. Did Dr. Fielding know that you were going to Paris with Mr. Findlay?

MISS F. No. Mr. Findlay wanted that to be kept quite secret from everybody.

M. W. Another question. Did Mr. Richard Findlay, the nephew, know of your friendship with his uncle?

MISS F. Mr. Findlay was terribly anxious that Dick shouldn't know. I never went to Tylecroft. Mr. Findlay told me once that Dick seemed to be nosing round a bit, and I dare say he did begin to put two and two together. But I don't see why he should have thought I was the lady.

M. W. Do you think Dick knew that Mr. Findlay intended to go to Paris with a lady?

MISS F. No. I don't see why he should have known that.

M. W. Do you think he thought his uncle was really going to Cornwall?

MISS F. He may have thought so. I shouldn't have.

M. W. Why?

MISS F. Oh, I don't know. It must have sounded a bit thin—just for a week-end you know.

M. W. Thank you very much, Miss Fillyan. One of us will come and see you later. Goodbye.

M. W. *puts the receiver down hurriedly.*

So much for Miss Fillyan. You may say I showed more luck than skill in spotting her as the lady. But Miss Crowne was unwittingly of great help to me. Let us deal with her now.

I first met her, you will remember, the evening I got back from Cornwall with Dick Findlay. She had wanted to see Dick in private, and resented my being there. I gathered at the time that they had been—shall we say 'friends'? And I gathered after dinner, when I asked Dick about Hilda Montaubyn's photograph, that the 'friendship' on his side had worn thin. His heart was now entirely elsewhere, though Miss Crowne's wasn't. She was still as much in love with him as she had it in her to be. I thought at first that her call at Tylecroft was due to a wish to reassure herself of his affections. We know now that she came to tell him Miss Fillyan's story. But I still think she came partly to keep a hold on him. No doubt she had felt him slipping away from her. Indeed, she had probably heard all about Hilda Montaubyn, who, as a former actress at the Garden City Theatre, would be well known to her by name, if not by sight. After all, it wasn't a weekly touring company, but a repertory company which hoped to settle down there permanently.

It seems clear that Miss Crowne left Tylecroft on that Monday evening (June 14th) far from happy in her mind, or satisfied with Dick. They may well have had another meeting, but so far from taking her or her story seriously, he was planning to go to France and meet her rival there. I think they must have parted on the verge of a quarrel. Finding her charms of no avail, she is reduced to threats. 'All right,' we can imagine her saying, 'I'll show you that I'm in earnest. I'll write to your friend, Mr. Warren, and tell him what Jane Fillyan said.' At this, Dick would tell her not to be a little fool. What did it matter what Miss Fillyan said? Uncle Hamilton had changed his mind. That was all. He had said he was going to Cornwall, and he had gone to Cornwall. If the other story was raked up, not only would it throw discredit on the dead, but it would still further delay Dick's receipt of his inheritance, and the good times he hoped to have—

Ah, but with whom?

Still peevish and unconvinced, she put her threat mildly into practice and wrote me the first of her anonymous letters. And I imagine that by the same post she sent a letter to Dick telling him what she had done. Then comes a reaction, and she is filled with remorse. Was this the way to keep Dick's affection, meddling in his affairs, and writing anonymous letters to his friends?

By the time I visited her in her shop she was fully repentant, and did her feeble best to prevent me from knowing she was the writer. Unintentionally, she did more. She drew my attention to Miss Fillyan. It was obvious, you see, that Miss Crowne must know something. Otherwise, I don't think the idea of writing the anonymous letter would ever have occurred to her. What was the most likely thing for her to know? The name of the lady in the case. It is true Miss Crowne may have hundreds of acquaintances in South Mersley, and it did not follow at all that her fellow shop-assistant was the sinister party. But Miss Fillyan was an excellent candidate. First there was her appearance, which no one could leave unnoticed. Secondly, her fondness (already noted) for rich old gentlemen. Thirdly, she was in close contact with Miss Crowne. Miss Crowne was in close contact with Dick, and Dick with his uncle. This provided an easy link—too easy, perhaps, to be sound; since Miss Fillyan has herself told us that Mr. Findlay picked her up outside the shop. I am willing to admit here that I may have jumped to the right conclusion for the wrong reason. But there was still another clue—Miss

Crowne's manner when I spoke to her about Miss Fillyan. It betrayed a mixture of spite and uneasiness. The spite could have been accounted for on other grounds. Not so the uneasiness. The more reticent and evasive Miss Crowne was, the more convinced I became that Miss Fillyan was the reason why Mr. Findlay 'went to Cornwall.' (I quote the words of the first anonymous letter.)

Then comes the second anonymous letter, a poor attempt to undo the mischief. Miss Crowne knows that I suspect her, and will go on suspecting her. The only thing she can do is to write an apology, and make me think that the first letter was simply the outcome of a lover's quarrel, as indeed, from her point of view it was. With that, she has played her part in the story, though it was not at all the part she would have chosen for herself to play.

Now I must tell you of two more telephone calls I have made this morning. One was to say that I shall not go to my office to-day. I shall be far too busy writing to you.

The other call was to Tylecroft, where I spoke to Mrs. Pressley. She told me that when she went to take Dick's early tea this morning, she noticed a smell of gas . . . you know the rest, or, if not, you can guess it. The usual notice on the bedroom door, 'Gas—don't come in. Call the police at once.' Poor woman, she was very much distressed. By the time I telephoned, the police had already been and taken Dick's body away.

I find this part of my letter painful to write. However, it isn't fair that I should bother you with my distress. He wasn't a great friend of mine. I don't think he was a *friend* of mine at all. But there was a lot to like in him. Let's leave this aspect of the case, or I shall become incoherent with self-analysis.

You will now want my version of why, how, when and where he killed his uncle. Very well, you shall have it.

Why?—Almost too many motives. First, the general situation. There he was, still brilliant, still fairly young, living at Tylecroft under his uncle's wing. What couldn't he have done with his uncle's money? And uncle went on living for ever, growing younger while Dick grew older. And Dick, who had solaced himself with suburban charms, suddenly fell in love with a star from another firmament. Fell in love, probably, for the first time in his life—hopelessly, desperately. A very different passion from the feeling he used to have for Miss Crowne, or the feeling she had for him.

Here you have all the substratum, if not the occasion, for a crime.

The two factors I have mentioned—Dick's dissatisfaction with South Mersley and his love for Hilda Montaubyn—would probably never have been sufficient to transform a murderous inclination into a murderous act. But there were others. You remember, he was employed in a chemical works owned, originally, by his mother's family. He must always have loathed his life there. But at least, he was fairly well paid, and had certain privileges. Then came a change in his position. The uncle (on his mother's side) who had befriended him somewhat grudgingly, dies, and the business passes into the control of unsympathetic cousins who soon decide to sell it to the Universal Chemical Combine. What are Dick's prospects when the deal goes through? Not very rosy. Henceforward his future and his hope of independence lie with Uncle Hamilton. But is Uncle Hamilton quite safe? Is it quite certain that, after living for ever, he will ultimately leave Dick his fair share? What if Uncle Hamilton should fall in love with some silver-haired young lady, and should not only fall in love with her, but marry her? The new mistress of Tylecroft, and her children, when they are born, will hardly allow Dick to inherit very much. Something must be done, and done quickly, before the infatuation goes too far.

At this point we come to something which I think even you will never know—that is, how far Dick knew of his uncle's fondness for Miss Fillyan. In my conversation with her this morning, she wasn't very helpful. On the whole I am inclined to agree with her view that he didn't know *she* was the lady. If he had known this, I can't think he would have been so bold. She was altogether too much in the South Mersley circle—too near home, and though he may have thought his plan was fool-proof, he would hardly have risked a scandal in the neighbourhood. 'Funny that Mr. Findlay was drowned in Cornwall the very week-end he had promised to take a girl to Paris.'

I may be wrong, but I think Dick knew neither that Miss Fillyan was the lady, nor that a trip to Paris was in contemplation. He probably imagined that his uncle's fancy had fallen upon some London girl, and that the honeymoon was to be spent in Brighton. In that event, there would have been small risk of a scandal, when Uncle Hamilton failed to turn up at the station—merely a disgruntled little Miss somewhere within a twenty-mile radius, who would shrug her shoulders, hope for better luck next time with another gentleman, and might never even hear that her intended protector had been drowned in unknown Cornwall.

This is my theory, and I am afraid it will have to remain theory. On the other hand, he may have been so keyed up, so desperate, that he took the risk, Miss Fillyan and all.

At this point, you may say, 'What grounds have you for supposing that Dick knew anything at all about his uncle's love affair?' I answer, I am sure that Uncle Hamilton betrayed himself. He betrayed himself by saying he was going to Cornwall. He overdid it. He should have said Bournemouth or Bexhill, not Cornwall. But he was thrown off his balance with excitement. I have no doubt he roused suspicion in a thousand little ways—furtive visits to the post, sentimental sighs, mysterious absences, changes of long-established habits. And, remember, Dick knew him through and through, and was watching. We even have a hint from Miss Fillyan that Mr. Findlay feared, for all his secretiveness, that he had given himself away. Poor, foolish, middle-aged man, how could he hope not to do so? And he had been forced to confide in Dr. Fielding—another foolish old man. How do we know that Dr. Fielding didn't give some involuntary hint to Dick? At all events, I think the easiest course is to suppose that, though Dick didn't know the lady's name, he knew there was a lady. And from this, the thought would at once occur to him, 'What if she gets him to marry her? What then?'

So much for motive.

How?—this is for you to discover. A blow with a blunt instrument, strangling, poison—I'm not particular. But I should guess poison. A quick-acting poison administered in Uncle Hamilton's coffee when he and Dick were sitting together in the loggia of Tylecroft after dinner on Friday, June 4th. You will no doubt analyse the contents of the stomach, in your dreary way, and you will also find out to what poisons Dick had access in the chemical works. You must remember Dick was a chemist.

I see that I have already answered *When* by my suggestion of after dinner. I ought not really to be so precise, and will amend my answer to 'sometime on the Friday afternoon or evening.' The poison may have been given in a glass of sherry before dinner, or even earlier, in a cup of tea. The limits to the period are: (1) Mrs. Pressley and her daughter must be safely away, and (2) Dick must leave himself time to complete his preparations. And he had a good deal to do.

Where?—Already answered. At Tylecroft. I suggest in the garden loggia, because it is secluded and handy for the garage.

Now I come to my general reconstruction of the whole case after the crime is committed. Many of my details must be guesses, but even if they are incorrect, they will only be like wrong touches of colour, and won't affect the picture's general design.

As soon as Mr. Findlay was safely dead, Dick disposed of the body. Here I must start with one of my bigger guesses. I think he put the body in the garage. The garage at Tylecroft is spacious and dates from the period when people built 'inspection pits' so that they could get at the underneath of their cars. Mr. Findlay had no car, and quite probably Dick alone had the garage key. I think Dick actually put the body in the inspection pit and covered it with some of the smelliest chemical fertiliser his firm could produce. You remember how a frightful smell of chemical fertiliser drove me away from the garage door, when I was prowling round the garden on June 14th. If you inquire from Garvice and Bagshaw, I think you will find that Dick ordered in a big supply of fertiliser from them not very long before. He would need enough to supply the gardener, as well as to shroud the body. I can imagine him saying to the gardener, 'This'll do for you to go on with. I'll store the rest in the garage. Let me know when you want any more. I don't mind the smell. I'm used to it.'

The most dangerous moment that afternoon or evening must have been when he took the body from house or loggia to the garage; for it was still daylight. However, Tylecroft garden is not overlooked, and we can, if you like, suppose that Dick had a wheelbarrow handy, put the body in it, covered it with sacking and wheeled it. Or he may even have induced his uncle to come to the garage on some pretext, and administered the poison there. But I mustn't waste time on too many of these conjectures.

Next he must pack Uncle Hamilton's holiday luggage. I think Uncle Hamilton had already begun his packing earlier in the afternoon, or at least, he had 'put out' some of the clothes he intended to take. He was, of course, packing for Paris, not Cornwall, and though his wardrobe was not very Parisian, it was more suitable for Paris than the country. I imagine that Dick either satisfied himself that the luggage was complete, or made it as complete as he could. On a chair, say, he would find an evening-suit.

That wasn't necessary for Cornwall, at the kind of hotel which Uncle Hamilton would choose. Put it back in a drawer. The evening shoes were already in a shoe-bag, and Dick mistook them for day-shoes, and packed them. His first mistake. But he was in a hurry. He had also to pack Uncle Hamilton's travelling suit, Homburg hat, wig, and the contents of the pockets of the suit in which he had just died, keys, money, wallet—and this mention of the wallet brings me to the draft letter to William Hicks, dated 6 vi. 37, which I found in it. We may as well deal with this draft letter now.

We know that William Hicks dined at Tylecroft at the beginning of May. Let us imagine this little conversation occurring during dinner, before Hicks put his 'business proposition' to his uncle:

DICK (*brightly*). You know Mrs. Pressley is deserting us for the first week-end in June?

HICKS. Is she? What are you going to do?

DICK. We're going away.

HICKS. Really? Where are you going, Uncle Hamilton?

UNCLE H. (*testily*). I rather thought of Cornwall, but I haven't settled anything.

HICKS. I've got to go to Cornwall then. There's a nursery-garden near Falmouth which is selling its stock, and if it's up to catalogue description, it should be well worth looking at.

DICK. Will you be staying in Falmouth, Bill?

HICKS. Yes, on the Sunday night.

DICK. Where are you staying?

HICKS. I'm told the Radnor is a decent place and not too dear.

UNCLE H. (*sourly*). I should have thought you'd better spend your time trying to sell the stock you've already got, rather than buying any more. How's your mother been keeping?

Henceforward, Falmouth takes shape in Dick's mind as

the place to which Uncle Hamilton must definitely go—or not go. Perhaps this is a little obscure. What I mean is, Dick begins to wonder from this moment whether or not it is wise to send Uncle Hamilton to Falmouth. At first he thinks, 'On no account Falmouth. Anywhere rather than that, provided the place is in Cornwall. It must be Cornwall, because my uncle has told so many people he's going there.'

But later, though probably not much later than May 6th, he changes his view. On that day he finds either in the waste-paper basket, or left carelessly on the writing-table, the draft letter to Cousin Bill, which I found, and read in Polgedswell Cove. Only, *then*, the draft was dated 6 v. 37 instead of 6 vi. 37. Dick, who is now continuously spying on his uncle with a view to riddling out his love affair, picks up the draft, reads it, and keeps it. He is not greatly interested in the negotiations which his cousin has been conducting with his uncle, but he is vastly interested in the date of the letter, 6 v. 37. If he were to amend it, with one stroke of the pen, to 6 vi. 37, what a piece of evidence it would be, if anything went wrong—if, that is to say, the police suspected foul play, and the crime had to be fastened upon someone. Why not send Uncle Hamilton to Falmouth after all? If he doesn't, the letter can't be used.

Dick is, in fact, hypnotised with his own ingenuity, and the ease with which the letter can be post-dated by a month is too much for him. Was there ever so conclusive or so simple a forgery?

He adds the stroke, and the forgery is complete. That is why Uncle Hamilton's wallet contained the post-dated draft letter.

No doubt your people have seen and examined it. I send you, herewith, the fair copy, dated 6 v. 37, which I got from William Hicks last night. I am sure you will agree that both letters, except for the stroke in the date of the draft letter, are in Hamilton Findlay's handwriting.

Next, Dick has to pack his own things, those which he is going to need (or, more correctly, those which he is going to pretend to need) in London, and the small minimum which he must have in Cornwall.

At length, everything is ready. One last look at Hilda Montaubyn's photograph, and he carries two bags downstairs—his own bag and his uncle's. From the hat-rack in the hall, he takes his cap—more compressible in a knapsack than a hat—and his own mackintosh. He has either forgotten that Uncle Hamilton will need a coat of his own, or Uncle Hamilton has no coat in any way suitable for a hiker in the country.

Then, after putting the two bags in the car, he drives to London—perhaps by a devious route, to begin with, just in case some acquaintance sees him driving alone. It would have been unfortunate, for example, if he had met Dr. Fielding, though even so he could probably have persuaded the old man that he was going on some preliminary errand.

Arrived in London, he goes straight to the mews flat in Chelsea which he has borrowed from his artist friend, leaves the two bags there, garages his car, and returns, to unpack his own bag. Most of the contents he spreads ostentatiously about the bedroom, but the small minimum which he will need in Cornwall goes into his uncle's bag.

Next, in case anybody calls, he must make the flat look as if it's lived in, and slept in. He will rumple the bed, make himself some tea, dirty some of the crockery and cutlery, leave a newspaper and a book on the table, use a couple of ashtrays. If he is thorough, he will even have brought in some milk, bread, butter, eggs and bacon, and put them in the larder—if there is one.

You may like a word or two about this secret retreat of Dick's. He only told me, you remember, that it was a mews flat in Chelsea, and belonged to an artist named Woodwell, whom he didn't think I'd ever met. I looked in the telephone directory on Saturday morning, but could find no Woodwell in Chelsea. Of course, that isn't conclusive, but I am inclined to think that Woodwell was not his friend's name. If I had probed the matter—and there was no reason why I should—Dick could easily have said that I had misheard him, and that the name was really Woodcock, Woodman or Woodgate, or, indeed, any name under the sun.

Chelsea, too, may have been a mis-statement for Clapham or Paddington, or any London borough. Personally, I should plump for Paddington, because it would be so handy for the Strafford Royal Hotel where the false Uncle Hamilton was to spend the night.

You may say, 'How do we know there was a flat at all?' I answer, he had to provide some kind of an alibi for himself, and he had to spend the Monday night away from Tylecroft. I imagine it was a flat without a servant attached to it. No one, except a chance visitor, would know whether it was inhabited or not. And a chance visitor wouldn't know that it wasn't slept in on the Friday, Saturday and Sunday nights. You'll have great difficulty in proving that he wasn't there then, even if you discover where the flat was. But you would have much less difficulty in proving that he was there on the Monday night, because he actually was there and would not fail to leave some memento of his presence, such as Monday's papers, and perhaps Tuesday morning's, too. Find Woodwell and question him. I think he'll tell you that Dick left something behind. I admit I never investigated this aspect of the case at all. When Dick told me he spent the week-end in London, I assumed he had some romantic purpose in view.

Another reason for the real existence of the flat. Where else was Dick to disguise himself? For, though he entered the flat as Richard Findlay, he came out as Hamilton Findlay, and as such went with Uncle Hamilton's bag to the Strafford Royal Hotel, where he signed the register in Uncle Hamilton's name.

We come now to the question of disguise. I have always

been sceptical of disguises myself, and have often laughed at Balzac for the way in which Europe and Asie deceive the gaolers in *Splendeurs et Misères des Courtisanes* by the most fantastic impostures. It isn't very hard, however, to disguise yourself when the people you're going to meet don't either know you or the character you are assuming. Dick, you remember, was a member of the O.U.D.S. at Oxford, and would at least know how to 'make up.' Also, Uncle Hamilton, thanks to his wig, was an easy subject to imitate. He was about Dick's height, and Dick was only too familiar with his appearance and mannerisms. Take as many photographs of Uncle Hamilton as you like to the porters at the Strafford Royal and the Trepolpen, and I bet you ten to one they swear that the original of the photographs stayed at their hotels.

Well, Dick goes to the Strafford Royal disguised as Uncle Hamilton, and from that moment I have no doubt that the false Uncle Hamilton's movements are exactly as the hotel porters have described to us.

The next day, after the railway journey, he arrives at the Trepolpen in Falmouth. Ormerod, the porter, received him, and you have had Ormerod's description of the man he received. I would only underline two little touches. First, Uncle Hamilton's suit was ill-fitting. At the time, I thought it quite natural that Uncle Hamilton should wear ill-fitting clothes. Since then, I have revised my judgement. I think that Uncle Hamilton bought very few clothes, but when he bought them they were good. However shabby his suits might be, they would fit. He would bully his tailor till they did. Presumably Dick couldn't wear quite enough padding to take up the slack.

The second touch is that Uncle Hamilton arrived carrying a mackintosh over his arm—Dick's mackintosh. Now you have the point of that sudden query which I put to myself as I was falling asleep at Neetham Priory: What became of Uncle Hamilton's mackintosh?

As to how Dick passed the Sunday, we have only Ormerod's evidence. And at this point I will let you raise a difficulty which you have been longing to raise for some time. 'Dick,' you will say, 'goes deliberately to Falmouth, disguised as his uncle, at the very time when he knows his cousin William Hicks will be there. Is it wise? Is it credible?'

Credible, yes, if not altogether wise.

I must insist yet again that when Dick found that draft letter and realised how easy it was to alter the date, he was carried away by his own brilliance. He felt an overwhelming temptation to complicate his own plan by devising a line of defence. If the accident theory couldn't be sustained, he would provide a suspect in the person of his cousin. To do this, it was essential to go to Falmouth, even at the risk (which he would take all steps to minimise) of meeting his cousin. And I have no doubt that if the meeting did unfortunately occur, he would have had plans for coping with the situation. You must remember what a coldness existed between William Hicks and his uncle. If the supposed uncle turns away and cuts his nephew in the street, the nephew will hardly be surprised. William Hicks wasn't the man to run after him shouting, 'Let bygones be bygones, and for heaven's sake lend me a fiver.'

There was a risk, I grant you, but Dick had decided to take it. And his luck held. He did not meet his cousin.

Now we come to the Monday morning. Dick packs his bag, or rather his uncle's bag, with the clothes which ultimately we are to examine together in the police station at Polpenford. He has by now undone the shoe-bag and realised that he has brought his uncle's patent-leather shoes to Cornwall. The piece of carelessness irritates him, but he doesn't like to risk throwing the shoes away. It isn't too easy to get rid of a pair of shoes. Besides, Mrs. Pressley might have inquired about them later. The incongruity of their presence has to be endured, and Dick packs them with the rest. Then he packs the knapsack which he bought, ostentatiously, at Jacka and Protheroe's on the Saturday afternoon. A good many things have to go into the knapsack—not only Uncle Hamilton's bathing-suit and towel, but a suit of Dick's own clothes, and the ingredients of a second disguise. Then, after his deliberately memorable conversation with the Trepolpen porter, he sets out on what we are meant to regard as Uncle Hamilton's last journey.

He reaches Brora Cove first, and considers it. But it won't do. It's too public, and the bathing is not dangerous enough. Then he comes to Polgedswell Cove, which is much more suited for his purpose. He finds a secluded cranny in the rocks, strips himself of the clothes he is wearing and the wig, and arranges them neatly in a heap, as Uncle Hamilton would have arranged them. Then he takes his own clothes from the knapsack, puts them on and—though this is a guess on my part—disguises himself afresh. This time he would probably assume the role of a youngish man, trusting, say, that a false moustache and dark spectacles will prevent anyone from recognising him when he revisits the scene of the supposed accident in his own person. He leaves the towel and the knapsack by the clothes, but he must, of course, take the bathing-costume with him, and destroy it at his leisure. And he also takes the mackintosh—which is his own. This was a blunder, and I am ashamed that I failed to notice it for so long.

I will not try to guess how he got back to London. Suffice it to say that he did get back somehow, wearing his second disguise, and gained the sanctuary of the mews flat, where he probably spent most of Monday night. It must have been a relief to him to emerge again on Tuesday morning as Richard Findlay, collect his car and drive home. That evening, as you know, Dr. Fielding came to dinner, and the alarms began.

I am not sure at what stage Dick conceived the idea of

making me his unwitting accomplice. There was always the chance that his uncle's clothes would be found quite soon, and reach coastguard or police. On the other hand, if they were not found, or if someone found them but did not report the finding, Dick himself would have to set inquiries in motion, and he felt a certain delicacy in fulfilling this task. Uncle Hamilton's home address was easily ascertainable from the visiting-cards in the wallet, and I think that Dick spent Tuesday, Wednesday and Thursday morning in hourly expectation that the authorities would ring up Tylecroft. But as they did not, it was for Dick to ensure that the clothes should be found, and his uncle's supposed visit to Falmouth corroborated. How much better it would be, if the story of the finding of the clothes and the corroboration of the visit could come from a third party! And for that third party he chose me.

I thought, at the time, in my vanity, that he really had chosen me to be his companion because of my previous experience of police-court cases, and my presumed talent for investigation. I realise now that he chose me for the opposite reason—because he thought I should be such a simple tool in his hands.

I told you, earlier, of our rivalry at Oxford, and how, till his father's death, he always came out top-dog. I have little doubt that he still felt for me the same contempt which he did not hesitate to show in the old days. Only, this time he was careful not to show it. How tickled he must have been at the way I lapped up his praises! And what a fool I must have seemed to him as, with my worldly-wise air, I fell into all his traps. I feel mortified when I think of it. For the sake of my *amour-propre* I will only add that he did, in fact, under-rate my intelligence to his own eventual undoing.

So he chose me to go with him to Cornwall. If I had not been available, or had refused his invitation to dinner (as I might easily have done if my experiment in mashing potatoes had been more successful), he would probably have tried some other friend—perhaps the Woodwell from whom he had borrowed the mews flat. In default of any friend, he would have had to do his own dirty work somehow. As it was, I did it for him.

I have already said that I can't tell you when I first began to suspect him. But I can tell you the moment when, almost subconsciously, I felt my first twinge of uneasiness. It was when he said, in reply to a question of mine, '*Oh, didn't I tell you? Uncle Hamilton mentioned the town he was going to—Falmouth.*' It was such an odd way of bringing out the name of his destination. I see now that this oddness was due to an inhibition on Dick's part. It was known to everybody that Uncle Hamilton was going to Cornwall, but Falmouth was Dick's own invention. That is why, during our earlier talk, he spoke of Cornwall with complete nonchalance, but when he came to the key-word *Falmouth*, he felt an embarrassment which betrayed itself in a verbal clumsiness. And it jarred upon me, though I couldn't tell why.

The next feature to note is Dick's behaviour when we got to Falmouth on the Saturday evening—his absurd fear that he might run into his uncle, and his eagerness that the investigation of the hotels should be undertaken by me alone. Not only did he want me to tell the story to the police, but he was anxious not to meet Ormerod, with whom he had had so many conversations when disguised. Note, too, how quickly I did find the right hotel. It was, of course, sheer luck that I came across the Strafford Royal in London (which there was no great point in finding), but it was Dick's careful guidance which led me to the Trepolpen. He must have felt like an adult watching a child play 'hunt the thimble,' and longed to say outright, 'Cold—warmer—boiling!'

And now we come to our little drinking-bout in the inn, when I celebrated my discoveries too freely. You remember I had a bilious attack that night, and on recovery from it slept well on into Sunday morning. I ascribed my queasiness to drink or Mrs. Pressley's sandwiches, but I didn't really have so much whisky, and I am convinced that the sandwiches, though distasteful, were not poisonous. I think it is far more likely that Dick put something in my whisky to make me sleep heavily. Not knowing how capricious my stomach is, he could not have anticipated that I should react by having a bilious attack—though from his point of view, the end justified the means; for I did sleep, and he was able, as he had hoped, to go out early in his car and make sure that the clothes were still where he had left them in Polgedswell Cove. In due course, we went to Polgedswell Cove, and it was neatly arranged that I should find the clothes.

I don't think it occurred to him, however, that I should be so bold as to examine them, while he went off to fetch the police. It must have been a shock, afterwards, when he learnt from my case book that I had not only opened the wallet, but read through the draft letter to William Hicks, and a still greater shock when he saw my observations, 'Query: Where is Uncle Hamilton's writing-block?' It was then, as we shall see, that he began to regard me not as a foolish friend, but as a potential enemy whose wits occasionally didn't gather wool.

There is only one more episode in our Cornish visit to which I need draw your attention—Dick's high spirits when he joined me at breakfast before we started back for London. You will remember, he had just been to Jacka and Protheroe's and found out that his uncle had bought a bathing-costume and a knapsack there. At the time I thought he was pleased with himself merely because he had taken a leaf out of my book, and in his humble way had successfully imitated my great exploits in detection. I see now that he was pleased because, for the first time, he had confronted someone to whom he had already talked when disguised as his uncle. The disguise had evidently been perfect, and the shopman showed no sign of identifying Dick with the old gentleman who had been his customer a few days before.

As it turned out, it would have been better for Dick to drive me straight home, instead of giving me a meal at Tylecroft. But he could not have foreseen that Miss Crowne would be there, waiting for him like a cat on hot bricks. I myself gathered nothing definite from Miss Crowne's visit, except that it was irksome to Dick and a matter of great importance to her. At the same time, it did occur to me that it was something of a coincidence that there should be two simultaneous 'states of tension' (to use a political metaphor) at Tylecroft—one created by Uncle Hamilton's disappearance, and the other by the importunity of Dick's girl friend. When, later in the evening, I saw Hilda Montaubyn's photograph and realised that Dick was in love with her, I put Miss Crowne's call down to unrequited passion. None the less, my mind did, somehow, link her with the major problem, and was thus the readier to suspect her of writing the anonymous letter—which, of course, was for me the turning-point of the whole case.

However, you will be more interested in Dick than in me. I think Miss Crowne's news was a great shock to him. So far, the visit to Falmouth had gone splendidly according to plan. Now he heard that Uncle Hamilton's intention had been to take Miss Fillyan to Paris. It would indeed be dangerous if that information leaked out. If a man says he is going to Cornwall alone, people will readily believe that he really intends to take a young lady to Paris. But if he says he intends to take a young lady to Paris (even if the young lady is the only witness), they won't be nearly so ready to believe that he really intends to go to Cornwall alone. Add to this danger the fact that I had found a Southern Railway time-table of the services to Paris in the hip-pocket of Uncle Hamilton's trousers. How Dick must have cursed himself for not going through Uncle Hamilton's pockets more carefully. I can only suppose that Dick had his own trousers made without hip-pockets. I seem to remember that when we were at Oxford there was some prejudice against them.

His next shock must have been the discovery of my case book in his car. (By the way, did I really leave it in his car, or did he take it from my room in Falmouth?) You remember how embarrassed I was when he returned it to me, especially when he said in his covering-letter that he had shown it to Cousin Bill. I have no doubt now that he never showed it to Cousin Bill at all. Our conversation of last night made that quite plain, and Dick's lie, designed to keep me from contact with his cousin, was a piece of intimidation which nearly succeeded. Indeed, if the silly Miss Crowne had not sent me the anonymous letter, I should have regarded the whole 'case' as closed.

You will notice that, from this point onwards, Dick, who had so far professed such eagerness to see me, began to avoid me, and that, in fact, we never met again.

Then came his visit to Blaireau-sur-mer in France. I imagine it was due to a half-invitation from Hilda Montaubyn. 'Oh, do come,' she would say, quite casually, 'I am staying with my friends the Whatnots. I know you'll like them and they'll like you.' The invitation, of course, was irresistible.

But he hadn't reckoned with Miss Crowne. (How, by the way, did she know that Dick was going to join Hilda Montaubyn?) But she must have known, or she would never have written to me.

Well, she wrote. And from that time my suspicions began to crystallise. I reviewed the whole 'case' many times, and each time I did so, I was struck with its incongruities and oddities, all of which could be explained, but needed explaining. That was the crux of the matter—why should one have to explain away so much, if the facts were as they purported to be?

I have told you when I felt my first twinge of uneasiness. I can also tell you when my suspicion became almost a certainty. It was when I lay in my bath last Friday evening, before dining with the Seymours. Dick's failure to ring me up then could only mean that he wished to avoid me. And for that there was only one reason. I need hardly say, however, that my suspicion was still in the nature of a 'hunch,' and that I had no evidence such as might make it my duty to go to the police.

I wish I could see the letter Miss Crowne wrote to Dick, telling him that she had written to me. I wish, too, that I could have seen him, during that gay visit—bathing, playing tennis, gambling, making unavailing love to his beloved, and all the time, despite sunshine and drink, haunted by the shadow of his crime, and the fear that, after all, he had failed. I picture him as alternating between ecstasy and despair. The jaunty letter he wrote to me—Hilda had smiled upon him. All might yet be well. With her as the prize he could risk anything. But without her?

Then came the inexorable hour, when he realised that he was not first favourite. His rival, the baronet's son, had triumphed. What was left? Nothing, except to die. The future couldn't be faced now. There was Uncle Hamilton's body, still in the garage at Tylecroft, waiting to be disposed of. There was I, perpetually on the alert. There was Miss Crowne, penitent but fatally guilty. There was Miss Fillyan, who any day might blurt out her sordid story to the police. And Hilda—Hilda wasn't there for him any more.

If human misery serves any purpose in the world, Dick served it greatly, I think, as he came back from France.

But there is still something he can do. He can make the supreme sacrifice—annihilate himself and yet leave his beloved one happy—and rich. I think you will find that Dick in his will has left everything he possessed to Hilda Montaubyn. And his 'everything' was now worth having, since it included half Uncle Hamilton's residuary estate.

But there is a law—is it a foolish one?—that a murderer may derive no pecuniary benefit from his victim. A last chance, a last gamble. Let the draft letter to Cousin Bill, now in the hands of the police, play its full part, and fasten the crime upon him. Then Hilda Montaubyn will have all.

I grant you, his technique becomes progressively weak. All along, he has been hypnotised by that draft letter, and the use he might make of it if things went wrong. I, at least, as he knows from my case book, have read it, and given my mind to it. But did he guess that I should decide that William Hicks could not have been the murderer, because it would have been the veriest lunacy on his part to leave the letter in his uncle's wallet?

And what did Dick make of my interest in Uncle Hamilton's writing-block from which, presumably, the sheet comprising the draft letter had been torn? It was the absence of that writing-block which first made me wonder whether the draft letter had really been written in Falmouth, as it should have been, on the basis of its date, 6 vi. 37.

Whether Dick followed my reasoning or not, we shall never know. If he did, it would only have rendered him still more desperate. But I think that he was already desperate enough. His plan, such as it was, must go through. He was in no mood now to devise another.

It was risky to bring poor Uncle Hamilton's mouldering corpse out of the garage and put it in the capacious 'boot' of his big car. It was risky to drive to the nursery at Sedcombe, take the body out of the car and drop it, weights and all, into the pond. What if Cousin Bill had seen him, or the dog had been loose? But Dick was now beyond considerations of common prudence, as his last gesture showed—the scattering of his uncle's visiting-cards on the grass verge of the pond. As he scattered those cards, he was writing, not his uncle's, but his own obituary notice for the whole world to read. It was as such that I read it.

He had decided to die in his gas-filled room at Tylecroft, and for the wretchedness of those last acts and hours, I can feel nothing but a shuddering sympathy.

In a sense, it was a love-death. There are worse deaths to die.

My hand is too cramped to write any more. But I think I have given you all you need. Probably a good deal more than you need. Excuse faults of spelling, punctuation and grammar!

When I have signed this, I am going to take it in person to Scotland Yard.

Yours sincerely,
MALCOLM WARREN.

15.
Wednesday, July 14th

[Letter from Detective-Inspector Parris, C.I.D., to Malcolm Warren.]

DEAR WARREN,

Many thanks for yours of the 12th.

No time to write you a long letter in reply. You were quite right, except over a few details, and they, being material and not psychological, won't interest you.

We found most of the body in Hicks' pond. Not all, because your friend had already disposed of some bits, somewhere. He must have intended to do it by instalments, till he lost his nerve. Our analyst will, in due course, declare the cause of death. At present he agrees with you—a quick poison.

We also found traces of body and a terrible smell in the inspection pit in the Tylecroft garage.

Interviews with Miss Crowne and Miss Fillyan confirm your theories. One little thing you did not know is that Sibyl, daughter of Mrs. Pressley, was a friend of Miss Crowne, and gave her information about Dick's visit to Blaireau-sur-mer. Hilda Montaubyn had tea with Dick at Tylecroft, and Sibyl eavesdropped. Mrs. Pressley was not in the secret, and disapproved of her daughter's friendship with Miss Crowne.

Hamilton Findlay's passport, a new one, was in his desk. Two seats were booked on the Paris train for Victoria, for the morning of Saturday, June 5th, by a Mr. Fenbury. He and his companion never turned up.

Dick's will left his whole fortune to Hilda Montaubyn, with the exception of a hundred pounds to you, who are his executor. You will get your hundred pounds, but, as you surmised, Hilda Montaubyn won't get very much, as the half-share of Hamilton Findlay's estate will not be allowed to fall into the estate of his murderer. If I were you, I should keep out of that young lady's way.

(Can't you picture her, if she had got the money, wiping away a discreet tear, and saying, 'Poor Dick! He was so charming, though I could never love him.')

Conversely, Hicks and his mother, who now get the whole of Hamilton Findlay's residuary estate, should be grateful to you.

Dick left a letter by his pillow saying he was sick of life, owing to a private disappointment for which no blame attached to anyone.

The Sedcombe police had an anonymous letter on Monday morning telling them to drag Hicks' pond. 'Peeping Tom' had seen someone throwing a body into it. The letter was posted in Sedcombe on Sunday afternoon. So Dick who, of course, wrote it, must have been prowling round the neighborhood, perhaps to see when the coast was clear.

You must have divined something of the sort when you told Hicks that the police would be calling on him next day. And may I make it quite clear to you that I fully understand why you refused to give Hicks a proper explanation of the mystery. You were afraid he would get hold of the police at once, and not give Dick time to get out of his muddle in his own way. You didn't breathe a word even to me until you'd heard from Mrs. Pressley that he was beyond our reach, and all through your letter I see a tendency to post-date your suspicions, so as not to appear an accessory after the fact. Well, I don't suppose any court of law would think you were. But no hint of this to my colleagues who don't, all of them, share my dislike for retributive punishment.

You will, of course, have to give evidence at the two inquests. I'll have it made as easy for you as I can. As to how far we should have got without you, I am wisely silent.

And now, I have two seats for the Sibelius concert at the Queen's Hall on Wednesday of next week. They are playing his fourth and seventh symphonies, and I know you enjoy them, as I do. I shall be so glad if you will come with me, and dine first *Aux Trois Pommes,* at seven o'clock.

When we meet, let us avoid crime and the international situation, and talk of music.

Yours,

H. A. P.

John & Emery Bonett

A BANNER FOR PEGASUS	P 554, $2.40
DEAD LION	P 563, $2.40

Christianna Brand

GREEN FOR DANGER	P 551, $2.50
TOUR DE FORCE	P 572, $2.40

James Byrom

OR BE HE DEAD	P 585, $2.84

Henry Calvin

IT'S DIFFERENT ABROAD	P 640, $2.84

Marjorie Carleton

VANISHED	P 559, $2.40

George Harmon Coxe

MURDER WITH PICTURES	P 527, $2.25

Edmund Crispin

BURIED FOR PLEASURE	P 506, $2.50

Lionel Davidson

THE MENORAH MEN	P 592, $2.84
NIGHT OF WENCESLAS	P 595, $2.84
THE ROSE OF TIBET	P 593, $2.84

D. M. Devine

MY BROTHER'S KILLER	P 558, $2.40

Kenneth Fearing

THE BIG CLOCK	P 500, $1.95

Francis Iles

BEFORE THE FACT	P 517, $2.50
MALICE AFORETHOUGHT	P 532, $1.95

Michael Innes

THE CASE OF THE JOURNEYING BOY	P 632, $3.12
DEATH BY WATER	P 574, $2.40
HARE SITTING UP	P 590, $2.84
THE LONG FAREWELL	P 575, $2.40
THE MAN FROM THE SEA	P 591, $2.84
THE SECRET VANGUARD	P 584, $2.84
THE WEIGHT OF THE EVIDENCE	P 633, $2.84

Mary Kelly

THE SPOILT KILL	P 565, $2.40

Lange Lewis

THE BIRTHDAY MURDER	P 518, $1.95

Allan MacKinnon

HOUSE OF DARKNESS	P 582, $2.84

Arthur Maling

LUCKY DEVIL	P 482, $1.95
RIPOFF	P 483, $1.95
SCHROEDER'S GAME	P 484, $1.95

Austin Ripley

MINUTE MYSTERIES	P 387, $2.50

Thomas Sterling

THE EVIL OF THE DAY	P 529, $2.50

Julian Symons

THE BELTING INHERITANCE	P 468, $1.95
BLAND BEGINNING	P 469, $1.95
BOGUE'S FORTUNE	P 481, $1.95
THE BROKEN PENNY	P 480, $1.95
THE COLOR OF MURDER	P 461, $1.95

Dorothy Stockbridge Tillet
(John Stephen Strange)

THE MAN WHO KILLED FORTESCUE	P 536, $2.25

Simon Troy

THE ROAD TO RHUINE	P 583, $2.84
SWIFT TO ITS CLOSE	P 546, $2.40

Henry Wade

THE DUKE OF YORK'S STEPS	P 588, $2.84
A DYING FALL	P 543, $2.50
THE HANGING CAPTAIN	P 548, $2.50

Hillary Waugh

LAST SEEN WEARING . . .	P 552, $2.40
THE MISSING MAN	P 553, $2.40

Henry Kitchell Webster

WHO IS THE NEXT?	P 539, $2.25

Anna Mary Wells

MURDERER'S CHOICE	P 534, $2.50
A TALENT FOR MURDER	P 535, $2.25

Edward Young

THE FIFTH PASSENGER	P 544, $2.25